"Is this what ~~down when it g~~

"Apparently so," Corey murmured. Drifting in emptiness seemed preferable to dealing at the moment.

All of sudden, she felt hands grip her shoulders. Her eyes snapped open and she saw Austin kneeling in front of her.

"You went to this place when you were seven," he said quietly. "There's no reason to do it now, Corey. You aren't alone."

"Who the hell do you think you are? Haven't you battered me enough for one night?"

His head jerked back, and his hands released her. She felt a momentary satisfaction. He'd been dishing it out all evening. Her turn.

He jumped up and started walking away. But he turned around suddenly. "Hate me," he said. "Even hate is better than nothing."

The words seemed to make no sense, but the next thing she knew, he lifted her off the couch and sat with her across his lap. Astonished, furious at being manhandled, she opened her mouth to yell at him, but the moment was lost as he kissed her.

Then she was lost, too.

DEFENDING THE EYEWITNESS

BY
RACHEL LEE

Published in Great Britain 2014
by Mills & Boon, an imprint of Harlequin (UK) Limited,
Eton House, 18-24 Paradise Road, Richmond, Surrey, TW9 1SR

© 2014 Susan Civil Brown

ISBN: 978 0 263 91420 7

18-0414

Rachel Lee was hooked on writing by the age of twelve and practiced her craft as she moved from place to place all over the United States. This *New York Times* bestselling author now resides in Florida and has the joy of writing full-time.

To those who love.

Chapter 1

Corey Donohue tossed the odd little note aside as she went to answer the doorbell.

I remember you but you don't remember me.

Exactly, she thought, the kind of joke she would expect one of her friends to play. They believed she was entirely too busy keeping up with the sewing shop she had taken over from her grandmother and thought she needed to shake up her life a bit. Well, that wasn't going to do it.

She hesitated, though, for just a second, looking back at the hall table where she had thrown the piece of notepaper. Anonymous envelope, typed... Wouldn't one of her friends have scrawled something like that with a pen?

But then she pushed the momentary uneasiness aside and reached for the doorknob. Whatever it was, it sounded teasing, not threatening. She supposed some old friend would finally call her to give her a hard time.

She was surprised to find the Conard County sheriff, Gage Dalton, standing there with another, younger man. The guy looked as if he'd just crossed the metaphorical train tracks from the wrong side—shaggy black hair, unshaven, wearing leather and denim, with dark eyes that looked like chips of coal. With bronzed skin and high cheekbones, he looked at once exotic and dangerous.

"Corey," Gage said, "meet a colleague of mine, Austin Mendez."

Austin nodded. She nodded back, wondering what was going on here. Strange men made her jumpy, and if Gage hadn't been there, she would have slammed the door.

"Austin's just come off an undercover assignment and he needs a place to decompress. I remembered your last roomer moved out, and while I know this won't be the long-term kind of thing you'd prefer, Austin needs a room for at least a month, maybe more."

Corey didn't at all like the looks of Austin. He was the kind a very young woman would find appealing, with his unkempt aura of danger, but she was long past that stage. She was also blunt. She turned to Gage. "You vouching for him?"

"Absolutely. He's law enforcement."

She wondered how much that really meant when dealing with a man who had been undercover. Someone had once remarked that the difference between a criminal and an undercover agent was that the agent had to lie.

She looked at Austin Mendez again. A man. In her house. But she felt the pressure of doing a favor for Gage, who had always been good to her. She couldn't just refuse. Gathering her courage, she said, "You get the whole upstairs. It's furnished. You can use the kitchen. I don't make meals for tenants because I'm usually at work. You can go on up and take a look, if you like."

It wasn't the friendliest she'd ever been to a tenant, but she didn't want to be friendly. She was accustomed to renting the space to women, one of the teachers, college students or nurses in the area. The last had been a student at the junior college, a truly nice young woman who had moved on to a four-year school. The fall semester had just begun, and she didn't have a replacement roomer yet. At this point, she probably wouldn't until the spring semester.

This was certainly going to be different, she thought as she watched Austin hike up the stairs.

She gave her attention back to Gage. "I just got home and made some coffee. Do you have time?"

He glanced at his watch. "Sure. Emma's working late tonight and the boys are thrilled to be ordering pizza. I'm a free man for a little while."

Which she took to mean that he wanted to give her a chance to get comfortable with the new tenant. She appreciated that and finally gave him a smile. "Kitchen or living room?" she asked.

"Kitchen's fine. We do everything in the kitchen at my place. I can't figure out why we even have a living room most of the time. These days the boys don't even watch TV. I can't pry them off their computer games."

She laughed. "If I had more time I'd probably get addicted to that myself."

The strange little note fluttered as they passed. She reached for it, intending to toss it in the trash, but then, on impulse, she tucked it, along with its envelope, in one of the drawers of the hall table.

As she poured them coffee, she looked up at the ceiling. "I guess I'm going to have to get used to heavy footsteps."

"That last tenant you had was a tiny sprite," he agreed.

"Just a few months, you said? Because I'm probably going to have to have students wanting to rent for the next semester."

"He just needs a little time and quiet. You pretend you're somebody else for a half-dozen years, and then you have to find yourself again."

"Was it like that for you?"

"Sometimes, but I didn't go anywhere near as deep. Austin doesn't have anybody just now. He went way deep from what I understand, and it leaves you a bit messed up. You also can't just pick up old relationships, not for a while. It could be dangerous if you get identified. But I don't know much I can tell you. Or even how much I know. Just rest assured that I wouldn't have brought him here if I hadn't vetted him."

She supposed that would have to do. Sharing a house with a man made her feel uneasy, though, and she questioned whether she should really agree to this. But she had already invited Austin to look around. Could she possibly look at Gage now and tell him she had changed her mind?

"He's DEA?" she asked.

"He's a friend of a friend," Gage answered. "I don't know which agency. I just know that apparently he spent a lot of time in the border towns in Mexico."

She blinked. While she wasn't up on all the details, she'd heard how dangerous it could be for undercover agents. "My God!"

"And I don't know whether he was involved in trying to stem the drug trade or the arms trade, but I guess it doesn't matter. Two sides of the same coin."

She looked up as she heard more footsteps. "That must have been hell."

"Life on a tightrope, for sure. Anyway, he shouldn't give you any problems, but if you have any, just call me. I'll make other arrangements."

She nodded, feeling a trickle of relief. "I've never taken a man as a roomer before." For good reason. While she couldn't remember her mother's murder, she had had a problem with men ever since, especially men she didn't know.

She returned her attention to Gage. "I take it you're doing a favor for this friend?"

"Sorta. I just suggested it would be hard to get a bigger change of pace. We're mostly quiet and peaceful and don't have the kind of triggers that could set him off."

"You would know. What do you mean, set him off?" She didn't like that phrase.

"Nothing violent. Just that there isn't much around here that ought to make him edgy. He should be able to start letting his guard down and maybe even take a few steps toward remembering who he used to be."

She shook her head and looked down. "If there's one thing I know, it's that you can never be who you used to be. Somehow you have to try to stitch all the changes into a new you."

Gage fell silent and drank his coffee. Corey supposed he was the last person on earth she'd needed to say that to. After all, this man had lost his entire family, a wife and two kids, to a bomb intended for him. Somehow he'd put himself together, remarried and built a family and a life here.

She wasn't sure she'd really finished stitching herself together. Nor was she sure that traumatic amnesia had helped with that one bit. The doctors said it was okay to forget, but she didn't always believe it. Yet it remained a horror she didn't want to look at.

Heavy footsteps on the stairs.

"We're in here," Gage called.

Austin Mendez appeared in the door and hesitated.

"Coffee?" Corey asked, determined to be polite no matter how uneasy he made her.

"Thanks."

She motioned him to a chair at the dinette and got him a cup. "Milk? Sugar?"

"Black's fine, thanks. That's a nice space you have up there."

Corey brought him his coffee and sat again, across from him and Gage. Somehow she was going to have to get used to this, at least for a few months. She decided to try to be chatty.

"Part of that has to do with my tenants over the years. They've fixed it up in various ways to suit them, from painting the rooms, to furnishings. When they move on, they leave a nicer place behind."

"I'm not sure I can do that, but I appreciate it."

He looked as if he was making an effort and it didn't come easily. South of the border? She'd bet he was more comfortable with Spanish than English right now. Unfortunately, her Spanish was more like Spanglish. But maybe that's the last thing he needed to hear now, fluent or not. How would she know?

He spoke again. His English was slightly accented, as if he'd picked up a new habit. Or maybe it was an old one. The longer she sat here, the more questions she had about him. "Gage told me the rent, Ms. Donohue. I'd like to pay a little more."

"Why should you do that?"

"Because Gage also told me you prefer to rent to women. I feel you're doing me a favor."

She blinked, then looked at Gage. "And what else did you tell Mr. Mendez about me?"

Gage smiled into his coffee cup. "Not much. I just told him that in case you said no. I didn't want Austin to take it personally."

That made sense, she supposed. She returned her attention to the male question mark beside Gage. "It's true, but making an exception isn't a favor. Just the regular rent, please." Maybe it wasn't a favor or maybe it was. But it certainly wasn't a favor to Austin. She owed Gage.

Austin Mendez nodded. "Okay. So what are the house rules?"

She hadn't really thought about that because she hadn't exactly needed to make rules before. "Buy your own food, clean up after yourself. That's all I ask. I'll give you a key so you can come and go as you like. I'm gone most days all day, so we shouldn't bother each other."

He nodded. "Fair enough. And I'm not looking to throw any parties."

"I've survived even a few of those," she remarked.

She was almost grateful when he smiled faintly. Not much of a smile, but she was beginning to get the feeling that whoever this man was, or had been, right now he was very much on edge and uncertain. Since she couldn't imagine him doing what he had done without at least a fair amount of confidence, it must be the total shift in gears that was bothering him.

Well, she could understand that. She'd spent a lot of her life trying to shift a gear that seemed to be stuck.

She also couldn't think of another thing to say. She'd never been one for small talk with strangers. So she looked at Gage. "How are the kids? I know how Emma is, I see her often."

"Ever since you got her into that quilting," he agreed, his eyes twinkling a bit. "Are there ever too many quilts?"

"Never." She laughed.

Gage turned to Austin. "Corey here owns the local sewing shop and gives classes in how to do all kinds of stuff from knitting to needlepoint to quilting. Emma's even talking about learning to make lace, though whatever for I can't imagine."

"There's something soothing about busy hands," Corey answered. "And when you get done, there's a sense of achievement."

"There's also a lot of kids in this town running around with hand-knitted caps and a lot of beds covered by Emma's quilts." His eyes danced. "It's kind of fun to watch her give one away. People are so overwhelmed by it and go on about how she couldn't possibly want to part with so much work. They should only see the stack in one corner of our bedroom."

At that, Corey laughed outright. "She did really get into it."

"Understatement," Gage pronounced. "You unleashed an obsession." He glanced at his watch again. "I gotta run. I know the boys are old enough to be by themselves, but every so often I still have to unplug them from their games and remind them there's a real world out here."

"Is there?" Austin's question fell into the conversation almost like a bomb. As if he realized it, he shook himself visibly. "Sorry." He stood up. "I need to go to the bank and get your rent. No checking account yet. If I could have that key?"

She rose immediately and went to get it for him. He thanked her and vanished out the front door and into the gloaming.

Gage stood in the kitchen. "Are you going to be okay with this?"

"You seemed to think I would be."

"That's no answer." He sighed. "I swear he's on the up-and-up. And if you want my guess, you'll hardly know he's here. But if you have any doubts, I'll find another way."

She hesitated. Part of her definitely wanted to say no. Since her mother's murder, she had trouble trusting men, especially strangers, even though she couldn't remember a thing about what had happened. Still… She thought of what Gage had told her about Austin Mendez and figured he'd earned some help with his return to regular life. Someone owed it to him, and she seemed to be the someone available right now.

"It'll be okay," she said firmly.

"But if it's not, let me know?"

"Promise."

He seemed content with that and took his departure after thanking her for the coffee. It was Saturday night, the classes at her shop were done for the day, and tomorrow she'd be open for only a few hours.

That suddenly seemed like an awfully long time away, before she walked back into the security of the shop her grandmother had left to her. She'd just pretended to a whole lot of confidence she didn't feel at all. But that pretense was embedded in her life.

She decided there was only one way to survive this evening. She grabbed a sandwich and a glass of milk, along with her e-reader and knitting bag, and headed for her bedroom. Once inside, she locked the door.

There would be a man in the house now, and she was not at all happy about it or comfortable with it.

Austin returned to the house a couple of hours later. He'd pulled the rent from an ATM, had dinner at the diner, where he noted an astonishing lack of tortillas, then grabbed his suitcase from his old beater and headed inside.

He realized immediately that his landlady had gone to ground. Her car was still in the driveway, but she had vanished. When he caught a glimpse of light from beneath a door at the back of the hall, he figured she had decided to vanish on purpose.

Not that he could blame her. He had a pretty good idea what he looked like, and she didn't know a thing about him. He could live with it. Right now, he wanted to be scarce, too.

Because only scarcity provided safety, and he'd been working without a net for far too long. He'd been initially relieved when they had pulled him out, but that was before he realized he didn't fit here as well as he had in the border towns. Here he had to be a different person than there. He had memories of being someone else, but in between lay six years of working himself into a position of familiarity and friendship with people he had never really wanted to know or become friends with.

The irony didn't escape him.

Nor did the way he had been treated after they'd pulled him out. A thank-you for all the intelligence he had given them, an endless debriefing, a pat on the shoulder, then "Get out of here and take some time for yourself."

They didn't know what to do with him, either, now. Hell, he'd been buried so deep that two of his fellow agents had beaten him up once, and another time one had shot at him.

Then when the joint task force rolled up the operation, they'd dragged him in just like all the rest of the bad guys, and the Federales had tap-danced all over him for days, leaving him with some broken ribs and other injuries before his own guys pulled him out in an ostensible "prison transfer."

Good for his cover, but he was quite sure all of that made his own team uncomfortable.

Well, he hadn't liked it, either, and frankly he never wanted to do it again. Job completed, time to move on. He just didn't know where yet.

He was still on payroll. They'd told him to take as much time as he needed. Even suggested a therapist, if he found the transition too difficult. He hadn't been back long enough to know if it was going to be too difficult. The only thing he knew for sure was that he could no longer stand a necktie.

He unpacked the few things he had brought with him and put them in the drawers of an empty dresser. He'd left behind the clothes in storage. The one suit he'd pulled out to wear to his debriefings had shown him that not only did he hate neckties now, but his body had changed. He was leaner now, his muscles in different places and shapes.

So that left him with his undercover garb and little else. He supposed he needed to do some shopping. If he wanted, he could fit in here pretty quickly. That was his gift.

And his curse.

Corey listened to the sounds of the stranger upstairs. He'd been gone a long time, but now he was back. Unpacking? She thought she heard the dresser move a bit. Then the unmistakable sounds of the shower upstairs.

She was having a serious problem with herself. She had been close to rude with a stranger, in defiance of everything she believed to be right. Strangers were to be welcomed, and while keeping a reasonable distance at first was okay until you knew them, you shouldn't be inhospitable. She'd come very close to that at the door, and now she was hiding in her bedroom as if her house had been invaded by some kind of freak.

She couldn't help her reactions to men. Eighteen years ago, one had killed her mother before her very eyes when she was seven and they were living in Denver. She knew she'd been there because of police reports. She even knew some of the awful details, again because of police reports. The man had never been caught. There'd never been a clue to his identity.

So whoever he was, he probably still roamed the world somewhere, and her memory of the incident was a total blank. It was a mercy, she supposed, that she didn't remember, and having been brought home to Conard County to live with her aunt and grandmother had given her stability and a loving home.

But she was still uneasy with men. Especially men she didn't know. That uneasiness had prevented her from going to college, except for some classes she had lately taken here, and prevented her from ever leaving this area. She knew almost everyone by sight, and she needed that.

But still, the guy upstairs had done nothing wrong, and the more she thought about it, the more she believed that the last thing he needed was to be treated like a pariah. Simple kindness required better of her.

It wasn't as if she needed to spend much time with him. Just some courtesy and an occasional smile. If there was one thing life had taught her, everyone had their own problems, and his, well, his might even be a private hell.

She noticed her knitting needles were clicking more rapidly than usual and that she'd stopped counting stitches at some point. Darn it, she was probably making a mess of this sweater. Sighing, she put the knitting on the bed and rose from her chair, wondering how she could handle this situation better. How she could make this man feel a little more welcome.

He must feel like a fish totally out of water. She could barely remember that feeling, she'd been ensconced here so long. She had to remember the days when the police had taken her to a social worker and then to a foster family, where she had waited for her grandmother to come. Had to remember how strange living here had seemed, how far from home it had felt.

A long time ago, but those feelings lived on. This man was no child, as she had been, but she had possibly found a point of connection with Austin. Fish out of water.

Gage had said that the man couldn't pick up his old relationships just yet, and she wondered what that meant. Might someone dangerous still come after him? Bringing trouble right to her front door?

She caught herself as her old suspicions started to rise up. Enough. The past was past, a very old past. There were limits to how much she could allow it to run her life.

She heard him come downstairs. Biting her lip, she hesitated, then unlocked her bedroom door and stepped into the hallway. Light spilled from upstairs and out of the kitchen door. She made her steps a little noisier as she approached. Startling this man struck her as unwise.

He was facing her as she entered the room, and she

could see the tension in him. Okay, he was *not* feeling safe. She froze on the threshold.

His body softened a little. He was wearing a black T-shirt and old jeans and walking barefoot. "I thought I'd make some coffee. Is that okay?"

"Of course it's okay. Are you hungry, too?"

"I ate at the diner." Then he gave her a crooked smile. "No tortillas."

"No…" Then she got it and smiled. "No, no tortillas, but you can get them at the grocery. Want me to make the coffee?"

"I make it strong."

"That's the way I like it." She gathered he wanted to do it himself, so she sat at the table.

All of a sudden he stuck his hand in his front pocket and put a folded stack of bills in front of her. "Rent," he said, and went back to making coffee.

"Are you going to miss the tortillas?" she asked, seeking something friendly to say even as her nerves kept coiling tighter.

"Fresh ones? You bet. The beginning and end to every meal. Stacks of them. Usually corn. There was one little stand I frequented and sometimes I just stood there watching that woman's hands fly. You wouldn't believe how fast she could roll a ball of dough, flatten it into a near-perfect circle and toss it on the grill for just a short time. Hot and always delicious."

"A real skill."

"Definitely. And it wasn't only her. I just happened to like her stand." His face darkened a bit as he spoke. Then, "Cups?"

She rose and went to open the cupboard. As she did, she accidentally brushed against him and nearly froze as a sizzle ran along her nerve endings. It was a feeling so rare in her life that it astonished her. She leaped away like a startled rabbit.

"Something wrong?"

Only then did she realize she'd been staring into the cupboard too long, and that he'd stepped away from her. She grabbed two mugs at random, closed the cabinet, then handed him one.

"Nothing," she managed to answer.

After he filled his mug, he remained standing as if he wondered whether she wanted him to go upstairs or remain. Be friendly, she ordered herself.

"Have a seat if you like," she invited as she returned to her own with coffee. Just before she sat, she changed her mind and went to get out a tray of raspberry-and-cheese Danish and two plates. She offered him some.

"Thanks. That looks good."

"It is. One of my friends finally fulfilled her dream of opening a bakery. It's an awful lot of work, though. Up well before the birds and all that."

Silence fell again. Apparently he wasn't in a mood to talk, and she didn't know what to say to him. Very awkward. Of course, she was used to hanging out with women at the shop or in the classes she hosted, but she knew most of them. Being confronted with a total stranger left her stymied. How in the world did you get past this when you came from such different worlds?

She supposed it didn't matter. She should just take her coffee into the bedroom and figure out where she had gone wrong on her knitting. Because she was sure she had. Knitting a diamond design into the sweater was not a mindless task.

"Well," she said, tired of the uncomfortable silence, and wondering what she was doing sitting here with a strange man, anyway, "I'll just get back to my knitting."

"Lo siento," he said, then quickly, "I'm sorry. You're trying to be friendly. I'm usually a friendly guy. For some reason, I've been finding that hard lately."

She hesitated. "Are you bilingual?"

"From the cradle."

"That's very cool. I wish I were."

At last he cracked a faint smile. "Being bilingual took me places, all right. My dad was from Mexico and my mom lived in San Antonio when they met. She was Anglo. Anyway, I grew up speaking both languages. Don't ask me how I sorted it all out, but at some point I did."

She laughed quietly. "Kids seem to be good at that. So, did you grow up in San Antonio?"

"Mostly. I spent some summers in Mexico with my father's family. They had a large *finca.* Country estate. Plenty for young boys to do there."

"What did your parents do?"

"Both of them taught at the university. That's how they met. What about you? Have you always lived here?"

"I grew up here," she said, shading the truth a bit. She could barely remember Denver at all.

"And you have your own business, I think Gage said?"

"Yes, it's kind of a crafts shop for women who like sewing, knitting, that kind of thing."

"Does it keep you busy?"

"Pleasantly so. I think we've become the up-to-date version of the women's sewing circle. We have all kinds of gatherings and classes."

"Sounds very friendly." He managed another smile. As his gaze drifted toward the Danish, she pushed it in his direction. "Help yourself. I can get more."

"It looks really good," he said. "I can understand why your friend is successful."

"I should ask her to make tortillas for you. I'm sure they'd be better than the stuff on the shelf in the store."

He looked surprised. "Why would she do that? She doesn't know me, and one person isn't a whole market."

"She'd do it because she's that kind of person."

This time his smile deepened, and some of the tension around his eyes eased. "Maybe it's not so different here, after all."

She wondered what he meant by that but wasn't sure how to ask. How much was she supposed to know? And she didn't have even a remote experience with Mexico. All she knew was this town and this county. Rightly or wrongly, she couldn't imagine a better place.

"Help yourself to anything you like," she said, rising. It was time to retreat behind her walls. "I know you haven't had time to go shopping yet."

He said something that might have been Spanish, leaving her perplexed as she walked down the hall. Then it occurred to her he'd probably been saying some form of good-night. Maybe she'd ask him tomorrow. Or maybe not.

He was a man, after all.

Chapter 2

Austin awoke in the morning considerably refreshed, knowing instantly where he was. He'd acquired that talent during his years as an agent. It was dangerous not to know exactly where you were and exactly what was around you, even when you slept. You never knew what you might wake up to.

He needed to rearrange the room a bit, but even as he sat up with the thought, he realized that would be overkill. He was in a safe little town in Wyoming, as far as he could be from anyone who might want to come after him…and no one should. They never knew his real name, he'd been whisked out of that damn Mexican prison so fast that the most his old compadres could believe was that he had been moved to another prison. Even if they suspected, they'd have no way of tracing him. Besides, by now, the rumor was probably running through the grapevine that he was dead. Killed in an escape attempt, maybe. That was the usual cover story when someone didn't survive manhandling by the Federales.

So it was needless to think of having another way out of here besides the stairs. He didn't have to live like that anymore. He repeated the mantra to himself several times. It was over. He didn't need to live like that anymore.

It should have been reassuring. Comforting. Something. Anything except make him feel utterly at loose ends.

He rose and headed for the bathroom, where he erased the beard he'd worn religiously for six years. Sometimes he'd let it become scruffy, sometimes he'd neatly trimmed it, but it had been like a mask, concealing his real features just enough. He didn't need concealment anymore, but by the time he got done, he looked at his unfamiliar reflection and could have laughed. The skin beneath the beard hadn't tanned along with the rest of him, and the paleness almost glowed. His skin had a natural olive tone, but right then, in comparison, it didn't look like it. He wondered how long it would take to catch up so he didn't look like a clown.

It was time, he decided, to get the lay of the land around here and figure out what kind of clothes he'd need to fit in. If it didn't involve a necktie, he'd be happy.

He heard a church bell ringing as he descended the stairs and realized it was Sunday. Hell, what did that mean for shopping around here?

He smelled coffee at the foot of the stairs and hesitated. Maybe he should just keep going and get breakfast somewhere.

But then he heard Corey. "I'm in here, Austin. Coffee's fresh."

Well, that drew him. He found her sitting at the kitchen table, newspaper in hands, a pair of reading glasses perched on the end of her nose.

"Help yourself," she said pleasantly. "There's cereal in the cupboard, if you like."

"I need to go shopping," he remarked. After the way she had looked at him yesterday, he wondered why she was being so friendly. At first sight, he'd been sure she wanted to send him packing.

She must have looked up as he went to get a mug, because he heard her say, "Oh, my gosh…"

He turned to look at her and she had clapped her hand over her mouth. Her blue eyes seemed to dance. For the first time, he allowed himself to notice what a pretty woman she was. Sort of like a Viking princess, maybe, with her long blond hair, milky skin and brilliant blue eyes. Even a nice figure, as he recalled, although it was invisible now in layers of thick blue terry cloth that seemed to cover a long flannel nightgown. He usually went for darker women, but this one was getting his attention. In the wrong way, considering.

He touched his cheek. "Beard?"

"You can't exactly call that a shadow." A laugh trembled in her voice.

"I know. I was thinking I looked like a painted clown."

A giggle escaped her then. "I'm sorry. Really. It was just so unexpected, but I should be used to it."

"Why?"

"We've got a men's club here and the members grow their beards every winter. I think it may have started as a lark, but it became a charity fund-raiser. You sign up to support someone and offer to pay so much for each inch they grow. Anyway, everyone around here recognizes that look, so don't worry about being mistaken for a clown. It's not that bad, anyway. I was just surprised."

He liked her laughter and didn't at all mind being the butt of it. Smiling easily for the first time in a while, he joined her at the table with his coffee. "I need to go shopping for clothes and food. Recommendations?"

"Nothing opens until noon today, I'm afraid. And your choices are limited. One grocery store, one department store."

"That makes it easy. Assuming they have everything, anyway."

"Freitag's is a good department store. I'm sure the big cities have better, but Freitag's is enough most of the time. If I need something they don't have, I order online."

He nodded, taking it in, taking her in. He wondered if she had any idea how lovely she was.

"What's it like in Mexico?"

He tilted his head. "It's a big country. It depends on where you are and what you're doing."

"I sometimes think I'd like to see the pyramids."

"Well, you could see some of them, anyway. There are a whole lot of them. The museums in Mexico City are great, too. But to get the most out of it, I would recommend hiring a good guide."

"Why?"

"Because he or she will know where it's safe for you to go."

Her eyes widened, and in spite of himself he grinned. "I could say the same about a lot of places in this country."

She flushed faintly. "You're right, of course. Like I said, this is the only town I know."

He sensed something then, and he always trusted his instincts. Something in this woman was locked up tight and for a very good reason. Fear held her caged in this town in the back of beyond.

He ransacked his brain for something he *could* talk about to get her mind off whatever disturbed her. Because, by the downward flicker of her eyes, he knew he had reminded her of something unpleasant.

He decided to return the conversation to Mexico. "The Tarahumara Indians are some people I'd like to help."

Her gaze met his again. "Who are they? And why?"

"They're some of the world's greatest runners. Amazing, really. They can run fifty miles without water. They have this game where they kick a ball along a path as they run up and down the mountains of the Sierra Madre. Until recently they managed to survive without the rest of the world, pure subsistence living, but they were making it. Then they gained international attention with their tremendous running abilities. They started having conflicts with people who wanted their land, with logging companies and finally with drug traffickers. They're poor, and they got even poorer after a drought started killing their measly crops. You can guess what happened."

"Tell me."

He had her full attention. "Because they're such great runners, and they're so close to the border, the drug cartels started offering them money to run backpacks full of drugs across the border."

Her hand flew to her mouth. "Oh, no!"

"Oh, yes. And some of the younger people did it because it was too much money to refuse when they and their families were starving, when they couldn't find jobs, or at least not jobs that paid enough. I mean, those who manage to find work are paid ten dollars a day."

"That's it?"

"That's it. Until recently, the Tarahumara were pretty much the people that Time forgot. They've had a really lousy introduction to the modern world."

"But what can you do for them?"

"I don't know. But now I've got some time to think about it, and I'm going to."

She was sitting there pondering, but he liked the way she kept nodding her head as if agreeing with what he had said. "I had no idea," she said finally.

"Most people don't."

"But you got to know them?"

"I sure did. Some of the mules make it back, but they're angry because they didn't get paid what they were promised. Others come back with tales of being arrested and sent to jail. Those are good cautions, but there are still youngsters who can't resist the idea of six months' pay for what they think will be a few easy hours of running with a backpack."

"God!" She drummed her fingers. "I've heard about all the violence, too. Is that getting any better?"

"Depends on where you are. Again."

"It must have seemed very different from visiting your family's—what did you call it?"

"*Finca.* And yes, it was very different."

She looked as if she was about to ask another question, then bit it back. He'd heard some of what Gage had told her about him, but not all of it. "How much did Gage tell you about me?"

"That you were undercover for six years in the border towns. He didn't say exactly what you were doing."

"Let's keep it that way."

"Fine by me." She gave him a pale smile. "Get some cereal. You've got to be hungry."

Corey had never had anything to do with drugs, although she was certain some of her friends had indulged. They made no secret of it, really, but this was such an out-of-the-way place that if there was a drug problem it remained relatively small.

What she had never thought about was the cost of those drugs, not in terms of money, but in terms of human misery. The news had made it clear that there was a lot of violence between the drug cartels in Mexico, but she had heard nothing about the people who got enticed into carrying those drugs over the border. She had always assumed they were members of the cartel, not innocent kids who were being tempted with desperately needed money.

Until this moment, all of that had seemed far removed from her. Somebody else's problem. But the way Austin had just described those Tarahumara boys sickened her. Their lives were hard, they loved to run evidently and were being drawn into terrible danger by amounts of money that must look like salvation.

Austin pulled a box of cereal from the cupboard. "What's this stuff?"

She looked at it and had to chuckle at his expression. "I call it my roots and twigs. High fiber. I think guinea pigs get better food."

He cracked a laugh. "This from a woman who brings home Danishes from the bakery?"

"The same. Who said I had to be consistent?"

He poured some into a bowl. "It looks like animal feed."

"It probably is. I eat it plain, but you might find it easier to swallow with some sugar on it."

"I can swallow just about anything, trust me. I wasn't raised on caviar. Thanks for sharing."

"Tell me that again after you've tasted it." Her tone was wry, and as she heard it, she realized she was becoming a little more comfortable with Austin Mendez. Maybe it had to do with the way he talked about those Indians.

"So, no idea how you could help the Tarahumara?" she said.

"Not yet. I don't mean to make them sound like the quote-unquote noble savage, because they're not. They fought the Spanish more than once. They fought the French and they fought us. Mining has long since destroyed a lot of their land, about half the original population simply integrated with the rest of society, and the remainder are not above putting on a good show for tourists. It's just that—well, I spent some time with them. The pressures on them from every direction are enormous and I'd kind of like to think there's some way to help them hang on to what's left rather than see them forced to raise opium poppies or run the border. Probably a pipe dream. Change, for good or ill, seems to be unavoidable."

She put her chin in her hand. "It probably is," she agreed. "You can't go back there, can you?"

He paused, then said, "To that part of Mexico? Not anytime soon. I guess part of what gets to me about them is that they make me think of grist caught between the grinding stones of a huge mill, drug cartels on one side, corporations and developers on the other."

"And you like them."

His smile was crooked. "Those I met, most definitely. But enough of that. It's a problem beyond a single man, there's another country involved, and I haven't even got a plan yet. Do you have to open your shop today?"

She nodded. "I'm always open for four hours on Sunday afternoon. When you need something for a project, you need it and you don't want to have to wait another week because you didn't discover the lack until Saturday night."

He flashed a smile. "I can understand that. This cereal is pretty good, by the way. Despite what it looks like."

"Roots and twigs, like I said."

So, all right, she thought. Maybe having him around wouldn't be so bad. She just hoped he didn't feel like being sociable all the time. She spent so much time being sociable at the shop, and while she enjoyed it, she needed her quiet time, too. Of course, she could always retreat to her room with her knitting or embroidery. It wouldn't be the first time she needed to hide out.

But Austin didn't linger much longer. He announced he was going to scope out the town, then go shopping. Ten minutes later, he vanished out the front door.

Her peaceful Sunday morning returned. She bent her attention to the paper again but realized she wasn't seeing much of it.

Instead, she was seeing Austin, hearing his voice as he'd talked about the Indians. She had no idea what kind of work he'd done in Mexico, and she wasn't sure she wanted to know. But whatever it had been, it hadn't hardened him. No, he wanted to help a whole tribe of people.

She couldn't think of a better recommendation of his character. Or anything that could have made him sexier.

As soon as that thought crossed her mind, she shook it quickly away and went to get dressed. She'd go to the shop early and take care of some busywork. It would be a good distraction, and right now she needed one.

A man had entered her personal space and left her wanting more. She'd think about how stupid that made her later. Right now, she just didn't want to think about it at all.

As she was walking to her shop two blocks over, she passed Good Shepherd Church. She hadn't attended since her grandmother's death, but before that she'd been in the pews every Sunday. What had changed? She honestly didn't know, but deep inside she was sure something had. Often enough, someone would invite her to return, and she had pleasant memories of the fellowship there, the potluck dinners, all of it.

It wasn't as if church had ever been a bad experience for her, but she still had no desire to go back. She glanced at the doors, saw a few stragglers entering and just kept on walking. Evidently, whatever she might feel was lacking in her life wasn't inside that building.

Not that she really thought anything was lacking. This was the life she had planned out for herself. She'd grow old like her grandmother, running the shop. She hadn't completely dismissed the idea of a family, but considering her trust issues with men, she didn't think it was very likely.

Regardless, she enjoyed her work, and that was more than most people could say. To her surprise, an hour before her scheduled opening, Daisy Loden was already waiting for her.

"Bless you!" Daisy cried upon seeing her.

"Me? For what?"

"For coming early. I made a lounging robe for my grandmother, her birthday party is in two hours, and I forgot to buy the buttons!"

Corey laughed and pushed her key into the lock. "I must have felt you calling me."

"Maybe. I almost went to knock on your door, but I decided that would be rude beyond belief."

"Next time, knock on my door," Corey said. "This is an emergency."

"Well," said Daisy wryly, "the worst case would have been explaining to Grandma that I still needed to put the buttons on it. I don't think she'd have been upset."

Corey knew that Daisy's grandmother was suffering from Alzheimer's and could sometimes be unpredictable. She also knew that caring for the woman was a severe strain on Daisy and her sisters at times, so who needed an upset because Daisy gave her grandmother a robe and then had to take it back? It might be okay, then again… "What kind of buttons?"

"Big ones, because her fingers are arthritic. And red because the whole robe is in the brightest colors I could find. She's always loved bright colors."

"I hope I have them." Corey honestly couldn't remember. Her shop was full of so many buttons and notions that she sometimes forgot exactly what she had.

"I know you do. You have *everything*."

Daisy's exuberance had always delighted Corey. The woman bubbled nearly all the time, and sometimes Corey envied her that. Daisy had her share of problems, but nothing seemed to squash her enjoyment for long.

Daisy hurried to the back to look at buttons while Corey settled behind the counter. There was a box on the floor at her feet that she hadn't opened yet, and a stack of mail from yesterday, most of which went straight into the trash. The bills she tucked into a drawer behind her.

Moments later she heard Daisy squeal. "Found them. Perfect."

She came up to the register holding two packets of scarlet buttons, big enough to go on a clown suit. "She'll be able to manipulate these," she said as she put them on the counter and started to pull out her wallet from her purse.

"It's on the house," Corey said swiftly. "My birthday present to your grandmother."

"Aren't you a sweetie!" Daisy leaned right across the counter and managed to give Corey a hug and a big kiss on the cheek. Then she scooted to the door, calling over her shoulder, "I'll bring you a photo of her in the robe."

The bell over the door rang as she left. It was only then that Corey noticed a man looking in the window. He appeared familiar, a local, so she waved cheerily. There were certainly lovely things in the window to look at. She used them to display the projects her sewing and knitting groups had made. Sometimes people even wanted to buy them, which meant some of the women made a bit of much-needed pin money.

The man didn't wave back, though. He just looked a moment longer, then sauntered on down the street.

"Well," she said to the empty store, "I bet he doesn't sign up for a class." Then she laughed and got to work.

Sundays were always a slow time, when a few women dropped in to pick up something, or to chat for a couple of minutes. It was a good time for catching up on things that she'd let slide during the week, from neatening her stock, to putting out fresh items, to sweeping floors and cleaning the bathroom. Her back office really needed some work, but she didn't feel like tackling it yet. She had a theory: once she put something away, she'd never remember where it was. Her stacks were her filing cabinet until she was certain she was done with an item. So far, the only way she'd managed to lose a thing was by putting it away.

Sometimes she thought she needed a highly organized

assistant, but the idea of giving over control of so many important things made her hesitate. Then she wouldn't be able to find anything at all, and what if something went wrong?

She was still shaking her head at her own hang-ups when she heard the bell again. Leaving her office, she went out front and was surprised to see Austin.

"Hi," he said. "I hope you don't mind, but I wanted to see your shop. It's bigger than I envisioned."

"Well, being in an old house has some advantages," she said. "We've got rooms in the back and upstairs for the sewing classes, and plenty of space up here for stock."

He nodded, hovering just inside the door as if he wasn't certain she wanted him there. Well, she wasn't, but this was a shop, for crying out loud, and he wasn't the first man to walk in here. "Look around if you like," she said when he didn't move. "I was just getting ready to close up."

"I don't want to keep you. I was curious. Now when you talk about it, I'll have a mental image."

She paused as she turned her key in the register, locking it. "Do you need mental images?"

"Don't you?"

"I never really thought about it."

"It's not only images. I keep a mental map. I like to know where everything is and what it's like, insofar as I can."

That made sense to her, given the job Gage had mentioned. "I guess I haven't thought about it because I've always been here. Seriously, feel free to look around. I need to take the trash out."

"I can do that for you. Where do I go?"

She pointed to the big wastebasket at the end of her counter. "Down the hall. Just outside the back door is a big bin. Be sure to use the doorstop or you'll be locked out automatically."

"Got it." He hefted the large can easily, with one hand and disappeared down the hallway. She returned her attention to tidying the last bits on the counter, but as she finished she found herself looking at the front window again. The day was still bright, the hour early, but that wasn't what she was thinking about. For some reason she remembered that man who had been looking in earlier, and tried to place him. She was sure she knew him. Well, sort of. She didn't claim to know everyone in the county or even the town, and she spent most of her time here in the store and with the women.

She sighed and shook herself. What did it matter who he was? Just a guy from around here who had probably noticed some item in the window.

Curiosity pushed her and she went to look at exactly what she had displayed there. It wasn't as if she'd forgotten, but she wondered what might have captured his interest.

Then she saw the beaded and embroidered purse Mary Jo Suskind had made. Golden threads, tiny silver beads, it was a work of art.

That was probably it. The guy might have seen it and been wondering if his wife would like it. She was sure he hadn't been attracted to the baby booties, kids' sweaters or even the brightly colored block quilt. No, it had to have been the purse. She hoped he came back and bought it. Mary Jo would be thrilled.

"All done," Austin announced from behind her. "I locked the dead bolt. Is that enough?"

"Around here it is," she said, turning toward him with a smile. He replaced the empty can, then came toward her.

"Anything else?" he asked.

"Nope. I'm finished." She flipped the light switches by the door, casting the shop into shadows except for one security light. Stepping outside with him, she locked the front door.

"Walk you home?" he asked.

Something inside her froze. Too friendly too fast. She tried to push past the feeling but it was too late.

"I know," he said. "I'm just the roomer you didn't want." His face shut as if a gate slammed down and he walked away, heading in the opposite direction of her house.

Damn it, she thought, suddenly furious at herself. Just how long was she going to let the past shadow her present? When was she going to become whole again?

Never, she thought grimly. Never. She ought to know that by now. Her mother had been murdered eighteen years ago, she couldn't even remember what she had seen, but to this day she was always on edge around men she didn't know well. And since she avoided men as much as possible, that wasn't a terribly large group.

She began to walk home, wondering how she should handle the matter with Austin. He'd made a casual friendly offer. She wondered what her face must have looked like to cause him to shutter that way and head in the other direction.

It did not at all make her feel good to think she had offended him. She might be paranoid about men, and with good reason, but she didn't want to hurt anyone needlessly. Not even a strange man.

Who wasn't quite a stranger any longer. He'd been forthcoming with her this morning. But that couldn't change her instinctive reaction.

Damn, she thought privately as she walked. She passed people she recognized, a few of the women who frequented her store, giving smiles and nods but not pausing. She had to get home. She wondered if she would arrive to find that Austin was moving out.

She decided she was catastrophizing what was surely a minor incident. If he left because of an expression on her face, then she was better off without any roomer at all. Its not as if she needed the money. She just didn't like living alone in a big, empty house.

Probably another thing she could trace back to her mother's murder. She sighed, feeling a whole bunch of self-disgust. She was grown-up now, and surely she should have conquered at least some of her childhood fears. It didn't matter that they were grounded in real events. What mattered was that they still ruled her.

She picked up her pace, trying to infuse herself with determination, although for what she didn't know.

She let herself into her house after waving to old Mrs. Bushnell across the street. The woman couldn't get around much anymore, but she did enjoy rocking on her porch on a sunny, pleasant afternoon.

Corey needed to get over there again soon, she decided. Mrs. Bushnell's children dropped by often to look in on her, but the woman had been one of her grandmother's dear friends, and from time to time Corey liked to drop by with some baked goods and a little conversation. It had been a few weeks now. Too long.

Inside, she almost froze as she closed the door. The house was silent, but she could smell someone else. A man. Austin, she realized, putting the scents together. Leather, man and a faint scent of bar soap.

Her heart had accelerated at her initial awareness, but she drew a couple of deep breaths and tried to calm herself down. This was stupid, she told herself. Absolutely stupid. After eighteen years?

In the kitchen, she started a pot of coffee, and after looking around, she realized there was no house key on the counter or table. Apparently Austin hadn't decided to move out. Yet. Considering her reluctance to have him here, her own relief surprised her. She didn't want him but she did want him?

Now, *that* was royally confusing. Maybe it was time to try some therapy again. Maybe it was time to pry that awful memory out of the place where she had buried it. Sometimes she wondered if having a face to put on the killer would make it easier to be around other men. Maybe she felt this way only because she didn't know what he looked like and he was still out there somewhere. Maybe she would have been better off if she had remembered the murder, gruesome though it had been.

She heard the key in the front lock. Austin. The coffee had just started brewing, so she moved quickly to the table and sat, hoping she looked casual.

He headed straight for the stairs. She hesitated, then called out, "I'm making fresh coffee if you'd like some." She had to smooth this over somehow.

She heard him pause, as if thinking her offer over, then his footsteps drew closer and he appeared in the kitchen doorway.

"Do you want company?" he asked bluntly. "Because really, I'm trying not to get in your way."

She felt her cheeks heat. "I'm sorry. Truly."

"Being looked at as if I'm about to hurt you isn't very enjoyable."

"Oh, my God," she whispered, and started to lower her head.

"I mean," he continued, "you don't have to like me, don't have to spend time with me. I get that I'm renting from you for a few months and we don't need to have a social relationship. Unfortunately, I'm cross-cultural. A gentleman offers to walk a lady home."

She winced, beginning to get a clear picture of her reaction to his offer. And understanding why he had responded as he had. Clearly, he was not one to pretend that nothing had happened. Maybe he was utterly through with pretense after his undercover work.

"Corey?"

She looked up. His face was still all hard angles.

"I just want to know what the hell you want from me. Leave? Stay? Stay out of your way?"

She motioned to the seat across from her and tried to find her voice. "Coffee. Then I'll try to explain a little."

He hesitated a moment, then went and filled mugs for each of them. He settled across from her and waited, his dark gaze firmly fixed on her. It was almost unnerving, that intensity, but she supposed he'd gotten very good at reading people, especially faces.

She cleared her throat, feeling as if her accelerating heart were trying to climb up into it. "When I... When I was seven, my mother was murdered."

At once he stiffened a bit, but at least he didn't try to say anything.

"Evidently I was there. I witnessed it. But I don't remember any part of it. Traumatic amnesia. It's been eighteen years, but I still have a problem with men I don't know well. It has nothing to do with you. It's just me."

"They didn't catch the guy?"

She shook her head. "Not a clue."

"So, he's still out there."

"Maybe."

"No wonder," was all he said.

But those two simple words seemed to free up something inside her. "I was thinking, after the way I reacted when you offered to walk me home, if I wouldn't be better in the long run if I *could* remember."

"I don't know," he said. "I honestly don't know. Overall it's probably best that you don't remember."

"I had therapy for a few years after, and the psychologist would agree with you. But I'm not so sure anymore."

"Why?"

"I know it was a terribly brutal murder. I'm glad I

don't remember that part. But if I could remember the guy's face…" She trailed off. This seemed like a remarkably intimate discussion to be having with someone she didn't know. Yet something about him invited confidences. Probably part of what had made him good at his job.

She sighed. "I may not remember, but it's left me with an indelible suspicion of men. Apparently that much didn't vanish into amnesia."

He nodded and sipped some coffee. "That's why you didn't really want to rent to me, and why you reacted the way you did when I offered to walk you home. It makes perfect sense. Would you like me to move out? I don't like the idea that I'm making you uneasy by staying here."

"I don't want you to move out." The words came with surprising ease. "It's getting easier for me, and I need that, if you can put up with my quirks."

At that he smiled. "I know quirks. Yours aren't that bad." Then his smile faded. "I'm sorry about your mother."

"I was actually lucky. My grandmother and aunt took me in. In fact, the scariest part I can remember was the three days I spent in foster care."

"Why three days?"

"Because they had to prove they were related to me and go through background checks. There was other stuff, too, I guess. The sheriff here even had to attest to their ability to care for me. I don't remember that part, obviously, but my grandmother and aunt told me about it. They wanted me to understand why I had to stay with strangers for so long."

"You must have been terrified."

"I was." She shook her head a little, as if she could shake off the memory. It wouldn't entirely shake away, though. "They must have wondered what they were getting into. I was placed with a family and I was terrified of the father. I hid a lot. When my grandmother came for me, they had to pry me out of the back of a closet."

He swore quietly. "Is your aunt still around?"

"No. She died of leukemia seven years ago. Grandma passed five years ago."

"Your father?"

"I never knew who he was."

"Damn," he muttered. "I have more family than I know what to do with. I can't imagine not having any."

"I can't imagine having a huge family."

"Maybe you've created one here. As I was out and about today, people wanted to know a little about me. When I explained I was rooming with you, I heard all about your sewing circles. You seem to be quite a social center in your shop. So you've got a family. Not blood family, but still."

She felt herself smiling at last. "That's how I think of them."

"And look at it this way," he said, leaning forward a little bit, "you aren't stuck with the ones who drive you crazy."

"Are you?"

"Of course. I can't be rude to Tío Reynaldo just because he's obnoxious. Not allowed."

She laughed. "Do you really think I could be rude to anyone in this little town?"

His smile widened and she almost caught her breath. My word, this man was attractive. Extremely so. His smile seemed to draw her in and make her heart skip a few beats.

"Well, you probably could," he said. "Just like I could be rude to Reynaldo. But there'd be hell to pay."

"It sure wouldn't help my business."

He laughed. "There's a downside to family. I could share some of mine with you."

"Starting with Reynaldo?" she asked archly. Amazement filled her as she realized how easily he had changed the subject and her mood. Relaxation replaced nervousness, and while she hadn't quite made up her mind, she rather thought that having Austin around for a while might not be bad at all.

"Of course starting with Reynaldo," he agreed. He glanced at his watch, a battered and inexpensive brand. "I need to get to the grocery. I picked up some clothes earlier, but I didn't shop for food. They close at six today, right?"

"Right." She glanced at the digital clock on the microwave. "You're running out of time. Why don't I drive you over there. I can show you where everything is." She surprised herself by making the offer, then realized she felt good about it. A major step forward.

"Will you be all right with that?"

She nodded. "Let's go. I need a few things, too."

Chapter 3

The man sat at the old computer. It didn't always work right anymore, but he had little use for it. He had begun to while away his evenings by composing messages in green letters on a black screen. He had known the first one he had decided to send would probably not bother the woman at all, but he was in no rush. These things needed careful planning.

Besides, he was going to have fun watching as the messages became increasingly troubling for her. He knew she didn't remember. She didn't need to remember until he reminded her. He liked knowing that he was in on a secret and she wasn't.

He'd been watching her for a few years now. At first, he hadn't thought much about it because she was so young, but now she was old enough that she should have dated someone, and if that had happened, he would have heard about it. Those things weren't secret in Conard County.

So she spent all her time with women. All of it. Her preference was unmistakable. The more he watched her, the more convinced he became that she was just like her mother. What was more, she'd quit going to church right after her grandmother had died. There could be no other reason for that change.

He'd had a brief moment of doubt when that man moved in with her, but then he'd watched through the window of the shop and had seen that woman hug her and kiss her.

There was no longer any question. She was what she was, and eliminating her revolting presence from this world had become imperative.

Cleansing was imperative, and this was his mission. He had no delusion that he could get rid of them all, but he could get rid of some of them.

Her mother had been a start. He had come back here thinking that was all he needed to do. But then her daughter had grown up and he'd begun to feel the irritation again. That woman shouldn't be walking the same streets with decent folk. It wasn't right.

But he wanted her to know what was coming. He wanted her to fear it. He wanted her to feel the trap closing in on her.

Because as he'd already discovered, the killing was too swift and too kind for someone so evil.

Empathy. It always struck Austin as a crazy descriptor for someone who could go successfully undercover, but at the start of this journey the psychologists had assured him it was essential. Part of being undercover meant being able to identify with the reasoning and motivations of the people you were investigating. Walking in their shoes, as it were.

Well, he'd walked in their shoes for six years, and the

results had left him with an internal mess. Yeah, he'd identified, all right. He'd understood. Clinging to his own values had sometimes become extremely difficult.

Had those psychologists even considered that part? Probably not. He'd not only walked the walk and talked the talk but he'd become one of them, all the while trying not to break the law or kill anyone. In that business, it was a dicey proposition.

He sure wouldn't be the first person to get so messed up by undercover work that he had to walk away. Austin still hadn't made up his mind about that. He'd never go covert again, but he wondered if he'd fit any other capacity.

He still often felt that he was on a spaceship, having departed one place, awaiting his arrival at his destination. Almost like being in suspended animation. Sooner or later, he was sure he would land. He just wondered where it would be.

He was troubled by Corey, though. It seemed to him her healing may have been truncated by her inability to remember, but he sure wouldn't wish those memories on anyone.

He understood her problem with men, though. Completely. It wasn't just empathy, either. After all, he'd been shot at on two occasions by fellow agents who had no idea he was on their side, and then he'd been left in that rat-infested cell being beaten by the Federales until they managed to identify him and yank him out. He wasn't feeling too fond of his fellow agents these days.

He could have gone home to San Antonio, but that was too close to the border, too close to the culture he was trying to shake away. Right now he needed to get his feet firmly planted in Anglo soil, his head firmly planted in this world.

As for his family...he didn't know exactly what the agency had been telling them all these years, except that he was alive and okay—okay being a relative term. They did know he was doing something highly secret, but after six years they must be wondering where the hell he had gone.

He supposed he ought to write or call, but something in him held him back. Maybe it was knowing they'd inevitably pressure him to come home, and he just wasn't ready to do that yet.

So he focused his attention on Corey. He doubted he could help her, and he wasn't a good bet for much these days. He'd discovered a streak of paranoia in himself that wouldn't quit. It had made sense during the operation, but now? He couldn't trust. He hadn't even really trusted the sheriff who had brought him over here, in spite of the fact that the man was his best buddy's friend. But then, he wasn't sure he trusted the old friend anymore, either.

Devil of a conundrum, he thought as he walked around town. He couldn't trust anyone except himself, Corey couldn't trust men, and he supposed he ought to find it amazing that they'd managed to get through a whole week now without any problems.

He tried to stay out of her way, which hadn't been too difficult considering that she worked long hours. Occasionally he drifted past her shop and was amazed by how busy she often was, especially in the evenings. At night and on Saturdays, the place filled to the rafters with women. The local churches would probably be happy with such high attendance.

The women came in all shapes, sizes and ages, they arrived with smiles and left with smiles. All of them carried big totes full of their projects and materials. When they left, the totes were fuller than before. Corey ran around looking happy, a tape measure draped around her neck, a big pair of scissors sticking out of her work apron.

He tried not to hang out in the vicinity too often. He didn't want to make Corey, or anyone else, nervous. He'd found Mahoney's Bar where he could get a shot of tequila and lime and one night had even gotten into a drinking contest with a couple of guys. He had a great head for tequila. He'd had to.

But that episode had had an amazing effect. Men nodded to him on the street now. Friendly town. But he didn't trust it one bit. He'd been in a lot of friendly towns the past six years. It was what went on underneath that mattered.

He realized he was scoping Conard City just the way he'd done with other towns across the border. Looking for a way in, looking to get clued in, looking to be taken as an insider. Damn. Would he ever get rid of the old habits?

Should he?

He almost laughed at himself. He hadn't landed yet, obviously. So he turned his thoughts back to Corey. Maybe not wise, given her distrust of men. Every time he thought about her, his brain ran to sensual and sexual activities.

She wasn't even his type, not that that seemed to be helping. Fair, blonde, blue-eyed... But while she didn't exactly flaunt it, she had a great shape, too. His eyes had a tendency to want to roam over her in a way that invariably left him hot and bothered. He thought he had pretty good control over his impulses because control had been essential to survival for a long time now. He couldn't afford distractions.

But Corey was proving to be one hell of a distraction. He had plenty of stuff to deal with, but his mind kept rambling right back to her. Like it or not, regardless of the number of times he tried to cross her off his mental list of possibilities, she kept bobbing right up in his thoughts.

When he watched her talk, he wondered how her lips would taste. When she laughed, something inside him sparked with pleasure. When she grew pensive, he had the worst urge to reach out.

She couldn't have been more off-limits if she'd been surrounded by barbed wire, but he kept wanting to jump that fence and bed her. He hoped she didn't suspect.

How could she? he reassured himself. He'd been staying out of her way, keeping their meetings as light as he could manage. If he'd been doing it right, he'd become the nearly invisible roomer in the background.

But he knew he wasn't entirely invisible. A time or two he'd seen an answering spark in her. A flicker of interest that she quickly buried. So he wondered just what it would take to get past that woman's fence. As near as he could tell, no one ever had. She'd come back to this town as a child, and nothing she said led him to believe she had ever left it again.

That struck him as sad. There was a whole world out there, good and bad, but mostly good, and she'd nailed herself to this tiny town because she was afraid of the dragons outside the gates.

He wished for her sake that they'd been able to catch the perp who had killed her mother. Maybe then, not being able to remember wouldn't be so crippling.

And what the hell did it matter, anyway, he asked himself irritably. He needed to find his own forgotten self, and he'd be moving on once he settled his own mental and emotional tab. Right now he was useless to everyone, himself included.

So leave Rapunzel safely in her tower, and get his head out of his groin.

Rapunzel? Really? He was losing it.

The thought made him laugh out loud, which drew a few looks his way as he strode down the street. He didn't care. A few of the people even smiled.

As long as he didn't run around town giggling like a lunatic, it would probably be okay.

Autumn just tinged the air and he noticed how much shorter the days had grown in the week he'd been here. Oh, they were still long, but the change was more noticeable here than down south. Maybe he was dealing with more than culture shock. Maybe he was dealing with climate shock, too. Desert nights at high altitude could get surprisingly cold, but he was used to hot days. No such thing up here, at least not now. People walked around looking perfectly comfortable in shirtsleeves when he was wishing for sweaters and a jacket.

Well, he'd been raised in places that rarely saw snow or ice. San Antonio had a kind of winter, but he suspected that if he stayed here for long, he might be in for some new experiences. After all, when he'd shopped for clothes, he'd seen some jackets that he had hitherto seen only in movies. He hadn't quite been able to bring himself to buy one yet, but inside the denim jacket he had chosen, he realized he had some adapting to do. What would have worked most places he'd lived was already failing him.

Amused by his own thoughts, he started whistling as he walked, cheered by the prospect of a totally different experience. Maybe that would help jar him out of the past.

He unlocked the front door of Corey's house and stepped into aromas that immediately snapped him back in time. He froze, working on centering himself, even as the scents called to mind another time and place.

"Austin?"

He closed his eyes, gathering himself.

"Austin?"

The voice came closer. He opened his eyes and drank in Corey, in all her Nordic beauty. She definitely didn't remind him of the past. Today she was wearing her golden mane in braids that wreathed her head. With a wrench that felt almost physical, he felt himself land in the present once again.

"Hi," he said.

"I've got a surprise for you." She was smiling with delight.

"I can smell it."

"Tortillas," she said, looking as pleased as if she were giving him a huge gift. "My friend made them. Some with white flour and some with cornmeal because I wasn't sure which you'd prefer. Come tell me if I'm cooking them right."

"Sure." He followed her, trying to shake off a sudden woodenness in his legs. Ridiculous reaction. Stupid reaction. Just some tortillas, for crying out loud.

Apparently she had taken him at his word about stacks, because there were large ones sitting on two plates. Another plate held the ones she had cooked.

"I don't have a grill," she chattered. "So I'm making do with a skillet. Will that work? And you said they were cooked fast, so I assume the fire was hot?"

"Just enough to heat them and maybe give them a touch of brown."

"Try one and let me know what you think."

He wondered if he would even be able to swallow. What had possessed her to do such a thing for him? What had possessed her friend? They didn't know him, and Corey had this thing about men, so what the hell? Suspicions began to arise in him. Strings were always attached.

But her face looked so open and pleased. Maybe she was just trying to be nice, although he couldn't imagine why.

Just as her smile began to shrink, he made himself go to the table and pick up one of the tortillas. White flour.

He'd loved them as a kid, but in Mexico he'd more often eaten corn. He bit into it, aware that she was watching, and in an instant was slammed back into his youth in San Antonio.

"Damn, this is good," he said truthfully. He looked at her again, and saw her smile had returned full force. She spoke. "Melinda says she'll be happy to make them whenever you want. And despite your doubts, there *is* a market here. She sold a bunch of them this morning. So, did I cook it right?"

"Perfectly." He forgot his manners and just shoved the rest of his tortilla into his mouth.

"Do you have a favorite thing to put on it? I didn't know about that for sure."

"I'll put almost anything on a tortilla." He pulled out the chair and sat, reaching for one made of corn. Another flash of the past as the flavor hit his mouth. "Wow. Just wow."

"Should I make more?"

"Lady, you can keep on cooking. But you might want to eat, yourself."

She laughed. "I'll get to it. They're really great this fresh, but I keep wanting to add something. Beans? Meat? Peppers? I mean, I guess people around here cook with tortillas, but I've never had any Mexican food. We don't have a restaurant here that serves any."

He gobbled down the corn tortilla, then rose and headed for the pantry. "I went shopping, remember?"

"How could I have failed to notice? My pantry is bursting."

"Well, here we go." He pulled out a can of green chilies, remarking that he wished they were fresh, a can of pinto beans and some seasonings. "Allow me to introduce you to refried beans. The best kind."

It apparently surprised her, but she let him take over her kitchen. Sitting at the table with coffee, she asked him questions about everything he was doing, and he was glad enough to share. "Just understand, I'm not a master chef. This came from the need to survive."

He liked the sound of her laughter, even as concerns niggled at the back of his mind. What had made her decide to be so friendly? "We're skipping a step here, by the way. The canned beans are already cooked, so basically I'm going to be doing only the last half of the job."

He pulled a half onion out of her fridge where it sat wrapped in plastic, then found the bacon. "Better yet. Fatback would be the choice in Mexico, but bacon... yum."

"Do you put the bacon in the beans?"

"Just the fat."

After he'd cooked a couple of slices of bacon, he set them aside on a paper towel, then tipped the frying pan. "About right. You don't need a whole lot of fat, just the flavor."

Corey watched with amazement. He might not be a chef, but he turned into a kitchen wizard right before her eyes. He tossed tortillas into one skillet while he flavored and stirred the beans in another.

"So what brought this on?" he asked.

"What?"

"Tortillas. Cooking them for me."

"Oh! Well, I was talking to Melinda, and I mentioned that you liked fresh tortillas and it seemed a shame that the only kind you could get around here were the packaged ones from the grocery. Next thing I knew, she was calling and telling me to pick them up. When I got home, I didn't know whether I needed to refrigerate them or whether they needed to be cooked right away, so…" She shrugged. "It just happened."

"Thank you both. Do you have a potato masher?"

Jumping up, she pulled it out of the drawer for him and watched him mash the beans. From time to time he added a little water.

"It was really nice of your friend to do this," he said again. Apparently he was nearly done, because a stack of cooked tortillas made its way to the table.

"She said it was easy. Not nearly as difficult as making a loaf of bread was how she put it. And I was kind of having fun experimenting."

"Sorry I took your experiment over."

"I don't mind. I'm learning."

Surprisingly soon, they were seated at the table with all the tortillas, a heap of refried beans that made her mouth water, green chilies in a bowl with a serving spoon and a jar of salsa.

"Wow," she said. "I never thought it could be that fast."

"Easy meal," he replied. "It works pretty good with eggs in the morning… Well, like I said, you can put almost anything on a tortilla. It's basically a rolled-up sandwich."

The fresh tortillas were so much better than any she had ever eaten. And the refried beans? She'd had them once or twice from a can, ready-made, but these beat any she had ever tasted.

"You made it look so easy," she said. "And it's so good!"

He smiled at her, making no apology for his large appetite. "Fresh is best," he agreed. "It wasn't a problem in San Antonio, or in Mexico. But I did cheat by getting canned pinto beans."

"Small cheat. You did everything else. I don't know where we could get you fresh green chilies, though."

"Oh, we could probably order them in a quantity suitable for a restaurant."

She had a mouthful of food and quickly snatched up a napkin as she tried to stifle a laugh.

"I could probably get a friend or a family member to mail some to me, but…" He let that trail off and she saw his gaze grow distant.

It was getting easier for her to be around him as time passed, and she considered that a positive sign. But there was still so much she didn't know about him, and she wondered how much she dared ask. It was none of her business, after all.

But in the end, she asked, anyway, because it seemed so important. "You aren't ready to make those contacts again?"

His gaze snapped back to her. "No." The word was short, but before she could recoil, or feel firmly put in her place, he spoke quickly. "Sorry. I didn't mean to snap at you. It's just that…" Again he hesitated and trailed off. "You know how it is with people you've known your whole life."

She nodded, not sure where he was headed.

"They'd be full of questions," he continued, reaching for another tortilla and covering it with beans, chilies and salsa. "I couldn't answer. They'd want to know what I've been doing all these years. Naturally enough. I'm not ready to go home and tell the necessary lies, not to people I care about. And if they suspected any part of the truth and it started to make the rounds...well, I need to wait a while. I wouldn't want to draw any trouble their way."

"Could you? Really?" The thought astonished her.

"Probably not. But I want some time to pass first. I want to be long forgotten by the people who knew me when I was undercover."

"That hardly seems fair to you."

"Life isn't fair. I think you know that."

She did, intimately, but she didn't want to think about herself right now. "So where do they think you've been all this time?"

"Officially I think I was assigned to a mission in Panama."

"Circles within circles," she remarked. "Like a maze."

"That's the general idea. Other agents on the ground had no idea who I was. That made for some, um, interesting experiences."

Corey forgot all about eating, instead trying to imagine all of this. If his own side didn't know who he was... "You could have been killed by your own people!"

"It was a possibility." His face seemed to go blank, as if there was more that he didn't want to reveal. She decided maybe she should just let it go. She didn't want to make him uncomfortable, or remind him of bad things.

"I can hardly imagine being so alone," she said finally. Although she could, if she let herself. Not for six years, but for a few days or weeks. Even after her grandmother and aunt had brought her back from Denver, she had felt alone. Separated. In an alternate universe. But at least she had been surrounded by people who cared about her. Austin had faced something very different. "So everyone was out to get you?"

"Not everyone, and not all the time." He managed a slight smile. "It was most dangerous at the beginning, then later at the end when we were getting ready to roll everything up."

"Did anyone know who you really were?"

"I had a couple of contacts."

That didn't seem like very many to her. Gage hadn't been exaggerating when he'd said Austin had been walking a tightrope. And without much of a net evidently.

"Why did you do it?" she asked bluntly.

"Someone has to and I was especially suited. Obviously."

"But did you really know what you were getting into?"

"Who does?"

She might have laughed if it hadn't been so frighteningly true.

"Look," he said finally, "it's really like the rest of life. We all leap and then look because there's no way we can really know what it's going to be like. We *think* we know, but we don't. Knowing what I know now, I'd never do that again."

She nodded, understanding. "Was any of it good?"

"Plenty. I met lots of great people who had nothing to do with my job. I made friends. I had fun."

"What about the bad?"

"I learned not to trust. I'm having trouble shaking that."

"I learned not to trust, too." She hated to say it out loud, but since he was being so forthcoming, she felt she should be, too.

"Ah," he said, "but you don't trust men. Me, I don't trust anybody."

Her stomach sank. She hadn't wanted to hear that, even though she had suspected it. But what difference did it make? she asked herself. She might be sitting here having dinner with him, but she didn't trust him, either. Not yet. Maybe never. All she felt was an attraction she didn't want to feel, an awakening of desires she had never actually experienced because she was afraid, yearnings that now troubled her sleep, all because of this man, a man she didn't trust. Not really.

Why *should* she trust him? They'd shared a roof for a week, but he'd pretty much stayed out of her way. She had tried to do something neighborly for him with the tortillas, and he'd been neighborly right back by making her a fine meal she would never have thought to make otherwise. But that was it. All of it.

She insisted on doing the washing up because he had cooked. He didn't argue, simply thanked her and disappeared upstairs. That gave her plenty of time to think.

To think about a man who must be good at making friends, at pretending to be something he wasn't. How else could he have inserted himself in such a way that he gleaned intelligence that could be gotten by no other means. After all, that was the whole point of going undercover. So if he wasn't a natural-born liar, he had certainly had to become one.

Who was the man living upstairs? He seemed honest with what he shared, but how would she know? And he'd certainly shared very little, really. Maybe that whole thing about those Indians had been meant to disarm her. It had worked fairly well, but how would she know truth from lie with this man?

She felt a welcome stiffening of her spine as she put away the leftovers, including two big stacks of fresh tortillas, and washed the pans. If she was going to work on breaking down her walls with men, Austin was the last man on earth she ought to try it with.

He had secrets upon secrets. *He* might not even be sure who he really was any longer. Gage had sort of warned her, hadn't he, with that stuff about finding the person he'd left behind. Well, Austin would never be who he used to be. Some things changed a person forever, as well she knew. He certainly hadn't had time to settle on the man he'd become.

He'd admitted that he didn't trust anyone anymore, and she wondered if his distrust included himself. It might. Six years undercover had probably taught him some things about himself that he didn't like. She couldn't imagine it wouldn't. Now he had to deal with that along with everything else.

In short, the guy was a mess. Gage had warned her. So why the hell had she begun to lie awake at night fantasizing about him? It hadn't happened right away, but at some point in the past couple of days, the initial attraction she had felt then squashed had returned big-time.

But maybe that was because he was safe in a way. He wasn't going to be here for long, he'd expressed no interest in her, other than an occasional look quickly turned away that she couldn't mistake even in her inexperience. So, yes, he'd evinced small moments of attraction to her, purely physical, but that was meaningless. She gave him credit for not acting on them.

Which left her exactly where? Indulging in fantasies as she lay in her lonely bed at night, fantasies that probably bore no resemblance to reality because she'd never even kissed a man, let alone gone any further.

Then she had a really ugly thought about herself. This whole tortilla thing. Had she done it to be neighborly or because she wanted his attention?

If she wanted his attention, was it only because he'd be gone in a relatively short time? Was she dancing close to the fire because she felt reasonably certain she couldn't get burned?

Was *she* using *him*?

She sat on the edge of the bed, surrounded by her comforting projects, and tried to figure herself out. Could she really be trying to batter down an old wall without regard to what that might do to him? Because he was pretty much in an emotional blender himself.

A wave of self-loathing rose in her. There were a lot of things she didn't like about herself, but now she had a new item to add to the list. She didn't like the way she was cowering from much of life. She knew she was a prisoner of her own fears, and it didn't make her very proud of herself.

In fact, sometimes it disgusted her, but not even disgust was enough to get her over the hump. Over time she had come to trust a small circle of men, like the sheriff and a number of others. Men she'd interacted with frequently for years. She could talk to them, share coffee with them, even invite them in once in a while as she had with Gage.

She was comfortable in this town, or comfortable enough, because the faces had become familiar over the years, but she'd let them just so close and no further. She only ever entirely relaxed with women.

It was a mental and emotional prison that not even a few years of therapy had been able to banish. Honestly, if she had seen Austin walking down the street before Gage had introduced him, she would have turned and walked the other way.

She didn't like being this way. It just was, and she had adapted as best she could.

So what was with the tortillas? She'd brought them home from Melinda's bakery when she could have just left a note for Austin that Melinda had made them. He could have picked them up tomorrow.

But no, she had decided to be nice, mainly to Melinda, who had gone out of her way to make them and deserved to sell them promptly. She'd brought them home, intending to put them in the refrigerator and leave a note for Austin.

Instead, for some unknown reason, she'd decided to try cooking some of them. Had she been hoping Austin would show up? She certainly hadn't expected it to turn into him cooking dinner and the two of them eating together.

All her reasoning at the time had seemed perfectly innocent, but it had ended in the most intimate time she had spent with a man ever: the two of them sharing a meal.

Maybe the most surprising part was that she hadn't run when he started cooking, rude or not. She wasn't incapable of it, although she was slowly getting better about it.

Still. She looked at herself and wondered if all her superficial reasons had been just that, superficial. There was no question that her subconscious controlled a huge part of her life. It made her afraid of strange men. It controlled her level of comfort or discomfort with people.

So how did she know what she'd really been thinking when she asked Melinda to make those tortillas, or when she had picked them up?

If it had been purely friendly, then she'd leaped a big hurdle and should be proud. If some other reason had been involved...

She sighed, her head whirling, and reached for her knitting. Was she ever going to get herself sorted out?

She'd been doing without many of the things that were part of a normal life ever since her mother's killing. Some of that was understandable, but after eighteen years, shouldn't she have come further?

And if she was trying to go further now, why had

she picked the one man who posed the most threat in every possible way. She didn't really know him, and he'd leave before long, which was a dangerous emotional game to play.

But maybe that was part of what she was doing here: trying to prove that she had good reason to avoid men, and any involvement with them. To prove that she was right to stay hunkered in her safe little hole.

It wouldn't surprise her. Not at all. But she had no business drawing Austin into whatever she was trying to do here. He had enough problems of his own.

She resolved then and there to firmly reestablish the distance between them. They'd both be better off.

Chapter 4

The Viking princess was driving him nuts. The thought amused Austin, but only mildly. After the tortilla thing, she'd pulled back into her tower and had taken to avoiding him as if he had the plague.

None of it made sense to him. He got her fear of men, which had led him to stay away as much as possible, then she'd reached out to him in the most traditional way imaginable: through his stomach. With food.

And now she was gone again. She worked long hours at her shop, but she seemed to have lengthened them. Unlike her baker friend, Melinda, she didn't have to get to work before the sun rose. But as soon as he stirred in the mornings, he heard her leave. By the time he came back in the evening, she was already hiding in her bedroom.

He didn't mind the long hours alone, walking around town and the countryside. They were settling him. But it was bothering him to be bothering Corey so much.

It also troubled him that he kept wanting to see her because she appealed to him so strongly. Physically, mentally, even emotionally, everything about her attracted him.

She was certainly beautiful. But apart from that, she

was in desperate need of something. So, was he stupid enough to imagine that he could rescue her? No, he didn't think he was that much of a fool. The kind of rescuing she needed was beyond him.

But that dinner…that bugged him. For a little while it seemed as if her fear had been gone. As if she'd been enjoying herself with him. Why should that frighten her back into hiding?

He tried to think of what he might have done wrong, but he couldn't imagine. She'd seemed willing enough to let him take over her kitchen. Not even the faintest sign of protest. She'd enjoyed the meal. She'd laughed and she'd smiled.

So what the hell?

Mahoney had a room over his bar he was willing to rent. If he could stand the constant odor of stale beer and the noise at night, anyway. So it would be possible to move out.

But he resisted the idea, mainly because he felt that whether or not Corey really wanted him in her house, she'd feel hurt or offended if he moved across town. He wouldn't be able to blame her for that. Nice place, kitchen privileges, reasonable rent…sacrificed to move above Mahoney's? Anyone would be offended.

But something had sure set her off. He wished she would talk to him, but she was staying so far away they'd need semaphore flags to communicate.

He still found her desirable, but he was long past the stage of life when that was a primary driver for him. Sex was fun, but laden with problems if you and your partner weren't on the same wavelength. Clearly, he and Corey weren't even at the same end of the spectrum.

He shook his head a little. Night was falling, he considered stopping at Mahoney's to play darts and have a few, but then decided he wasn't in the mood for it tonight. Nor was he in the mood for the backroom poker game.

Sometimes, he thought wryly, he wasn't too fond of the company of men, either.

He turned the corner and almost froze as he saw Corey at her front door. She was juggling a stack of mail and her keys. Oh, well, he thought, and closed the distance, anyway.

She started at the sound of his approaching footsteps, and some of the mail slipped from her grasp.

"Just me," he called out. "Let me help with that."

"Thanks." Her voice sounded a little wobbly.

Concern instantly filled him, and he quickened his step, trotting up onto the porch. "Are you okay?"

"Fine…" But her voice sounded thin. Then she gave an uneasy laugh. "I just got unnerved."

"I'm sorry."

"It wasn't you."

Curious, but keeping his questions to himself, he gathered the fallen mail from the porch planks while she unlocked the door. He followed her inside and when she dropped her armload on the hall table, he followed suit before he closed the door behind him.

Then he looked at her in the hall light. Her face was pinched and tight. "What's going on?" His tone made it clear that he wasn't going to let her get away without answering.

Her blue eyes finally settled on him and he couldn't mistake the worry in them.

"Corey?"

"It's probably a joke," she said.

"What?"

She picked up an envelope from the stack and passed it to him. Then she headed to the kitchen and he heard her making coffee.

He checked the envelope, noting that it had no return address but had been mailed locally. Then he stuck his fingers in and pulled out a small rectangle of paper.

I know about your mother.

If that was a joke, he thought, it was an unkind one. In fact, it was cruel. Disturbed, he followed Corey into the kitchen. The coffeemaker was already brewing and she was sitting at the table with her head in her hands.

"Are you okay?" he asked, not knowing what else to ask that wouldn't sound even stupider. He needed her to talk, explain. Say *something*.

"Yes. No. I—" She broke off and raised her head, looking absolutely haunted. "It's not funny."

"No, it's not funny at all. Not even a little bit. In fact, it's cruel. I can't imagine why anyone would do this."

Her lips trembled. She covered them with her hand, then said in a muffled voice, "I thought the first one was a joke."

"There's another one?" He felt everything inside him skip into high alert. "Do you still have it?"

"Drawer in the hall table."

He went to get it and found it immediately on top of some other papers. It looked exactly like the one that had just come, but he could see why she had thought it a joke. Alone, it would have seemed innocuous. Joined with the second note, it became anything but.

He carried both into the kitchen. "How long ago did you get this first one?"

"The day you moved in. I put it in the drawer just after Gage brought you here."

He put the letters facedown on the table, and without waiting for the pot to finish brewing, he poured her a cup.

"Here."

"Thank you." She cradled it without drinking, though, as if she needed to warm her hands. He sat across from her and turned the notes and envelopes over. "I should just burn them," she said.

"No, don't."

"Why not? They don't really say anything. Whoever the writer is just wants to upset me. I don't know why, but that's all they do. They bother me. It's not a threat."

He hesitated, reluctant to worry her more, finally settling on something relatively innocuous. "They're like puzzle pieces. If you get any more, we may figure out what this is about. Or who is doing it."

She shuddered and finally sipped some coffee. "I don't know if I want to know who's doing it."

"I think you do," he said firmly, wishing he had more to offer her. Given the way she looked right now, he'd have loved to give her a hug and tell her everything would be all right. It might be a lie, but the hug might comfort her. If he weren't a man, anyway.

"Why?" she asked, showing some of her normal spark.

"Because they're being mailed here in town."

He watched understanding wash over her. Her pale skin paled even more as she realized her castle was no longer a safe place. "It's got to be a joke," she whispered.

"I sure as hell hope so. But anybody who'd think this is funny deserves a good lesson."

"We'll never know," she insisted quietly. "No return address. Fingerprints? If any are left, do you think the sheriff is going to waste time on something like this?"

Probably not, he thought as he studied the notes and envelopes. She was right, there was no threat here. It could just be a sick joke. This might be the end of it, too.

He looked at the notes side by side. Ink-jet printer, unrevealing. Cheap paper. Cheap self-sealing envelopes that you could buy just about anywhere. Self-adhesive stamps. Lifting the envelopes, he sniffed them, smelled only paper and glue. The notes themselves were no better. Paper often picked up odors but this offered none.

Which, he supposed, could be a clue itself. A useless clue at this point. No aftershave, no tobacco odor, no scent of marijuana, not even a cooking aroma. Then he sniffed the newest note again, and caught a faint whiff of something.

"Corey? Is there a smell on this paper?"

Surprise widened her eyes, but she took it from him and brought it to her nose. "No. Why…" Then she paused and sniffed again. "Beer?" she asked finally. "But it's so faint I'm not sure."

"Me, neither." A bazillion people drank beer. Useless. When she handed the paper back to him, he tucked each note in its proper envelope. "It was worth a shot," he said more to himself than her.

"It's just somebody's idea of a sick joke," she said again. "Probably some teenager with a warped sense of humor who just heard about what happened to my mother. It's been a long time, Austin. There's no reason anyone else would bring it up now. Anything people wanted to say about the murder was said a long time ago. It's practically forgotten."

Except by one person, he thought, looking at the envelopes again. *No, make that two.* How likely was it that some teen would be hearing the story at this late date? Eighteen years was a long time. Corey was right about that. Collective amnesia had probably set in among the people of this town quite a while ago. Yesterday's news, and all that.

Eighteen years didn't even add up to any kind of anniversary to be recalled, unless someone remembered it every year. The only person likely to mark that anniversary annually was Corey herself.

His apprehension should have been easy to dismiss unless something else happened, but some instinct wouldn't allow him to let go of it. Too many years of living a paranoid life? Maybe.

He studied Corey again, deciding he didn't at all like the way she looked. He had to do something to lift that cloud from her face, but the distrust that lay between them, especially on her side, wasn't going to make it easy.

That part of him that had been so carefully nurtured all these years undercover reminded him that she could have sent these notes to herself. To what end, he wasn't sure. Looking at the postmarks, he could clearly see that the first one had been sent two days before he arrived in town. So it couldn't be to get his attention.

Or the sheriff's, it seemed, because if it were, she'd be on the phone to him right now. So what purpose would she have in doing this herself?

He hated thinking this way, but this kind of thinking had kept him out of a wringer more than once. Very little was what it seemed, including Viking princesses. Everyone had a public face and a private face. He knew that as well as anyone, and he knew very little about this woman. How could he, when she avoided him?

All right, then. He didn't know what was going on here. He had no idea if this woman had the kinds of problems that would cause her to seek attention this way. No idea why anyone else should want to upset her.

Lacking information wasn't new to him, but it never made him feel comfortable. So he'd hang and watch, and see what developed, if anything. In the meantime, he could do himself some good just by finding a way to try to bring her smile back.

"Quesadillas," he said.

She stopped staring at the envelopes long enough to give him a confused look. "What?"

"I'm going to make some quesadillas. They're easy. And it just so happens that my favorite baker sold me some very nice tortillas this morning. They're in the fridge."

She started to rise, reaching for her coffee cup. "I'll get out of your way."

"No, you don't. If I'm going to make them, I can make one for you without any extra trouble. The nice thing about being stateside again," he said, flashing a smile he didn't quite feel, "is how many things are more convenient. You won't see me shredding the cheese, for example. Or making the green-chili sauce. You have a very accommodating grocery."

"I do?"

"Yeah. He ordered the exact green-chili salsa I wanted. And a few other items. So let me get you some fresh coffee and I'll get to work."

After he freshened her coffee, he took the letters out and put them back in the hall table. He would think more about them later. Right now, he wanted to see Rapunzel smile.

Hell, he ought to get himself out of here before he let those thoughts go any further. Then he wondered why his mind should even run in such a direction. He'd faced a lot of danger, much more realistic danger, than any this woman could pose. So the only excuse he could have was that he had his own problems to work through so he could find his way back to some kind of life, and that didn't leave energy for Corey's problems. That was so selfish he could hardly believe it occurred to him.

Was that the man he had become? God, he hoped not.

When he got back to the kitchen, he thought Corey

looked a little better. Her color had returned and her face had relaxed.

"What can I do to help?" she asked.

"Admire my culinary expertise."

Corey laughed quietly at that, and he figured they'd gotten over the rough patch, at least for now. The real joke was how simple it was to make quesadillas.

"This is another one of those cool, anything-goes recipes, but tonight it's going to be straight cheese and salsa. Another night I might make them with chicken or other veggies."

It didn't take him long at all, and soon she had a folded quesadilla, sliced into triangles, in front of her. "Don't wait for me. I'll only be a minute here."

He made a couple of them for himself, then sat with her at the table. She was still poking at it with a finger.

"Too hot?" he asked.

"I think it's almost cool enough." She shrugged. "Melted cheese. I got burned on it once, and it sticks. So you put the green salsa inside?"

He nodded, surprised that he was impatient to see whether she liked it. Finally she lifted a triangle and bit. A smile dawned on her face as she chewed.

"Good?"

She nodded. Satisfied, he began to eat his own.

"You're going to change my whole diet," she said between mouthfuls. "I love these tortillas, and you make some really tasty food with them."

"Mexican, Texican, Tex-Mex, they're all good. Maybe someone should serve some of it around here. Do you like hot foods? Because I've been missing some really good chili peppers."

"How hot?"

"Well, in Mexico a pepper isn't hot unless it brings tears to your eyes. And when you've been eating them your whole life, that's got to be a really hot pepper."

"I don't think I'm ready for that." But she was smiling again, looking comfortable again. In fact, more comfortable than he could remember her looking around him. More like the way she looked in her store among her friends.

Good? Bad? Only time would tell. Apparently they'd found common ground over tortillas. A smile danced across his face. Tortillas. Of all things.

"I like your friend Melinda," he remarked. "Very nice lady."

"She's a doll," Corey agreed.

"She said she's amazed how popular the fresh tortillas are. She's thinking about adding burritos to her lunch menu. I gave her some tips. I don't know if burritos will be such a big deal around here, but I'm glad she's not making tortillas just for me."

"Give her half a chance and she'll be making burritos for breakfast, lunch and dinner."

"I was in a lot of homes where beans and chilies were always simmering over the fire. Like a stockpot, only better. It was never turned off, and ingredients were continually added. Occasionally, extra chilies for flavor. People just walked by, grabbed a tortilla, scooped some of that concoction on it and kept on walking and eating."

"So there's no exact mealtime in Mexico?"

"Oh, there is. It's not that people don't have full dressed-out meals when they can afford it. But it's not so easy for the hardworking lower-income groups. You can eat anytime of day if you need to, get right back to your work and nothing gets wasted. Some of the best food in the world is peasant food."

"I've heard that before."

She had nearly finished her quesadilla, and he asked if she would like another. She immediately shook her head. "It tasted so good I could just keep on eating, but I'm stuffed."

Which exhausted the entire subject of tortillas and quesadillas. He wanted to sigh. He couldn't seem to get started with this woman, an unusual state of affairs for him. By nature, he could be gregarious when he needed to. He made friends easily. That was part of what had made him so good at his job. But this woman kept impeding him. Something about her was so closed off, he couldn't seem to really get past the barrier. Everything remained superficial.

Except for her reaction to those notes.

She really *was* locked in a cage or a prison, and calling her a princess and likening her to hiding within a castle didn't really get to the root of the ugly turn her life had taken. Not a princess in a castle, but a prisoner behind a moat that was guarded by the unknown dragon who had killed her mother.

However he tried to look at the situation for his own comfort, the fact remained that this was no fairy tale, and Corey might as well be locked in a cell, emotionally speaking. She had her friends, she had her shop, but a big chunk of her resided in an ugly jail. A barren jail.

Damn. All his readjustment difficulties seemed paltry by comparison. Self-indulgent, in fact. Time would sort him out. Even eighteen years hadn't been enough for Corey. Maybe the thing she needed most was to put a face to her mother's killer, but at this late date that didn't seem likely to happen.

His mind wandered to those notes again. If she had really managed to dismiss them as a sick prank, more power to her. But he'd lived on the underside so long that he couldn't do that. Pranks like this occurred for a reason, and none of the reasons he could think of were innocent.

Someone wanted to upset her and eventually scare her, if he hadn't scared her already. Austin just had to hope that was as far as this *cabrón* wanted to go.

She offered to do the dishes again because he had cooked, but this time he refused to be sent on his way so easily.

"No, I'd like to help," he said, brooking no argument. "It's not like I just put out ten courses of five-star cuisine."

"It *was* five-star cuisine," she said, but her smile didn't quite reach her eyes. His fault? Or the fault of those notes? No way to know, no way to ask. He wondered if he'd ever had such a hard time with anyone. Even working his way into a gang had seemed easier than this. At least he had gotten feedback, whether good or bad.

He washed while she dried, which gave his mind

the opportunity to dance back over the years. At first, when he'd arrived in Mexico as an agent, familiarity had washed over him. It was a big and varied country with pockets of culture that reached back further than the Western history of the place. It was possible, still, to get far enough off the beaten track to places where almost no Spanish was spoken and religion was a mish-mash of Christian and much older beliefs. But along the border, that often wasn't as obvious, at least not in most of the places he'd had to hang out. Just as Mexican culture had seeped into Texas, the North American way of life had seeped into Mexico, creating a colorful, interesting blend.

So, for a couple of days he'd felt quite at home, settling in, meeting people, establishing a background of having come from a town near Mexico City, re-creating himself as someone who liked adventure and money both. He'd sounded out a few people about work opportunities north of the border, leaving around little bits that might attract attention.

But this time he had not just been a *turista,* and that had changed his perspective hugely. He remembered being acutely aware that things were going on around him, things he wasn't supposed to notice, things he couldn't ask about, things he shouldn't know. As if there was a layering in the bright, seemingly friendly and sunny world. Beneath it lay darkness.

It was the darkness he'd been after, but it was sealed off from him, a big, blank steel wall. He'd bided his time, working on becoming part of the background, all the while losing his sense of having come home. Instead, he sharpened himself and waited.

He finally met a *coyote,* one of the guys who led people over the border through the desert. They'd danced around for a few weeks, until finally the guy had offered to help him cross the border for a huge sum of money. At that point, Austin had sent up the flare he'd been waiting to fire.

"I don't need you, man," he told the coyote. "Me, I'd rather spend the money on a gun and take myself across."

Then he'd asked quietly where he could buy one, and not just any gun. No *pistola* for him. Money had exchanged hands and he'd been given an address.

The moment he crossed the threshold, he knew he was in the middle of it. There were only two ways that could end, and one of them was with him being buried in the desert sand.

"Austin?"

He looked up, recalled to the present, and he realized he was standing at the sink, soapy water in front of him, dishes all washed.

"Are you okay?"

"Fine," he answered. "I was just remembering." He turned slowly to look at Corey. She appeared calm now, easier within herself, but a crease of concern etched itself between her brows.

"I was remembering," he said, "the day I met up with the gunrunners for the first time. Everybody's got their turf, you know? I stepped on somebody's turf and they thought I might be from the competition."

Her eyes widened. "Were you scared?"

One corner of his mouth ticked up. "Only a fool doesn't get afraid. I was there on purpose, but I knew the dangers. I was a walking corpse when I passed through that door. I just needed to make sure I was still breathing when I came out."

Corey dropped the towel, then sank onto a kitchen chair. "I can't imagine being that brave."

"More likely you aren't that stupid."

She shook her head quickly. "Don't put yourself down like that. You knew you could have been killed but you did your job, anyway."

"So I was brash, young and a bit of an adrenaline junkie."

"How old were you?"

"Your age right now. Twenty-five. Young enough to feel a bit invincible, I guess."

"I don't feel invincible," she remarked. Her voice seemed to tighten.

"But you're a woman."

Her head snapped up. "What does that have to do with it?"

"Women seem to grow sense earlier than men."

To his relief, she relaxed again and actually laughed. "I wouldn't know."

"Take my word for it. Ask me today if I'd take the job I just finished, and I'd say no. For a lot of reasons, but mainly because I damn well know I'm not bulletproof."

Again, the landscape of her face changed, reflecting shock. "Did you get shot?"

"Close enough. But no, I didn't get shot." He'd had

plenty of other bad experiences, though, enough to drive some real sense into his head.

She put her chin in her hand. "You've certainly had an adventurous life."

"Do you wish you had?" It was the bluntest he'd been with her, and he waited to see if her drawbridge would slam into place. After all, she'd been frank about her distrust of men.

But she didn't react immediately. Instead, she seemed to think it over. "I guess," she said slowly, "some part of me does. I told you I wanted to see the Mexican pyramids."

"Then go. Get some of your girlfriends together and go."

The drawbridge slammed closed right then, with an almost audible bang. "You just don't get it, do you?" she said angrily.

"Get what?"

"I've been away from here. There's a world out there, all right. I've experienced it. It killed my mother."

A few seconds later he was sitting alone in the kitchen, the aroma of quesadillas still hanging in the air, listening to the silence of a graveyard full of dead dreams.

Chapter 5

Corey awoke after a restless night. Sleep had turned into a battle, leaving her feeling exhausted. Her head ached and her body felt as if she had slept on rocks.

Fragments of dreams sifted through her mind as she sat up, none of them making any sense. It was as if she were skipping through a disorganized photo album, a flash of this, a flash of that, with nothing to piece it together. Austin making the quesadillas. Her shop. Her quilting group, which provided some of the greatest fun because the women liked to work together on projects. The sheriff. Her grandmother Cora. Her aunt Lucy. Austin again, this time looking like a huge black shadow of risk.

God! She threw the covers back and climbed out of bed, hoping to shake off the images. It was as if her subconscious had opened in her sleep and tossed up a hodgepodge from her life.

She had barely taken a step when another image from sleep grabbed her, freezing her. Austin. Holding her. Murmuring something to her. Her insides sizzling in response. Her entire body reaching out for him.

Oh, boy, she was losing it. She headed for the shower,

telling herself her dream about Austin was an aberration, even though she knew it really wasn't. She might be afraid of men, but that didn't make her immune to a desire for all the things women wanted: a husband, family, children.

Sex.

The thought of that at once made her toes curl and her entire body shudder. Austin definitely turned her on, but the idea of letting any man that close to her turned her off almost as quickly. Somewhere in a place she couldn't remember, she had seen what at least one man was capable of. Argue with herself as she might, she couldn't mend the scar that had left deep within her. Men could be nice. She knew a handful of them around here that she'd let get close enough to know a bit. But they were all safe men, married men. They posed no threat. A stranger was a whole different level of concern.

For all he seemed nice enough, Austin had spent six years in a dangerous job. A job that probably meant he could be dangerous, too. Possibly even violent. A flutter of panic passed through her as she stood beneath the shower spray. She had let him into her house, and a little way into her life, yet he was a huge unknown. Being in law enforcement was no guarantee that a guy was trustworthy. She could watch and read the news like anyone else. Bad apples existed everywhere.

Possibly right inside her house. What the hell was she thinking?

She rested her head against the wall beneath the spray and let the water beat on her shoulders and back. If she was trying to break through her intractable fear at last, she could have chosen someone safer to try it with.

She needed to get out of here, get away, get to her shop. She didn't want to see Austin. Somehow they had gotten too close for her comfort last night. He'd be gone in two months, so she just had to figure out how to avoid him. No more cozy meals while he talked of Mexico.

He'd gone through a door as a *walking corpse?* He'd really said that. It had shocked her, but now the expression penetrated. It was a measure of the kind of life he had lived. The way he had lived. He might have been one of the good guys, but she couldn't begin to imagine the things he must have seen and done to survive. What was she doing trusting him even a little bit?

You're losing it, said that cockamamy voice in her head that occasionally popped up, often with unwanted commentary. If she wanted to build her first real bridge of trust, she should have chosen better. She should have chosen someone who'd been around her entire life. Someone she'd gone to school with. Anyone but a smoldering, dangerous undercover agent.

Dang, did he smolder. She'd been pushing that awareness away successfully since she'd met him, but his mere presence lighted the long-ignored and -buried libido that nothing could take away. Normal women had normal needs. Sooner or later they were going to escape the bondage of her determination.

Stepping out of the shower, she toweled off and thought she heard Austin leave. Good. Breakfast in peace. Well, as much peace as she could muster after that note yesterday.

She gave Austin credit for not dismissing her reaction to it. Even now she felt a creeping unease, like something cold and slimy were climbing her spine. Who would write something like that and why? Worse, why a second note? The first one had caused her barely a ripple, but the second seemed to place weight on both of them.

She hated to think that someone around here might simply be toying with her for their own amusement, but it was possible. As with any community on the planet, Conard City harbored all kinds of people. Probably even people sick enough to think this was funny.

The culprit had to be a kid. Someone who had no idea how her mother's murder had impacted her. Someone who had no idea of what it was like to lose a loved one. Someone with a warped sense of humor who meant no serious harm.

The voice in her head popped up again. *I've got a bridge I could sell you.*

"Oh, stop it!" She snapped the words out loud and finished dressing in khaki slacks and a royal-blue polo. Jogging shoes followed since she'd be on her feet most of the day.

The scent of coffee met her nose the instant she stepped out of her room. Austin must have made some before he left.

As she turned the corner into the kitchen, however, she got a shock. He was sitting at the table with a mug of his own. It looked as if he was waiting for her.

She froze. "I thought you'd left."

"I went out to get the paper for you."

"Thank you." Feeling as if her joints were stiff, she

walked over to the pot and poured herself a cup. "Thanks for making coffee, too."

"No hay problema."

"Does that mean no problem?" she asked, tentatively sitting at the table.

"Oh, sorry. Yeah. It's not a problem. No problem. You're welcome. All purpose." He shook his head, giving her a crooked little smile. "I think I was dreaming in Spanish again."

"Do you do that? Really?" Some of her tension slipped away.

"Sure. I always have, on and off. My dreams are bilingual. But dreaming in Spanish was a good thing when I was in Mexico. Imagine the consternation if I'd started speaking English in my sleep."

A totally unexpected bubble of laughter rose from her stomach and popped out. "Not good."

"Very not good. I'd have had a lot of explaining to do. Nobody's ever told me I talk in my sleep, but you never know. It only needs to happen once."

She was amazed to feel a tiny spark of jealousy at the idea that anyone had shared a bed with him long enough to know whether he sleep talked. But, of course, people had. Women had. He was thirtysomething and probably had had at least a few girlfriends.

In fact, she couldn't imagine that he didn't have to fight women off. She looked down at the newspaper, afraid her face might reveal something. It wasn't just that he was good-looking, but that he had that smoldering look. The Latin lover. She might have laughed at herself if this train of thought wasn't making her so aware of her own inexperience.

He saved her with an unexpected comment. "You said your grandmother and aunt brought you here?"

She nodded.

He sighed. "You've sure had your share of loss. I guess I've been damn lucky. Both parents. Check. Two brothers, check. Too many cousins to count, check. Nieces and nephews. Check. When we get together, we make half a town."

She lifted her head, interested. "Do you all get together often?"

"Annual family reunion that I've been missing for a while. One year at the *finca,* the next in San Antonio."

"Your mother's family, too?"

"Of course. Let me tell you, *chica,* that when you marry into a Latino family, you're *family.* You and all your relatives, at least those who want to be part of it."

"So your mom's family wants to be part?"

"As far as I know, all of them always did. My dad jokes that they were a little reserved at first, but the Mendez family cured them."

"That's really neat."

"That's the way it is. Of course, when we fight we can get just as passionate." He was smiling, his dark eyes dancing. "No Hatfields-and-McCoys stuff, but I had two uncles who didn't speak for ten years."

"How'd they get over it?"

"Their wives had had enough. I never got all the details."

Another laugh escaped her. "It sounds amazing."

"It can be. It's not perfect. Nothing is. But we hang together pretty well. We squabble, we spit, we make up and start all over again. We're very passionate people."

A shiver ran through her as he said that, but it wasn't at all unpleasant. "But you got both sides of that?"

"Let's just say I can play the reserved bit when I need to. But it general I don't think people are naturally reserved. I think it's cultural, what's acceptable and what's not."

"You might be right."

"Now, I don't know you very well, but so far, you seem pretty reserved to me. Stiff upper lip, soldier on, all that. Very ladylike and upper-crust."

She blinked. "Me? No way."

He laughed quietly. "I'm not criticizing you at all. Maybe I'm just experiencing some more cultural transitioning, and noticing things I wouldn't otherwise notice."

She bit her lip, then asked, "Was it hard to come back?"

"Depends on what you mean by hard. I came back pretty angry, I can tell you that."

"Why?"

"Because they left me rotting in a Mexican jail long enough that I got severely beaten several times and had three broken ribs. I got carted out on a stretcher."

Shock and horror rippled through Corey. "Why so long?"

He shrugged. "They didn't want to blow my cover."

"My God." All she could do was shake her head at the dreadfulness of his experience. Her stomach knotted just thinking about it. "I can see why you wouldn't want to do it again."

"It wasn't all fun and games, but the job needed doing. Right now I'm glad I did it, and I'm glad I don't have to do it again."

"So what's in your future? A desk job?"

"Or training position. I'm not sure."

"But you can't go home yet?" She knew she'd already asked about that, but conversation over breakfast was definitely something she wasn't used to. Any subject would do.

"Not for a while. I'd hate to run into someone on the street who recognized me."

There was so much more she wanted to know but was afraid to ask. She figured he probably couldn't get into much detail about what he'd actually done, and, very likely, he didn't want to. "I'm sorry you can't go home."

He surprised her with a wink. "Well, I could bleach my hair and grow a mustache. Think I'd look like a surfer?"

Despite what he'd told her, the instant she pictured him with blond hair and a mustache, a giggle burst out of her.

"No way, huh? Oh, well." Then he dropped the rakish grin. "What about you, Corey? Do you have anyone?"

"Not anymore," she admitted. "Friends, but no family."

"And you don't know anything about your dad?"

"I must have had one." Discomfort began to fill her again. This was not something to discuss with a stranger. Then what he had said about her reserve hit her. She *was* reserved. Maybe too much. It felt awkward when he'd opened up about his own family. "I don't know who he was. I suppose my mother did, but he wasn't from around here. Apparently she got pregnant when she was out of town. I don't know. Then a while after she had me, we moved to Denver."

"I don't know whether I should say I'm sorry."

"I gather she wasn't. Grandma and Aunt Lucy both said she was happy to be pregnant and didn't seem at all concerned about my father. So maybe he was a mistake. Anyway, my family were all black Irish. Dark hair, blue eyes. They joked that my mom must have met up with a Viking." She touched her long blond hair.

He smiled. "I've been thinking you looked like a Viking princess."

That remark reached past all her walls and barriers, settling into her guarded heart with heat. Even as alarms went off, reminding her that she had so many problems dealing with men and this could lead nowhere at all, another part of her welcomed the totally unique thawing inside. Maybe she could get past her hang-ups? Just once?

Sheer craziness. It wouldn't happen. On the few occasions she'd been asked on a date, she'd struggled to say yes but always said no. Her psychological block was too big to get around.

Finally, she'd just started freezing men out of her life. It had been a long time since any man had asked her out, almost as if her aura deflected them. It had been a relief to her to be left alone and not have to deal with those awkward moments any longer.

So what the heck was she doing now? Toying with

something she knew to be an impossibility? Austin was attractive, all right. Women probably swooned as he walked down the street. But he was not for her.

She rose. "I need to get to work."

"You haven't eaten," he said mildly.

"I'll get something at the bakery." Then she grabbed her lightweight jacket and wallet, and scrambled out the door.

The man was confusing her, making her want and need things she didn't want to want or need. This was not good.

Austin sat in her wake, bemused and maybe a little concerned. Had he gone too far too fast by talking about his family, then asking about hers? It seemed like such an innocent conversation, the kind of thing most people talked about willingly enough. All he'd been trying to do was encourage her to be more comfortable with him.

She was an extraordinarily attractive young woman, though, and the way she was living her life told him all he needed to know about her trauma. Men around here weren't blind. They should have been beating a path to her door. Instead, there was nary a one in sight.

Remarkable.

He ate a few tortillas, finished another cup of coffee and then set out. Today he had a mission, one he was sure Corey wouldn't like. Too bad. While she was insisting on remaining in her cell, someone needed to deal with the big bad world.

Ten minutes later he entered Gage Dalton's office in the rear of the sheriff's department. Gage wore his full tan uniform, except for the cowboy hat that hung on a coat tree in one corner. He leaned back, the springs of his chair creaking, and waved Austin to sit across from him in one of the two battered chairs.

"You see what's on my desk?" Gage remarked.

Austin nodded. A stack of papers on one side, a computer on the other. In between were writing instruments, a family photo and a nameplate that looked as if it made a habit of falling to the floor.

Gage pointed. "Paper." Then he pointed again. "Computer." Then he waved to the corner where a printer stood on a stand. "Printer."

"So?"

"Back twenty-five years ago, maybe thirty, someone told me that switching to computers would eliminate paper."

Austin started to laugh before the sheriff finished.

"Exactly. If you ask me," Gage said, "all they've done is multiply the amount of paper. Why? Because you can't really trust this dang machine not to flip its lid. Lose things. Crash. Whatever. So we fill out our reports, print them out, file them in a good old-fashioned filing cabinet, and all I can say for this machine is that it's made carbon paper and correction fluid obsolete."

Still laughing, Austin said, "Ah, but email."

"Nuisance." But then Gage paused, his dark eyes twinkling. "Enough of being a curmudgeon. What do you think of our town?"

"It's growing on me. The longer I'm around, the friendlier people get. Pretty soon I'll be part of the background."

"I bet you're good at that. Getting along okay at Corey's?"

"Fine. But I want to talk to you about that."

"Depends on which that."

Austin nodded his understanding. "I want to know about her mother's murder. I need to understand. She doesn't remember, but it certainly left her terrified."

"Makes her a bit difficult to deal with sometimes," Gage agreed. "She keeps her circle tight and mostly confined to women."

"You knew that when you took me over there. So why did you inflict me on her?"

Gage frowned. "Is she making you feel that way?"

"No, but I've got a picture of what's going on here and I need to understand. You put me in play for a reason, Gage. There's a room over Mahoney's, and I'm sure you knew it."

"Of course I did. I used to live there."

"So maybe you can tell me why you took me to Corey knowing she's afraid of men."

Gage sighed. "Hope."

"Hope?"

"Yeah, hope." He leaned forward, wincing a bit, and put his crossed arms on the desk. "That woman needs to break out of her shell. I watched her grow up, and it's really bothering me that she can't seem to get past what happened."

"So why me?"

"Lots of reasons. Handy excuse because you needed a place to stay. After I checked up on you, you seemed to be trustworthy. You're someone she doesn't know and already have a pattern with. Plus, you must be pretty good at getting into closed circles."

Austin wasn't at all sure he liked this. "So you manipulated the two of us?"

"You could say that. Or you could just say I was hoping she might find a wedge so she could peek out of her shell. I'm not asking you to do anything. I was just hoping it might turn into a good mixture. There's always that room over Mahoney's if you're furious."

"You wanted me to con her."

Gage slammed a hand down on his desk, clearly angry now. "Absolutely not. If I had for one minute thought that was possible, I'd never have let you stay in this town, let alone Corey's house."

"Then what the hell do you mean by me being good at getting into closed circles?"

"That's what you did in Mexico, wasn't it? It's a gift. How you use it can make it a con. But you're not a con artist. You were a freaking agent doing a god-awful job, which I well know since I did it myself. I pretended a lot on the job, but never off the job. Did I mismeasure you?"

Austin glared right back. "No."

"I didn't think so. And what you do or don't do with Corey is between the two of you. I'm not working any angle at all here, just hoping like I said. Nobody in this damn town was getting past her walls, and she sure as hell isn't traveling. I figured you might get her interested enough to come out of her shell a bit. I also figured you must be sensitive enough not to break the eggs, so to speak. If that's a crime, leave."

Austin wanted to stay angry. He was feeling used.

He figured Corey would feel the same if she guessed, not that he was going to tell her. But he also saw Gage's point. The man was concerned about a young woman. Evidently he'd been concerned for some time. So he'd taken a flier. He even understood Gage's reasoning, because he was the last person on earth who wanted to inflict harm on some innocent person. He'd just spent six years avoiding that with every means at his disposal, six years trying to protect people he didn't know and would never meet.

"I just wish you'd have told me."

Gage gave a crooked, humorless smile. "That would have worked real well."

Probably not, Austin admitted to himself. In fact, he'd have found another place to try to get himself together again. Instead, he'd found Corey, and her whole mess was focusing him again in a way he thought he'd lost indefinitely. He might not be doing her much good, but she was doing some for him.

"Let's move on," he said finally. "Tell me about the murder. About Corey."

"You have a reason for that?"

"Yeah. I'll tell you when I have the picture."

Gage told him, and it wasn't pretty. A gunshot would have been bad enough, but as a child, Corey had witnessed her mother being stabbed over thirty times. The assailant had left no clue at all. Corey, covered with blood, had been taken out of the room in a nearly catatonic state. She hadn't spoken for days, hadn't cried, had spent all her time trying to hide.

Austin swore fluently in two languages. "And no leads?"

"Zip."

"So the murderer might have even been a woman?"

"The Denver P.D. is pretty sure the culprit was a man, from the angle of the wounds and the strength of them. Then, there's Corey's fear of men."

"True. Well, from the sound of it, it's probably better that she can't remember anything."

"A blessing," said Gage. "Besides, what if she did remember? Any description of the assailant she might give us would probably be useless. She was a child, she was in shock, and I doubt she'd remember much except what happened to her mother. The guy might even have had his face concealed."

Austin sat pensively for a few moments. "Does everyone here know that she can't remember?"

"I can't answer that factually, but if you want my suspicion, then yes, most folks probably know that. Her grandmother Cora talked about it some with her friends. I imagine it made it to the furthest reaches of the grapevine."

Austin was intimately acquainted with rumor mills like that. They'd served him well and often. "Well, there went that, then."

"What?"

"The day I arrived, Corey got an anonymous note in the mail. She dismissed it as a prank, but at the same time she was uneasy enough to keep it. It was mailed in town here."

"What did it say?"

"'I remember you but you don't remember me.'"

Gage's eyes narrowed. "Why do I think that's not the last of it?"

"Because it's not. She got another one yesterday. Same M.O. This one said, 'I know about your mother.'"

"Well, damn," Gage said sharply.

"She's trying to treat the notes as a sick joke, but I don't think she truly believes it. I can't dismiss it."

"Hell, no," Gage agreed, drumming his fingers rapidly.

"The thing is, there's nothing in these notes that couldn't probably be said by anyone who knows about what happened. It's the two of them together that make me worry. No threat, just a kind of torment for Corey. Frankly, Gage, I have little patience for tormentors."

"Even less when they might keep it up, or make it worse. She doesn't need this, joke or not."

Austin didn't answer. This was Gage's town. He knew it inside and out. Austin was on the outside here and needed a whole lot more information than he had right now.

"Did you bring the notes?"

"No. Got a warrant? They're not mine, I'm not operating in an official capacity, and anyway, I don't want to betray her trust. I did look them over pretty closely when she and I talked about them last night. No identifiable markings, cheap paper, cheap envelopes, self-sticking stamps. Hell, even the envelope flaps are self-sticking. They appear to have been printed on an inkjet printer."

"Address, too?"

"Yes."

"So what you're saying is this guy may have taken great steps to ensure he can't be traced. No DNA, no fingerprints…"

"That's a hunch based on the fact that he wouldn't have had to lick the envelope. But what does it mean, anyway, Gage? How likely is it that if you got a print or DNA off those letters that it would be useful? You know most of that stuff is only of use once you have the perp."

"But it does make me wonder about the intent behind the notes. Anything else?"

"We thought we smelled beer on one of the notes, but it was so faint we couldn't be sure. That means about half the population."

"Great." Gage again drummed his fingers briefly. "We have similar backgrounds, you and I. If your nose and mine agree, we're going with our noses."

Austin nodded. "I'll keep sharp. I definitely don't like the way this smells."

"Me, neither, but I've been wrong before."

"Let's hope we both are." Austin rose, but Gage stopped him just before he opened the office door.

"Austin? When she was in high school, Corey took gym classes in the martial arts or something. I won't go into all the psychological claptrap about why she probably did that. I'm sure you can figure it out yourself."

"Pretty much. And?"

"There's a gym over at the high school and another at the junior college. Try to persuade her to refresh a bit. Maybe with you. Just let me know, I'll make sure she can use one or the other during off-hours if she doesn't want to be in a crowd."

That was a good idea, Austin thought. He was sure he could talk her into it. He was starting to get the measure of Corey.

Then he thought of the child Gage had described, nearly catatonic, not speaking for days, hiding from everyone. A crack opened wide in his heart. It wasn't that he hadn't seen children who had suffered similar experiences. The world was full of them. But to do his job, he'd had to keep his focus on other things. Trust other people to take care of the world's waifs.

Now he had a waif of his very own. He was absolutely certain that Corey would hate knowing he thought of her that way for even an instant, though.

She'd be right, of course. Hunkered down though she might be, she was no longer that traumatized seven-year-old. She'd built herself a decent, if limited, life and seemed to handle things very well.

But there was still a monster in her closet, and all of a sudden, for no evident reason, it seemed to be trying to creep out.

Damn, what was going on here?

Austin had evidently decided that whether she liked it or not, he was through keeping out of her way. He was in the kitchen when Corey got home, and delicious aromas filled the house. Dropping her sewing bag near the door, she wandered in and found him at the stove, wearing a bibbed barbecue apron. He turned when he heard her and flapped it at her. "You like? I thought about getting one covered with tulips because I liked the pink frill around the edge..."

Her laughter interrupted him.

"Okay, I guess this was the better choice. How was your day?"

"Great," she said, actually touched that he'd asked. "We started a new quilt. It'll be embroidered butterflies, each set in a white block edged with blue. The butterflies are going to be a challenge, but it'll get more of my ladies involved."

"Why is that?"

"Because we'll have the sewing group make the butterflies, the embroidery group decorate them and the quilting group piece it all together."

"That sounds like some kind of project."

"It's going to be auctioned for charity, so it's worth it. Plus, everyone is having fun. I like it when we come up with projects that everyone can participate in."

"You forgot your knitters and crocheters."

"They're working on a different project. What are you making?"

"A feast. I hope you don't mind, but I'm craving my native cuisine again. Tamales tonight, along with chili con queso, guacamole and some corn chips."

"Um, wow."

"I hope that's a good *um*."

"It is. What's in a tamale?"

"Basically cornmeal. Think of them like dumplings, except I found some chorizo to add to them."

She sat with a thump. "You found chorizo *here*?"

"Like I said, you have a very friendly grocer. Now he's asking me for recipes."

She gaped at him. "You should have gotten the apron with the tulips."

He laughed so hard she thought she saw the sparkle of a tear in his eyes, and she joined him, holding her sides.

"Actually," he said when he caught his breath, "I may be in danger of being asked to give cooking lessons at the market. I made extra tamales so I can bring some by in the morning."

Amazement filled Corey. Conard County was a friendly place, but it generally took strangers a little while to knit themselves in, and a lot of them never came to be regarded as "locals." This guy had been here just a short time and the grocer was asking him for recipes? Food as an international ambassador, she thought. She realized she was catching a glimpse of the man who had gone south of the border undercover. He'd had to knit himself in there, too.

She supposed that ought to make her suspicious of him, the ease with which he fit himself in, but she actually admired it. This was her hometown, yet she had never felt as if she really fit. More like a puzzle piece that didn't quite press into the hole that it had once been part of.

"He also got me some poblanos, too. They're a mild pepper, and I may make chiles rellenos tomorrow. That recipe goes back maybe five thousand years, but it hasn't lost any flavor in the meantime."

She giggled again, and gave herself up to the experience.

"Although," he added almost ruefully, "I might have gotten carried away with tonight's dinner and we may have a lot of leftovers." He glanced over his shoulder. "Cooking for my family did not teach me how to cook for two."

Another little laugh escaped her.

"I hope you don't mind me taking over the kitchen," he said.

"I thought kitchen privileges were part of the deal. I just didn't expect to enjoy the fruits."

"Well, I'm certainly not going to go to all this trouble just for me. In fact, if you want to invite some of your friends over sometime, just let me know and I'll put out a spread."

"Is that part of your culture?"

"It was how I was raised. If you get a group of us together, it's an excuse for a party, and everyone brings something. Potluck. Anyway, none of this is terribly difficult or I wouldn't be doing it. I have limits." He glanced at her again. "I was wondering if you could do me a favor?"

All of a sudden she felt uncertain. Guarded. "If I can."

"I need to work out. Walking and a few calisthenics aren't doing it for me. I feel like rust is creeping into my joints."

"What a description. We don't have a commercial gym. Do you need some special kind of equipment?"

"Not really. Gage said he'd get me the key to one of the school gyms if I wanted to get in when they were closed. I mostly need space to practice my martial arts, limber up and all. It'd be great if I could find a sparring partner, too."

She hesitated a few moments. She was sure there

were plenty of people around town who knew something about the martial arts, most of them former Special Ops, and they were probably rusty, too. A lot rustier than Austin, maybe. But for some reason those creepy notes wafted up to the front of her mind, and on impulse she said, "I can spar with you. I haven't really kept up with it for the last few years, though, so I might not be good enough. I mean, I took it as a high school gym class."

"Really? That would be great. I wasn't especially practicing when I was in Mexico. I got in some, but not enough, so the rust is probably burrowing deep by now."

What in the world was she thinking? Butterflies settled into Corey's stomach as she realized what she'd just offered to do. Spar with a strange man? Spar with *any* man? She looked at her hand and realized it was trembling. She tried to find words to say she'd changed her mind, but something prevented them from emerging.

He wasn't really a stranger anymore, she told herself. He'd been open about his family, more open than she had been. Whatever problems he had from all that time undercover, she couldn't see them.

Those notes. She kept flip-flopping about them, sometimes dismissing them as an ugly joke, sometimes getting frightened, wondering if someone who knew her past was stalking her for some reason. But it didn't make any sense. After all this time?

She looked at Austin, who was humming almost under his breath as he wrapped dough and sausage in corn husks. He made her want new things. He made her aware that the life she had created for herself was missing important elements, no matter how hard she tried to tell herself it was a perfect life, exactly what she had planned.

So she sat there, her mouth a little dry, anxiety filling her, and faced the fact that in some ways she was a total failure. She'd built a life all right. Half a life.

That didn't make her feel exactly proud. So, okay, maybe it was time to take a step out of her cocoon. Austin provided a way, a relatively harmless way. Gage knew who he was. Sparring with him at one of the gyms should be safe enough. It wasn't as if they'd be the only people there. Surely other students would be there if they went early enough in the day.

"What kind of martial arts did you study?" Austin asked, rolling yet another husk around some dough.

"Well, not exactly martial arts," she said. "I might not be a very good sparring partner for you. I tried dribs and drabs of things, but I was mostly interested in self-defense."

He glanced over his shoulder. "That's cool. I didn't exactly go black belt in anything myself. For my job I needed to be good at things like street fighting. Some martial arts went into that, some self-defense... Anyway, the important thing for me is that I need to work some kinks out and get my reflexes back in the zone."

"Have you been home that long?"

He paused, then wiped his hands on a paper towel and turned to face her. "I told you I was beaten. I spent some time recovering from broken bones. Ribs, my arm. Everything's okay now, but I was moving more gingerly than a hundred-year-old for a while, thanks to the ribs. It even hurt to breathe."

She winced in sympathy. "I've heard that's terrible."

"It's certainly not comfortable. I had what they call flail chest. I had three broken ribs and had trouble breathing. There was also some organ damage. So I spent time in the hospital, went through a bout of pneumonia because I wasn't breathing right, and when they finally let me go I was breathing but hurting." He shook his head and gave an almost puckish smile. "Some way to end a storied career."

"But your career isn't over, is it?"

His face turned hard, almost flat. "That part of it is." Then he turned back to cooking.

Whoops. She guessed she had put her foot in it. "I guess I shouldn't have said that."

"No, it's okay." But he didn't look at her. He just kept wrapping methodically until he had a baking dish full of tamales. "I apologize if it sounded like I was snapping. I guess I have some issues. It'll pass."

Hers hadn't passed very well. She hoped his did.

Regardless, when he was done rolling the tamales, he returned to the easygoing guy she was getting to know. The smoothness of the switch made her nervous. Who was the real Austin Mendez?

"So everyone is excited about the quilting project?" he asked.

She recognized deflection when she heard it. After all, she did it often herself. "Very," she said. "We even got started cutting the pieces. I think I'll go change."

She didn't say she'd be right back because she wasn't sure she would. Or could. She needed to think about what he'd told her, but mostly she needed to think about that sudden change in him.

She had thought she was getting to know him. Now she wondered if anyone could truly know this man.

Chapter 6

Several days later, the man sat at his computer again, looking over the list of possible notes he could send to Corey. Evidently the first two hadn't even rippled the surface of her life. She hadn't changed one thing. She still walked to work, stayed late, walked home, all by herself.

At least she didn't have a lover living with her. He'd thought that last college student might have been, they spent so much time together, but now she was gone and there was a man living there.

Well, she rented out her upstairs. That didn't mean a thing, not against the number of women who had lived there. Fast and loose was the way he had evaluated her. Always girlfriends.

No, the guy didn't count. He was a friend of the sheriff's according to word around town, just looking to stay a few months. Between jobs, they said. A lot of people were "between jobs" these days.

So the guy had no connection with Corey at all. They didn't go anywhere together, didn't do anything together. That meant he wasn't wrong about her.

Because it was very important to be right. He couldn't

preserve decency and condemn sin unless he was right. There were rules, ways to keep himself pure so he didn't become a sinner himself. A lot of people didn't understand that, but he did. Unless he remained pure, he couldn't sit in judgment.

He reached for the one beer he allowed himself each day. Some thought alcohol was sinful, but he'd read about it right there in the Good Book. The important thing was moderation, so he moderated.

Unfortunately, he might have been too moderate in his first few notes. Part of the punishment for iniquity was to understand your sin. To be faced with it and know you were about to pay for it.

It did no good to claim the penalty from someone who didn't understand why it was being meted out. Her mother had understood. He was sure of that. She'd gone running to Denver to escape her punishment.

At first he'd felt sorry the child had to see the mother's punishment, but later he'd come to understand why it had happened that way despite his plan. It was so Corey would be steered to the path of righteousness.

But that hadn't happened.

Like mother, like daughter.

Those words seemed to glow brighter than others on the screen. He wondered if she would get it then.

There was still a chance she could change, see the error of her ways. It was always possible. Maybe if she saw that, she'd change her life, save herself.

But he didn't believe she would. Her mother hadn't changed, she'd just run. With a child. A misbegotten child from a loveless or unnatural coupling. He wasn't sure which, but it didn't matter. Corey's mother had been selfish enough to want a child despite her perversion.

Perhaps that was an even greater sin, having the child. But whether or not it was, it had brought yet another perversion into the world, one that had to be erased.

He had watched long enough to be sure he was dealing with the same thing. He had waited patiently, hoping the child would grow up decently. It wasn't as if she had come from a tainted family. Not until her mother.

But she evidently hadn't escaped the snare. She was discreet, but so had her mother been. In fact, it had actually been harder to figure out her mother, but the child... well, these times were so much more brazen.

But Corey might not know about her mother. Might not have any idea what she had been.

Still, the words that glowed brightest on the screen arrested him. They appeared to be the next step. Vaguely threatening, but nothing overt. Not enough to call the police. Or if she did, not enough to alarm them. But he hoped they'd be enough to alarm her.

He settled on them, highlighted them and started the printer. It was old and sluggish, but the message was short. He reached for his beer, taking only a small sip because he had to make it last.

He needed to remain a fit instrument of judgment.

Corey looked at the envelope with horror and growing fear. She recognized it now: plain, white, no return address, computer printed with her address. There was no question there'd be some kind of message in it, and she didn't want to know. Her hand shook as she held the envelope, then she dropped it quickly on the hall table.

At this rate, she thought bitterly, she was going to let the mail pile up outside the door and never look at it again.

Why would anyone want to do this to her?

That bothered her more than the messages. Someone wanted to scare her and unnerve her, and she couldn't imagine why. Out there in this friendly, familiar town was a sick mind. No longer could she think it just a teenage prank. She'd reacted in no way to these letters, and surely any "fun" wouldn't have gone out of it by now.

Yet another one had arrived. She stood at the counter, trying to collect herself, trying to think this through in some way that would make sense. Some way that would make her feel less threatened. Because she *was* feeling threatened. Stalked. The object of some kind of awful intention.

Part of her wanted to run back to her shop, the only place she felt safe, truly safe. After all these years, only being surrounded by people, women, could make her feel safe. But the shop was closed now, the sewing circle had finished early, and it was after six. How would she find safety there?

Just because it wasn't here, where the letters kept arriving? That was stupid. If he knew where she lived, he knew where she worked. Everyone in town did.

Regardless, she hurried around the lower floor, making sure all the curtains were tightly closed, even though she seldom opened them. They'd been the first change she had made after her grandmother's death. Heavy, light-blocking curtains over the downstairs windows. Because once she was alone, she feared the idea that someone could look in. She'd turned the lower part of her house into a cave. Even recognizing what she was doing, she couldn't stop herself.

Finally she managed to sit at the table and give her wobbly knees a break. She tried to tell herself she was overreacting, but that didn't work. Someone was trying to make her miserable. Maybe even trying to scare her.

It was all too much. She felt drawn as tight as a bowstring, and she didn't think it was just the letters. It was having Austin in her life, a man who had been inserted into her carefully constructed world. He was nice, he was fun, he'd gone out of his way to make her comfortable with him, but his presence caused tension. It broke the smooth surface of her life with thoughts of a different life, with awareness of how much of an emotional mess she was. He reminded her of her failures and her weaknesses…and her desires.

He alone was enough. But the letters, too?

Then she heard Austin's key in the lock. For the first time, the sound filled her with relief. Huge relief. He was home and she didn't need to be alone with all this anxiety. She didn't even question her reaction. He might be a source of tension, but he was also something else at this instant: protection. A friend. Someone to break the solitude that offered her no comfort at all.

He entered and headed for the stairs. She called out, stopping him. "Austin?"

He backtracked and came to the kitchen doorway, smiling. "Hey," he said by way of greeting. Then his face changed. "Corey? You're pale as a ghost. What's wrong?"

"Another letter."

He swore. At least she thought he did, but it sounded like Spanish. It also sounded like cussing. Before she realized what he was going to do, he closed the distance between them and dropped to his knees beside her chair.

"Don't panic," he said.

An instant later, his powerful arms wrapped around her and hugged her tightly. She stiffened instinctively, ready to pull away. She *never* let a man get this close. But all of that vanished swiftly as she realized something else: it had been a long time since anyone had hugged her and she missed the feeling, the warmth. What's more, she actually *liked* the strength of his arms surrounding her like a bulwark.

Oh, God, was she making a terrible mistake? But the emotions overwhelmed her, the need overwhelmed her, driving the stiffness from her body until she surrendered to his embrace.

He just held her. He did nothing to frighten her, nothing to make her uneasy. It was as chaste as any hug her aunt or grandmother had given her. She closed her eyes, accepting the comfort he offered, and discovering it wasn't so very difficult to do. In fact, it was easy.

She should have been disturbed by that, but she had other things to be disturbed by. It was just a hug. A simple hug. The kind people gave each other all the time.

She drew a long, shuddery breath, then expelled it, and with it a very old tension. It would probably return, but for now it evaporated in the warmth of his arms, and she was reaching a point where she desperately needed someone.

Going it alone all the time, even with a circle of friends, wasn't easy. She needed someone to share this new circle of hell with her, to walk with her through it. Yes, that was selfish, but who else could she turn to? Her friends were all married. They wouldn't have the time or even understanding of what she was going through now. After all, murder hadn't visited their lives.

Austin, at least, seemed to understand. He was no stranger to dark places. Her friends would either laugh the notes off or tell her to go to the sheriff. But she so far had nothing to take to the sheriff, and she couldn't laugh this off. She was long past that now with a third note sitting on her hall table.

Then Austin spoke again, and she heard his voice rumble in his chest against her ear. "You're not alone," he said.

Had he read her mind? Or maybe he just got it. Before she could figure it out, though, he loosened his hold on her and began to pull away. She wanted to stop him, but didn't have the temerity. Losing the protection of his arms made her ache, made her feel empty. Oh, man, she could get into trouble here.

She blinked rapidly, reaching for her self-control as he stood.

"Coffee?" he asked. "Or something else."

"Coffee," she decided. "I'm not going to sleep tonight, anyway."

He paused halfway to the pot. "What did it say?"

"I haven't opened it. I recognized the envelope and

then started to fall apart. Sorry. It's just that it's the third one. I can't tell myself it's meaningless any longer."

"No, of course not. And don't be sorry. You weren't exactly hysterical, but if you had been, I wouldn't have blamed you."

"Why not?" she asked, wondering why she all of a sudden felt angry. "You've faced far worse things without getting hysterical, I'm sure."

"I get hysterical quietly, deep inside. I've also never been stalked like this. Getting angry? Good. You should."

She should? But there it was, fury flowing hotly into the places so recently filled by fear and a sense of failure. Like white fire, it felt as if it would melt her from the inside out. "What good is anger?"

"It's a helluva lot better than hopelessness or fear. It's quite a powerful fuel, actually. As long as you use it right."

Her hands clenched. Her mouth felt dry, her insides wanted to push a primal scream past her lips. Angry? Oh, hell, yeah, she was angry. She wanted to shred something with her bare hands.

Austin readied the coffeepot, then came to sit at the table. "Have you ever gotten angry about anything before?"

"Well, of course."

"No, I mean really angry. Killing angry. When your mother died? I doubt it. What about your aunt and grandmother? Did you ever want to tear the heavens apart?"

"No," she admitted, closing her eyes.

"I figured. Well, go ahead and rage. God knows, you

have plenty of reason. If it gets to be too much, let me know. Gage gave me the key to the gym at the college. I hear they've got a few punching bags."

She took a moment to process that as her nails dug into her palms. "Gage? Key? Why?"

"I mentioned that you and I wanted to try a little sparring, but with your work schedule I figured Sunday morning would be about your only free time. Next thing I know, he gives me a key."

"Oh."

"Nice guy, your sheriff. When did you eat last?"

Food? She couldn't even think about it. The worm of anger was gnawing at her insides, consuming her. "I don't know."

He didn't say another word, just left her to deal with the rage that had filled her. She didn't deserve this, she thought. After all she'd lost, she didn't deserve to be hounded like this by some sick twist who probably thought it was amusing.

As soon as she had the thought, her anger started to die. "Deserve?" she said aloud. "Why don't I deserve this? Things happen to people all the time that they don't deserve."

"True," he said, popping some leftovers in the microwave and pushing the buttons. The beeps sounded loud. "But that doesn't keep us from feeling that way. Nor does it help to short-circuit our feelings by telling ourselves someone has it worse. Of course they do. The world is full of people who have it worse. If they ever find the guy who has it worst of all, I want to meet him."

Amazingly, that made sense to her. It was as if he

could enter her mental conversation and finish it. Damn, he was something else. "You're good at reading my mind."

"I just hear what you say."

Soon he'd filled two plates with leftover pulled pork and yellow rice. He had found a bag of prepared salad mix and dumped that into a bowl, placing it along with two bottles of dressing on the table. He added small plates for the salad and mugs of coffee.

"Eat," he said gently as he sat. "You're going to need it."

"For what?"

"Getting through this. No time to go on a diet."

She wasn't hungry but she forced herself to eat, anyway. At least she was emerging from the emotional storm that had beset her since she saw that letter. She'd visited nearly the entire emotional map, she realized. As she settled into a calmer frame of mind, her appetite returned and she ate a healthy portion of everything.

"You're a great chef," she said. "That was as delicious tonight as it was the first time."

"I enjoy cooking."

"You're spoiling me."

He flashed a quick grin. "I don't mind. Feeling any better?"

She pushed her plate aside and reached for her coffee. "Yes. Much. I was caught in a whirlwind."

"I thought so, but I wasn't sure." He cleared the dishes to the counter quickly and returned, facing her across the table. "You've been holding a lot in."

"What else is there to do?"

"Share it."

"Do you share it?"

"Believe me, I do and did. I left some people at the agency feeling pretty scalded about the treatment I got while I was undercover. The agents who thought I was one of the bad guys and tried to take me out I could deal with. I *was* undercover. But leaving me in the filthy, stinking jail getting beaten to a pulp? I didn't much care how many good reasons they had."

"I guess not."

"But I don't want to talk about me. Not now. I want to talk about you. You've been holding in an awful lot, haven't you."

"We all have to cope." But even as she spoke the sensible words, she felt her eyes begin to sting. No, please. She didn't want to break down now.

"Sure we do. But that doesn't mean burying our feelings. You've had a lot of loss for someone so young. People who should still be with you."

She stared at him from burning eyes. "You've never lost anyone?"

"I didn't say that. I've buried *mis abuelos,* two of my grandparents. I lost an uncle in a car accident. But there's a huge difference. I had a big family to share the grief with. Who did you have?"

"Well, when my aunt died, I had my grandmother."

"How did that go?"

"I think she felt pretty badly. I mean, it was her *daughter* and she had lost both of her daughters."

He sighed and sat back. "So you were the strong one,

eh? You helped her as much as you could because her loss was so great."

"Well, of course! I lost my aunt, but she lost her only remaining daughter!"

He nodded. "So you measure loss? You weigh it on a scale? Losing a daughter is a bigger loss than losing an aunt?"

She felt the spark of anger again. "I didn't say that."

"Yes, you did. And maybe for some people it's true. I wouldn't know. Losing a child is a terrible thing. I feel for your grandmother. But I also feel for you. You lost someone important, too, and then you lost your grandmother. I bet you did a good job of carrying on."

"You have to."

"I agree." One corner of his mouth lifted. "I'm really not arguing with you. What I'm trying to get at is…well, did you leave space for yourself to grieve? Did you have someone you could cry with when it hurt too much? Or did you lock that part of yourself away?"

She opened her mouth to dispute him, then realized she couldn't. His words were opening a sinking, hungry maw inside of her, full of monsters and demons she had locked away. Her eyes closed, her breaths came more rapidly, and her chest began to feel as if it would crack open.

"I didn't have a big family," she said, her voice breaking. "When my aunt got so sick, I had to help my grandmother with everything. I took over most of the store so she could sit with Aunt Lucy. There wasn't anyone else to do it, Austin."

"Lo entiendo." He paused. "Sorry, I keep slipping languages. I get it."

"Then it was as if…as if the heart were cut out of her. After my aunt died, my grandmother just…lost her zest completely. She was just going through the motions and practically faded before my eyes."

"Nice for you."

Her anger sparked. "What's that supposed to mean?"

"Was she sick?"

"At first, no. Depressed, I think."

"Of course she was depressed. Everyone gets depressed over the death of someone they love. Maybe it's just the way you describe it, but *you* were still here. Didn't she care for *you?*"

"Of course she did!"

"But she didn't make you feel that way, did she."

He didn't ask it as a question, he stated it. And the way he said it, with such certainty, lit the engine on the rocket of her anger again. She wanted to jump up and shout at him, and tell him he didn't know what the hell he was talking about.

But even as her body started to stiffen, as she began to push back from the table, the justice of his statement hit her like a gut punch.

All the air whooshed out of her and she bent forward, wrapping her arms around herself, trying to ease the devouring ache. True or not, she *had* felt as if her grandmother had given up and abandoned her. Fair or not, watching Cora fade had left her feeling deserted, not cared for.

"I hate you," she whispered between her teeth.

"I don't blame you. Truth is a painful thing."

"You don't know! You *can't* know."

"I hear you," he said quietly. "I hear the words you speak, every one of them, and how you speak them. I am not going to say that's exactly what happened with your grandmother. She was getting older, she may have had a sickness they didn't find. But you felt abandoned, *chica.* And you weren't wrong. *Escúchame,* listen to me. Your feelings *are* reality. They are as real as a physical event. Maybe they're even more real. And I wish I could settle on one language."

"You don't usually have trouble," she answered, her voice muffled.

"I seem to be getting a bit emotional myself."

"Why?"

"Because I give a damn."

The words seemed to explode inside her head. He gave a damn about her? Caught in a maelstrom of other emotions, she didn't know what to make of that or her reaction to it.

"You're a nice lady," he went on. "Very nice. You didn't want a man in your house, but you've been kind to me. You've been through a lot of loss, but you've remained strong. And you've been terribly alone."

"I have friends."

"Lots of them," he agreed.

"They helped me as much as they could. They really tried."

"But did you let them?"

"What's that supposed to mean?"

"Exactly that. Did you turn to them, or did they have to come to you? Did you hold it inside because you didn't want to impose on them? Did you feel as if your sorrow would become a drag on them, too? Did you put on a bright face even when you weren't feeling it?"

She glared at him as the truth of his words struck home. "Do you think you're some kind of psychologist?"

He shook his head. "I watched my mother do these very things for years after her best friend died."

"So maybe you're projecting."

"It's possible. So tell me I'm wrong."

But she couldn't. The worst of it was, she couldn't deny any of what he said. *Be strong.* It had been her mantra ever since she could remember. Sitting hunched over, hugging herself, she couldn't even move. It was as if her entire self-image had been exploded and lay in smoking scraps around her. When she looked inward, she saw a bleak landscape.

"Why are you doing this to me?" she whispered. "Why?"

"I told you. I care. I've been with you for a few weeks now. I see a strong woman who tries to rely on no one. I also see a woman who's been acting as if nothing is wrong when I know damn well that those notes disturbed you. Then another one came and you couldn't even open it. Now here we are, that note is waiting out there, and I want something very clear before we open it."

Something inside her chilled at the very thought of that note, but given the huge tide of feelings he had ripped open in her, it didn't seem like such a big thing. "What's that?"

"That with me you're not going to hide your feelings or your fears. You're going to be open so we can deal with this together. I can't do that if you're always hiding behind a smooth facade."

"What difference does it make?"

"It lets me know you trust me enough to scream or cry. If you won't trust me, that's your choice. But without trust, things'll be a whole lot harder."

"It might be nothing," she said quietly.

"I hope so. But with a third note, I'm not betting on it. Are you?"

Slowly she shook her head.

"Then let your feelings rip, Corey. Whatever they are. Be honest about anything and everything, including what a pain in the butt I am and how wrong I am about you. Just quit being a stranger."

Exhaustion from the extreme emotions that had torn through her since she saw that letter, since Austin had dissected her with surgical finesse, began to creep through her. She put her head in her hands and thought that she ought to hate him. He'd peeled her open and revealed all the hidden pain within.

She really ought to hate him.

But somehow she couldn't. In the wake of the storm came something like a summer breeze, blowing away all the painful detritus, at least for now.

She heard him push back from the table, but she didn't look up. The damn note.

But instead, he emptied their coffee cups and refilled them. She nearly jumped when he briefly stroked the back of her head before resuming his seat.

"You're not my type," he said.

Startled, she forgot everything else and raised her head. He was actually smiling at her. "What?"

"A Nordic princess." He shook his head. "Cool, reserved and blonde. My type is darker with a touch of salsa and a helping of peppers."

How was she supposed to take that?

He leaned toward her and winked. "My type could be changing, though. You never know. There's fire inside you, Corey. Let it out."

"God, you're impossible!"

He shrugged, still smiling. "I know. I just like everything on the table, out in the open. I spent too many years wondering what was under the table and if it would get me killed. No more of that for me."

That at least made sense to her, although she still couldn't understand why he had thought it was so important to get to the root of her feelings, especially about her grandmother and aunt. Why should he care?

Then it struck her what he had meant about trust. He wanted her to trust him with the devils inside her so that he could trust her. Given where he had been and what he had done for six years, that actually made sense to her. Whether she wanted to give him that kind of access was another question. He was right about how rarely she opened up to anyone. If she ever had.

But God, he had come so close to the bone, and hearing it from his lips had hurt. Was she really that broken?

Did any of that even count as broken? She had done what she had to do, and she'd remained strong for a lot of good reasons. Was he suggesting that she should have sobbed all over her friends?

But no, she didn't think that was it. He was going for something deeper.

She looked at him again. "I called for you when you came in. Because of the note."

"Yes, you did. I was touched, and I want to help. Will you let me?"

She didn't know how he could help, but one thing became blindingly clear in her mind. She wasn't alone. For once, she wasn't alone. Austin was barreling into places she'd never shared, and letting her know that he was there for her no matter what. "You're a bit of a battering ram."

He chuckled. "Sometimes delicacy just won't work."

She had to give him that. She also realized that deep within her heart of hearts, she was sick of facing everything alone. Sick of always having to be strong. Sick of always having to pretend that everything was just fine.

Nothing in her life had been fine since her mother's murder. Nothing.

End of story.

"Get the note," she said. "Please."

Chapter 7

Austin went to get the letter from the hall table. She was right, he was a battering ram. He had surprised himself by the way he had pushed her, but he understood why he'd done it. He'd been feeling the pain in her the whole time he'd been here. On the surface she seemed amazingly well-adjusted, but other stuff seeped out around the cracks. She couldn't really claim to have dealt with the death of her mother because she'd been a child and couldn't remember it. Hell, she could probably hardly remember the woman.

Then there were her other losses, her circumscribed life, friendships that didn't extend much past her shop. When it came to that, there was her shop. She kept killer hours and he didn't think that was entirely from necessity. She worked herself into forgetfulness so she wouldn't notice the lacks in her life.

Alone, that all would have been disturbing enough, but now there was another note. A third one. At this point he wasn't about to dismiss it as some sick jackass enjoying a bit of torment for the hell of it.

Then, of course, there was the other thing. The sexual thing. With each passing day he wanted Corey more.

He managed to bury it pretty good, but it was there and growing, anyway. He'd have bet his last dollar that she was a virgin, and while he avoided inexperienced women like the plague, Corey was making a shambles of all his good intentions. He wanted her, and the only way he was going to get her was to break down the castle walls and pull her out of the dungeon.

Great imagery. It sickened him actually, to think of her living that way, even though it was close to the truth. But more than desire was goading him. He was truly coming to care about this woman, and even if he never bedded her, he'd at least like to know he'd opened up her world. Someone should have cared enough to do it long ago.

Evidently no one had, and while he'd never say so to Corey, he wondered if anyone had ever put *her* first. Apparently not even her grandmother had.

He picked up the envelope, wondering if they should open it tonight. She'd been afraid to do so earlier. What had changed? Was she deflecting him? Did the potential threat of these notes seem more welcome to her than any more out of him?

Probably, and he couldn't blame her. Standing in the hallway, he held the letter and stepped back from what he had just done, reviewing his own behavior.

Then he dropped the envelope and went back to the kitchen empty-handed. This conversation wasn't done.

She was still hunched in on herself, and it hurt to see it. He had done that to her.

"No envelope?" she asked as he sat again.

"Not yet. First, I'm going to apologize. I had no right to be so hard on you. I wasn't kind."

"No, but you were right," she admitted. "It's the way I am. I'm not like you."

"What's like me?"

"You're very open and frank."

"Not always." He sighed and passed his hand over his face, trying to collect some thoughts here that wouldn't turn him into a battering ram once again. "I couldn't be open and frank when I was undercover. Did I like it? No. I was living a lie and I hated it. I used people and I hated it. But it was an important job. Gunrunning across the border is helping to escalate the drug violence. You sit up and take notice when you face the numbers. Over fifteen thousand people were the victims of drug-related violence in Mexico last year. It's hard to conceive of. It wouldn't be as awful if it were just the drug gangs killing each other, but unfortunately it never ends there. Innocents get in the way. Reporters get shot. Decent cops trying to protect people get shot. Nobody's safe when the violence reaches that level."

She drew a long breath, and he was relieved to see that she uncurled and sat up straighter. She was letting go of the hurt he'd inflicted. It would come back, of course. Pointing it out wasn't a cure. It was merely an opening.

"And then there are those Indians you spoke of."

"The Tarahumara. Yes. A people who've been fighting since the Spanish arrived just to be left alone. Now too many of them are caught in the drug wars, too."

"And you just merrily tripped your way into the middle of this."

"*Merrily* wouldn't be the right word. I oozed in like slime, very slowly and carefully."

She blinked, and then a sound escaped her that made his heart ache. "Slime? You oozed?" She actually laughed, broken though it sounded.

"Best way to describe it," he admitted. "I had to become familiar before I could get anywhere I needed to go. Anywhere at all. Undercover work takes time and care. Finesse. Exactly what I haven't used with you."

"I don't need finesse," she said, but her face drooped again. "Look, Austin, I'm sorry, but I'm feeling as shredded as the pork we had for dinner. At least to some extent you're right about me. I need to deal with it."

"The way you always deal with it? Or are you going to let someone help you?"

"You seem to have already started the process. You may be stuck with the results."

"I can live with it."

"I guess we'll see. In the meantime, let's just look at that note. I won't sleep tonight wondering, even if I won't sleep because of what it says. It's sitting out there like a ticking bomb."

"I'll get it."

He brought it back to the table. "Do you want to open it, or do you want me to?" He tossed it on the table and pulled his chair around so that he could sit closer to her.

She was being too calm, he thought. She had pulled back inside her walls and was locking things out again. Maybe he'd been wrong to even try to breach them. If she built her walls higher and stronger because of him, he'd go beat his head on something and clear out of town before he made matters any worse.

"You open it," she said tautly. "For some reason, I don't even want to touch it."

Well, he could understand that, and at least she wasn't trying to be tough about it. He twisted around to pull a knife from the drawer, then slit the top of the envelope. "I suppose I should wear gloves."

"There are some rubber ones under the sink. I don't know if they're big enough for you, though."

"Then I'll do it differently." He spread the envelope open a bit with the knife and peeked in. "Same scrap of paper." Then he used the knifepoint to tease it out of the envelope until it lay on the table between them.

Like mother, like daughter.

They stared at it a moment. Corey gave a truncated laugh, almost as if she couldn't believe it. "What the hell is that supposed to mean?"

"I don't know." But given what had happened to her mother, he found this note infinitely more threatening.

"My mother? This creep keeps bringing up my *mother?*"

He was glad to see her anger, not fear or despair. But then she jumped up. "I've had enough. Really. I'm going to my room. Maybe I'll sit there like Madame Defarge and knit all night."

She stormed out of the kitchen and down the hall. He heard her door slam like a punctuation mark. She was mad, with every right. And he didn't think it was just because of this note.

He slipped his hand into his shirt pocket and dug out his cell phone. He punched Gage Dalton's personal number.

Gage arrived twenty minutes later with evidence-collection materials. "You didn't touch it?"

"Not the note. We both handled the envelope, but so did the post office. I slit the top with a knife and used the knifepoint to tease the note out onto the table."

"Good." Using tweezers, Gage lifted the paper and slipped it into a clear plastic evidence bag, which he sealed and wrote the date and time on.

"What the hell," he muttered as he looked at the note through the plastic. "This is purely ugly."

"No kidding."

"The other notes?"

"Corey has them tucked away. And no, I'm not going to get them. This is her place. I already trespassed enough by calling you, but I didn't want to risk losing prints. You'll have to ask her for them."

"I'd have appreciated it," said Corey from the door-way, "if you'd asked me about *this*."

Her eyes looked hollow, but there was a flame deep in them. He saw a woman at the breaking point, and he'd helped put her there. "Sorry. You'd gone to your room and I got the distinct feeling you didn't want to be bothered."

"You were right," she said sharply. "I'll get the other notes, much good they'll do."

Gage looked at Austin. "Why do I feel like I just stepped into a heap of manure?"

"Because you did. My fault."

Gage frowned. "I didn't put you here to cause trouble."

"No." But Austin wasn't going to argue with him. Gage had been hoping that having a guy around would loosen up the steel bands that held Corey in their grip, but nothing was that easy. Hence tonight's manure.

Corey returned with the other two envelopes and handed them to Gage. He read them, then tossed them in another evidence envelope.

"Okay, then," he said. "I can see why you didn't think the first two were worth calling me about, Corey, but this one is an escalation."

Pale, rigid, she folded her arms and gave a short nod. She gnawed her lower lip. "Is this guy dangerous?"

"I honestly don't know," Gage answered. "But I get the feeling he's trying to scare you. He knows about your mother? Most everyone in town with a memory who is old enough knows about that. This last one, though… that's directed at you. It's meaningless enough on the face of it."

"Except that someone went to the trouble to send it," Austin remarked.

"Exactly," Gage answered. "But the meaning is anything but clear. Did the writer know Corey's mother? Does he just mean they're alike in some way? Looks? Personality? Or is he trying to say something else? Damned if I know. But this note does seem more threatening somehow, especially given that it's the third one. I'm going to run it for prints. If we find any, we'll see if we can find a match on the federal database, but that could take weeks, and we might not find anything at all."

"I know," Austin said. But his attention was no longer on Gage. He was staring at Corey, and he didn't like the way she was looking. As if she had been hollowed out. He felt a sharp twinge of guilt.

"Just be careful, Corey. If anything at all seems out of the norm, let me know. Austin, keep an eye on her. This might just be some idiot who needs a good psychiatrist, but there are no guarantees." He paused. "These are being mailed here in town. That means we're not going to get some easy lead, like some stranger who started hanging around." He gave Austin a crooked smile. "You're the only stranger right now."

"But I arrived after Corey got the first note." His statement was weak and he knew it. He could have arrived a couple of days earlier and mailed the first note before introducing himself. "I'll leave if it'll make things better."

Corey surprised him by speaking. "No," she said. "It won't make anything better."

After Gage left, Corey retreated to the front room. She used it seldom because she was rarely home. Another mark of her messed-up life, she supposed. After a minute, Austin joined her, hovering as if he wasn't certain of his welcome. Without a word, she waved him to the chair facing the couch she sat on. Old furniture, ripe with memories of her grandmother and her aunt, of her childhood here with them. Behind the couch there was a place where her mother, as a child, had written her name on the wallpaper. "Olivia." Nobody had ever bothered to repaper the wall.

There were also photos. She watched Austin look around at them. Maybe those photos were part of the reason she didn't spend much time in this room. Her grandmother had framed quite a few, including a couple of larger frames that held multiple photos, one for her, one for her aunt and one for her mother. Three generations, but only one remained.

"Your family?" Austin asked.

She nodded. Deep inside she felt hard and tight, withdrawn somehow. As if she wasn't really there.

"I'm sorry I called the sheriff without asking first," he said. "I guess I'm too used to making my own decisions."

"It doesn't matter." At that moment, very little seemed to matter. She felt as if she stood on a high, dark pinnacle in the middle of nowhere. As if she had been plucked from her familiar life. Crazy thinking, but it was how she felt.

"Yeah, it matters," he said. "All I could think of was the importance of preserving possible evidence, and with the way you had gone to your room, I thought you wouldn't want to be disturbed. I was wrong, focused entirely on the wrong thing."

"No," she said. Even that word seemed to take a lot of energy.

His dark eyes settled on her, seeming to measure her. "Is this what you do?" he asked. "Just shut down when it gets to be too much?"

"Apparently so," she murmured, closing her eyes. Drifting in emptiness seemed preferable to dealing at the moment. She'd get back to dealing, she always did, but right now…not right now.

All of a sudden, she felt hands grip her shoulders. Her eyes snapped open and she saw Austin kneeling in front of her. His gaze was so intense that it seemed to burn right through her.

"You went to this place when you were seven," he said quietly. "There's no reason to do it now, Corey. You aren't alone."

Anger, like lava, poured into the quiet dark that had surrounded her. "Who the hell do you think you are? Haven't you battered me enough for one night?"

She saw his head jerk back. His hands released her. She felt a momentary satisfaction. He'd been dishing it out all evening. Her turn.

He jumped up and started walking away. Not a word, just leaving her. Good. She needed some time to deal with the shambles he'd already made of her. Time to find her bearings, raise her defenses…

But he turned around suddenly. "Hate me," he said. "Even hate is better than nothing."

The words seemed to make no sense, but the next thing she knew, he sat on the couch and pulled her into his lap. Astonished, furious at being manhandled, she opened her mouth to yell at him, but the moment was lost as he kissed her.

Then she was lost, too.

Austin was quite sure he was losing his mind, but he didn't care. He'd had enough of feeling as if this woman's barriers were keeping him at a distance, preventing even a genuine friendship. He'd had enough of seeing her occasionally peek out from behind the bars that imprisoned her, of seeing the longing flicker across her face only to be quickly banished.

He couldn't have begun to explain why her carefully cultivated indifference bothered him so much. It wasn't just that she was living a half life, it was that she was treating him as if he had no reality. Polite, superficially friendly, willing to share a bit of laughter and a meal, but almost never to actually share herself.

A smart man would have looked at Sleeping Beauty here and moved on, but he couldn't move on. Those letters kept him nailed firmly here because he wasn't the type of man who could ignore the fact that she might be facing real trouble.

Or maybe he wasn't the type of man who could walk away when defied by a nearly blank wall. Which probably made him some kind of creep, but he was past caring. He'd fought to sweep away that facade tonight, and he wasn't ready to quit.

He hadn't been kidding when he'd said hate would be better than nothing. Her hate would at least be real.

He didn't examine his need to get a real response from her, a real feeling about him. He'd seen the cracks earlier when she'd called him a battering ram, but then she'd pulled back. Back into her safe dark place.

Back into superficiality, where they both pretended everything was just fine.

Nothing was fine. Not her, not him, not those notes. He'd been somebody else for so long now, maybe his entire problem was that he needed somebody to really see *him*. He certainly felt a strong need to see *her*. The real Corey, not the icon of friendly tranquillity she pretended to be.

Because he could feel in her that there was no real tranquillity. There sure as hell wasn't any in him.

Even as he seized her and kissed her, he knew this was all wrong. She'd have every right to throw him out. To have him arrested. And he just plain didn't give a damn.

He needed *something* from her, something real.

At first she was stiff. He could sense the fight building in her, but shortly after he clamped his mouth over hers, he felt the change. She softened as if something hard had been yanked out of her. She melted as if feeling a new kind of warmth.

And then slowly, astonishingly, he felt her arm slip upward to wrap around his neck. Her head tipped back a little to rest against his arm.

Here came that reality he wanted.

Her mouth had been open when he started kissing her, but only now did he take advantage of that fact. He plunged his tongue into her, the way he'd have liked to plunge his staff into her. Taunting, teasing, showing her things he was absolutely certain she'd never experienced before. Like how many sensitive nerve endings there were in a mouth and the delicious shivers that a carefully wielded tongue could send racing through her body. He sought gentleness, sought to take his time, but in truth need was beginning to pound in him like the beat of his blood.

His tongue moved in and out of her as he tasted her.

He snaked his tongue along hers, then traced her teeth and the insides of her cheeks until she shivered. Only then did he pull out and ever so lightly lick her lips. Her breathing had speeded up, her arm around his neck tightened as if she didn't want to let go.

He should have felt triumphant, but he knew there was going to be hell to pay for this. He'd crossed into territory where she had never let anyone go before. Just this simple kiss. She was going to be mad at him, and mad at herself because this was one wall she'd never be able to erect again.

Her curves felt luscious pressed to him, and she turned into him, granting him even more sensation, the fullness of her breast against his chest, the roundness of her hip against his swelling erection. When she squirmed on his lap, he groaned deep in his throat and knew she must feel his hunger for her. Too late to hide it, too late to take anything back. He shifted a little, too, cupping her hip with one hand as he raised the other to stroke her hair and her cheek.

No further, a smidgen of sense warned him. Too soon. But he could steal just another little kiss and he did exactly that, tasting her anew. His head spun with delight as he felt her respond this time, trying to mimic his movements. When her tongue entered his mouth, everything inside him exploded with pleasure. He sucked on it, as he wanted to suck on other parts of her, and heard a soft sound escape her.

Time to stop. Now. Before he forgot himself and her inexperience. It felt like tearing away a piece of his own body, when every cell demanded he continue, but he wasn't so far gone he didn't remember who and what he was dealing with here.

Slowly he lifted his head, breaking the kiss, trying to make his reluctance obvious. Then he wrapped his other arm around her, waiting for his body to quiet, his heart to slow.

Waiting for whatever vengeance she wanted to take.

Because he was sure to the core of his being that he'd given her enough cause just this one night to hate him forever.

But she didn't seem to be in the mood for vengeance. She stayed where she was. Minutes ticked by and he didn't mind. Frankly, he hadn't let anyone come this close to him either in a long time. Flings with easy women, well, they'd been part of his persona, though one he hadn't been fond of practicing often. When you'd known the real thing, the pretense wasn't very satisfying, unless you were built differently than he was.

But just hugging a woman like this? More than six years. At least. He didn't want to give this up quickly.

But finally she stirred and dropped her arm from around his neck. He tensed a little, waiting for the fire to rain on his head.

Then she amazed him. "I liked that," she murmured. "Grab me again sometime."

All the apologies that had been bubbling up inside him, starting with how hard he had been on her earlier, burst like an overfilled balloon. Um, wow? "You're okay?" he asked, almost unable to believe it.

"Very okay," she said shyly.

"Not mad at me?"

"I suppose I should be, but I'm not."

Caveman tactics win the day, he thought, shocked. Who would have thought? "Really? You're really not mad? After the way I've carried on tonight I couldn't blame you if you told me you never wanted to see me again."

An eternity seemed to pass while he waited for her to speak.

"You hurt me," she said finally.

He tensed. Here it came. Nor could he deny that he deserved it.

"I've never had anyone talk to me that way before," she continued. "Never. I felt gutted."

Part of him wanted to apologize, but part of him held back. Rightly or wrongly, someone needed to kick her out of the safe little cocoon she lived in. Especially now with these notes. There was a chance that denial could be deadly. Besides, after accepting her on her terms the past few weeks, he could no longer stand it. It actually hurt to see her locked up inside herself. Nobody should live like that.

"Other people," she said quietly, "just leave me alone. Take me as I am. Assume that what they see is me. Why can't you do that, Austin?"

"Because it's painful to watch."

The thought seemed to appall her. But she was still sitting across his lap and making no attempt to escape. "I wonder if anyone else sees me the way you do."

"Some do, probably. I don't have a corner on seeing behind the obvious."

"I don't know." She sighed and closed her eyes. "Certainly no one else has your gall."

"I've got plenty of that." True enough, but he wasn't sure he liked it. "Maybe I need to learn to keep my mouth shut."

At that, the oddest smile came to her mouth and her eyes opened. "I'm glad you didn't. It hurt like hell. I still need to evaluate what you said, but at least now I'm going to evaluate it. I probably should have taken a hard look at myself a long time ago."

"Maybe you were hurting too much."

"Maybe I was hiding too much."

She stirred and he let her go, aching as she pushed herself from his lap to sit beside him. Was this the distance returning? But no, she kept talking.

"Some of what you said…well, I know it's true. And like you said, the truth hurts. I told you, for days after they pulled me out of the…the murder scene, I hid in a closet. My grandmother and aunt got me out of the physical closet, but I guess part of me is still there."

He didn't speak. He'd talked enough for one night. Maybe more than enough. Instead, he held out his hand and waited.

Slowly, ever so slowly, she reached out and laid her hand in his. At once, he clasped her fingers and squeezed gently.

"Maybe," she said quietly, "it's time for me to grow up."

"I think you're grown up. I also think you've been traumatized. There's a difference."

"I guess." She sighed and let her head fall back against

the sofa, revealing a slender neck he would have liked to cover with kisses. But this was definitely not the time. He looked at their clasped hands, and realized he was looking at a minor miracle. Maybe even a major one.

"You were right, though," she said. "I never let anyone help me very much. I didn't trust them. Or maybe I was afraid."

"Losing a mother can do that, I imagine. Especially losing one the way you did. But you saw a therapist."

"For a while. I don't remember it very clearly, except that it seemed very important to become normal."

"Normal? Why?"

"I was afraid of the therapy. Maybe I was afraid I'd remember things. I don't know, I was just a kid."

"So you fooled everybody?"

"I learned to act like most everyone else. That seemed to make everyone happy."

That hit him like a hammer blow. So everyone was happy when she started acting as if nothing was wrong? What a great message to send, yet he could understand how it came about. People wanted her to be better. When she started acting as if she was, they heaved a huge sigh of relief.

Leaving Corey broken in a new way. Man, it was hard to keep his mouth shut. But he didn't need to, because Corey spoke again.

"I guess I learned some of the wrong lessons."

"You were a kid."

"Yeah. Amazing how kids think, huh? Not remembering the murder was a good thing. I heard that because it frightened me not to remember. The psychologist insisted that it was a kind of protection, that if I ever needed to remember I would, but it was okay to forget. But then she'd ask questions like she didn't really believe I'd forgotten. Those were the questions that scared me most. I didn't—and still don't—want to remember what I saw. When I was in high school, I went to Gage and asked him what had happened, and he gave me as sanitized a description as he probably could. It seemed like enough."

"It probably is."

"I don't know. I just knew that the only way I was going to stop going to therapy was if I acted like I was okay in every way. So I became okay. But, not really."

"Look, about what I said…"

She turned, hushing him. "You were right. People tried to help me and I didn't really let them. Then it kind of faded away. Everything seemed all right until my aunt got sick. Folks tried to help but I'd put on a smile and say I was doing fine. I was always doing fine. I guess I even persuaded my grandmother that I was doing fine. But that was the whole game, you see. To be fine."

She surprised him then by looking down at their linked hands. "Funny, but right now I feel better than I have in eighteen years." Her fingers tightened, holding his hand as if she feared he might pull it away. "Do you realize that no man has ever held my hand? I like it."

"I'll gladly hold your hand anytime you want."

She smiled at him. It wasn't a bright smile, but it was genuine. "I may take you up on that."

"Feel free." He was amazed that an evening that had been headed for catastrophe had turned out so well, but he didn't entirely trust it. Eighteen years of learned habits wouldn't be easy for her to overcome.

Nor would the desire he felt for her make any of this easier. He still couldn't believe he had grabbed her and kissed her that way. Nor could he argue that he had done it for her sake. No, he'd done it for his own. An utterly selfish need to penetrate her walls had driven him to it, and now he was going to pay for it. Now he didn't have to wonder what it would be like to hold her and kiss her. Now he knew. This whole situation was apt to drive him nuts.

She was fragile. Rapunzel had peeked outside her tower. So far she liked what she had seen, but it might take only a small thing to drive her back into the safety of her fortress. She'd been trying to go there right before he grabbed her.

She could do it again, and how he was supposed to prevent that, he had no idea.

"Corey?"

"Yes?"

"Just don't lock me out. Hate me if you need to, but don't lock me out. I'm here for you, and I don't want to have to batter at your walls again."

"I've been shutting people out for a long time," she admitted. "Keeping everyone at a safe, friendly distance. I don't know how good I'm going to be at this whole trusting thing. But I'll try."

"That's all I can ask."

"But if you see me slipping, bring out the battering ram." A crooked smile accompanied the words. "I have a feeling that I'm going to be very grateful to you."

He didn't want her gratitude, but he didn't say so. He'd done enough for one evening. Whether anything good would grow out of this, only time would tell.

Then she squeezed his fingers and withdrew her hand. He searched her face to see how far she was withdrawing, but she looked calm. Back into her shell? He couldn't tell.

"I'm really tired and I have a lot to think about. So tomorrow we beat each other up?"

"I was thinking we could beat up some punching bags."

She surprised him with an almost impish grin. "That, too. See you in the morning."

Then she was gone, leaving in her wake only her faint scents, scents that he somehow knew he would never forget.

Chapter 8

Corey was feeling pretty wiped by the time she left the gym in the morning. Austin had wanted to jog home, but she didn't have time. She needed to shower and get her store open for the afternoon.

It turned out to be kind of funny, though. Given the number of stop signs and turns, he nearly kept up with her, and once even passed her, waving as he went. It brought a giggle to her lips, a sound she was relieved to hear.

Last night had been hell. Well, except for the kissing and hand-holding part. His method of just grabbing her and doing it was clearly wrong, but she couldn't hold it against him. She never would have let him do it any other way, but she savored the all-too-brief experience he had given her. He had shown her something that hitherto she had only been able to imagine. Her fingertips touched her lips briefly and she couldn't smother a smile.

Was it wrong to hope he'd do it again?

But the moment of delight faded as she recalled the rest of the evening. He'd been ruthless in calling her attention to her shortcomings. She had been so angry with him at first, she had wanted to hate him, but unfortunately, her self-delusion didn't extend to denying a truth that was as plain as the nose on her face. The brief time she had spent in her bedroom, trying to stay angry before Gage had arrived…well, the anger had started fizzling rapidly. Truth had pummeled her and it hurt.

Part of her was still that child who had hidden in a closet after her rescue. She didn't know much about what had happened before that, except that she had been described as nearly catatonic. When they'd taken her to a temporary home, she'd found an isolated closet, climbed in and refused to come out. Even her grandmother and aunt had had trouble getting her out of there, until finally Aunt Lucy had just reached in, pulled her out and said, "You're coming home with us, Corey. You'll be safe at home."

Maybe a bad choice of words, she thought now. Home. Where was home? With the mother who was gone? It certainly hadn't felt like coming home with her grandmother and Lucy.

Her memory of that time was blurry and broken, little pieces that didn't string together, like snapshots out of order. She remembered the closet. She remembered being torn from its safety. She remembered snatches of the drive up here and of the weeks following. It was as if her memory stuttered. Or perhaps a seven-year-old's memory just wasn't that good to begin with.

Regardless, she needed to face up to the fact that part of her had never come out of that dark closet. She had felt ripped from safety by her aunt, and so she'd built her own little closet inside. A place nothing could touch. Where nothing could get at her.

Then she had realized they wouldn't leave her alone

until she seemed normal again. She had hated going to the psychologist. It had threatened her in some way she supposed she ought to think about. Had she thought the psychologist would tear away her closet? Expose her to all the things that terrified her? Or bring back her memory?

She didn't know, but she remembered very clearly the moment she had realized what they all wanted: for her to act as if nothing was wrong, to be like the other girls in second grade. They wanted her to appear to be okay, even if she still had the dark closet inside her, a closet she wasn't going to give up.

Pretending had been a whole lot easier than letting anyone get inside her. Thus, the psychologist's conclusion that amnesia had benefited her, and that she was better off not remembering. Everyone had seemed happy with that.

Maybe she'd been happy with that herself. The therapy visits had tapered off and she'd thrown herself with a vengeance into being just like the other girls.

Except she wasn't and never would be.

But appearances were everything, right? Wrong, evidently. Austin had pierced right through them last night, leaving her feeling exposed, raw and full of demons she'd never dealt with.

Maybe it was time she considered a return to therapy. There was a new psychologist in town, a woman who seemed nice enough.

But no, she wasn't ready for that yet. She wanted to think some things through first, decide whether she really wanted to change.

Because any way she sliced it, she hadn't been doing that badly all these years. She spent an awful lot of her

time with women, listening to them talk about everything under the sun, and if there was one thing she had
figured out, it was that every single one of them had
problems. Sometimes they were quite open and talk-
ative about it. Other times, she just got hints that things
weren't quite right in someone's world.

Nobody had a perfect life. Nobody was pain-free. The
important thing was coping with it somehow.

She already did that fairly well. At least until Austin.

No, she needed to be fair. Until the notes. She doubted
anything would have happened last night at all except
for her reaction to that note. She'd finally reached out to
someone and had gotten more than she had bargained
for.

He'd held up a mirror, showing her that she apparently didn't seem as "okay" as she'd been pretending.
Or maybe he was just unusually perceptive. Either way,
she'd looked at herself in a fun-house mirror and now
had to decide how much of the reflection was true. And
once she decided that, she needed to figure out whether
she wanted to do something about it.

Goading her, though, was the memory of his kiss.
The memory of having her hand welcomed by his much
larger one. If she ever wanted that kind of stuff to be part
of her life, then she would *have* to change.

For the first time in her life, she truly sensed what
she had been giving up. Just a taste of all that she was
passing by in her determination to avoid men and remain "okay."

Damn. By the time she pulled into her driveway, she
was mad again. She couldn't remember the face of a

single man, so she didn't trust any man. Well, except for a very small handful, like Gage Dalton. She doubted she would have allowed him within her protective circle except for the hours she had spent at the local library with his wife, Miss Emma. Getting to know Emma inevitably meant getting to know Gage. Even after all this time, the two were a classic pair of lovebirds. Sitting in the library on any given Saturday afternoon often meant Gage would be hanging around, sometimes with their two adopted sons, sometimes by himself. Emma sparkled when he was around, and he smiled a lot.

So she'd gotten to know him well enough, and a few other guys. Just a few. Nor would she ever forget the time Gage had stood as a bulwark with her when those detectives had come up from Denver trying to discover if she remembered anything at all. They'd been careful, but even at her young age she had remembered that Gage had hovered protectively and kept them not only careful but kind.

She glanced at her watch and realized she still had some time. She had started backing out of the driveway again when Austin startled her by rapping on the side of the car.

"Where are you going?" he asked. "I thought you wanted a shower."

"Cemetery," she said shortly.

He frowned. "Can I ride along?"

She shook her head. "I need to be alone."

"I'll follow you, then."

Damn. She cussed under her breath and pulled out. Let him follow. She couldn't prevent that.

The cemetery lay on the eastern side of town in one of the flattest areas around. Though the mountains rose abruptly from the high plains, as one approached them the ground began to roll gently. The farther east one went, the flatter the land became.

From the cemetery, though, you could see for miles. The caretaker kept it in fairly decent shape, keeping the grass trimmed if not manicured. She vaguely remembered when someone had suggested they plant trees out here, but the idea hadn't flown well. The area was drier than most and besides, everyone claimed to like the unobstructed view.

Without trees, however, the prairie wind keened ceaselessly, pulling her hair loose from its ponytail, whispering in her ears as if to share long-forgotten messages. She heard Austin's car pull up as she walked down the rows, knowing exactly where she was going.

Three canted granite stones lay side by side, one for her mother, and identical ones for her aunt and grandmother. Nearby was a bigger stone, for her grandfather. He'd left a place for his wife, but before she had died she had told Corey to bury her beside the girls in the same way.

She dropped to her knees and sat on her heels, studying the headstones. She hadn't known her grandfather at all. He had died before she was born. That left three she had known, all she had known of her family, and she couldn't remember one of them. Not really.

Oh, she had photos of her mother to remind her, but it wasn't the same. She had only the merest snatches of memory, the slightest fragments of speech or lullaby, and after all these years she couldn't know if she remembered that correctly.

What she *did* know was that not having a mother had left a gaping hole in her life. Memories shared by Cora and Lucy hadn't been enough to fill the emptiness Olivia had left behind her. Reaching out, she brushed some dried grass from her mother's tombstone. It was an old hollow inside her and the years had made it familiar. It didn't eat her alive anymore. Lots of kids lost their mothers.

But this was the last of her family, lying here in a row beneath the ground of the place her grandparents had come to settle so long ago.

Looking at the row of tombstones, she faced the fact that all life ended here. All around her stood markers to lives that were gone, some of which were probably forgotten. All those experiences, all those years, and it came down to a gray slab that marked nothing except that a person had once lived.

Olivia's life had been dreadfully short. As far as Corey knew, the only mark her mother had left on this world was a daughter.

Look at that daughter now. Somehow Corey didn't think her mother would be especially pleased with her. After all, Olivia had taken life by the horns as a single mom who had moved to Denver with big dreams. She had dared to have a child in this little town without revealing who the father was, or marrying. All she had ever said about the man was that he was someone she had met on a trip to the West Coast. Clearly he hadn't been black Irish.

It was all very odd, but Corey could also see how very brave it had been. No one would have blamed Olivia if she had left her daughter behind with her mother and sister while she struck out on her own. In fact, Cora had often assured Corey that she would have been glad to raise her from birth. Maybe she had even wanted to.

Questions would never be answered now. Sighing, Corey kissed her fingers and pressed them to each headstone in turn. Life always ended here.

Maybe it was time to take more advantage of the years she had been given.

Austin watched from afar. He sat in his car and kept an eye out, but apparently no one else had any desire to visit the cemetery this morning. Nor to even drive by, although it didn't seem to be on the way to anywhere. It was set off by itself in a place that appeared desolate, the town disappearing from view behind a bit of rolling land.

He wished he knew what Corey was thinking. She'd had a rough time last night, thanks to him, yet she hadn't shared a single thought this morning. If he'd hoped to break down her walls, he was now wondering if all he'd done was to raise them higher.

The workout this morning had been good. She apparently remembered a lot of her self-defense training and merely needed a tune-up. She'd certainly pummeled the punching bags in a way that suggested she was dealing with something unpleasant. But not a word. A few smiles, an occasional laugh, but otherwise she talked about nothing except the moves they made and how to do them better.

Then a trip to the cemetery? This didn't strike him as a good thing, but how would he know? Maybe she came out here frequently. Some people did. All she had now was memories, after all. Maybe this was Sunday dinner with the family.

Damn, that sounded awful. He shouldn't have even thought that. But looking at her over there kneeling by some headstones made her loneliness stand out as if it were limned with neon.

He had a big family. Huge by some estimations, he supposed. Growing up, his best friends had been his cousins and brothers. He'd straddled two worlds while all the time being swaddled in family. He couldn't imagine what life must be like for Corey, surrounded by people but none of them family. Not anymore.

Of course, he'd also seen cases where family wasn't such a great thing, either. What was that saying? Family aren't necessarily people you would choose for friends. Probably true. Maybe he'd just been blessed.

Still, she looked awfully alone, and he had to batter down an impulse to go to her. She had said she wanted to be alone out here, so maybe he should respect that. He'd respected little enough last night.

At last she rose, brushed off her knees and returned to her car. At once he turned and headed back to town, giving her the space she wanted.

Had he made things worse for her last night? The glum question followed him all the way back.

The store was quieter than usual, even for a Sunday afternoon. Corey felt disappointed, then realized she'd been hoping for an unlikely flow of customers so she wouldn't have to think about anything.

"Coward," she said aloud. And maybe that was the definition of everything she'd become since her mother's death. Hiding, always hiding inside herself. Afraid of things she had no reason to fear.

Really, to be afraid of almost all men because of one she couldn't remember? Maybe Austin had been right when he said she might be better off if she could remember the man who attacked her mother.

But how could she do that? The entire episode had been firmly walled off by her brain. Protection, maybe, but useful? Maybe not. Probably not.

For heaven's sake, she was twenty-five, nearly twenty-six, and she hadn't even dated. Until last night, she'd never held hands with a man or kissed one. She'd blocked out a huge chunk of her life because of fear.

Didn't that make her feel proud?

She cleaned the store with a vengeance. By the time four o'clock rolled around and it was time to close, she was sure the place had never sparkled quite the way it did then. Working with fabrics tended to create perennial dust and little bits of thread and lint, but they were all gone now. She figured it would last about two or three days.

She didn't think again of the mysterious notes until she was walking the three blocks to her house.

Like mother, like daughter.

What in the world did that mean? All she knew was that it felt seriously creepy. Even though it was still daylight and people were about, she quickened her step. She wanted to get back to the safety of her house, and hoped Austin would be waiting there.

A little shiver of nervousness hit her as she realized she hoped a man would be waiting for her. She hoped this was a sign she was growing out of at least some of her shell.

This morning she had kept their conversation to the purely impersonal, avoiding any possibility that he might penetrate her defenses the way he had last night. He was no fool, and probably realized exactly what she was doing.

That note hovered at the edge of her mind, then burst to the foreground, making her seriously uneasy. It felt like a threat, and made stepping out of her hiding place even scarier. But how would hiding within herself make it any better?

Austin's car was parked out front when she arrived home, but as soon as she entered she realized he wasn't there. Disappointed and despising herself for it, she went to shower and change. Cleaning the shop had created a need for her to clean herself. The thought amused her somehow, and lifted her mood.

After she dressed, she picked up her clothes hamper and headed for the laundry room beside the back porch. After she started her first load, she went to make a pot of coffee and started when she saw Austin there already making it.

"Do you mind?" he asked.

"Not at all. I was just about to make it."

"Good. How was your afternoon?"

"Quiet. No customers at all, so I cleaned the place."

He nodded and turned around, leaning back against the counter as the coffee brewed. "Dinner tonight."

She waited, looking at him uncertainly. "Yes?"

"Well, I don't know if you've tried it before, but your grocer makes his own Polish sausage." One corner of his mouth tipped up. "I think we've gotten to the point of dueling ethnic foods."

In an instant everything else vanished and a laugh escaped her. "Seriously?"

"Seriously. He gave me some of his smoked stuff to sample and told me how to cook it. Have you eaten it before?"

"I didn't even know he made it."

"Well, something to do with health codes and all that. He can't sell it in the meat case, so only those of us who are blessed to be considered trustworthy are offered any. The only Polish sausage I ever had was made by a big company. He assures me this is the real thing, that it's much better, and we'll love it. Given the hour, I guess we'll eat it like hot dogs. I got bakery buns."

"Sounds good." She was still smiling, and liked the way his eyes seemed to hold warmth for her.

"Great. Next week he's going to teach me how to make cabbage rolls. And I promised to teach him how to make chiles rellenos. Cooking class begins."

Turning, he filled two mugs and brought them to the table.

She realized she liked the way he had fit into this town. "Food must be an international language."

"It's certainly at the core of most socializing." He

sat facing her, still smiling. "Nothing like exchanging recipes."

Another giggle escaped her. "Do you know how funny that sounds coming from a man?"

His smile widened. "Pardon me, but we're *chefs*."

"Excuse me." She was still smiling, and unreasonably happy. This development both amused her and warmed her.

They ate the sausage on buns, the mood cheerful. She enjoyed the break from all the heavy thoughts she'd been having. Austin was good at diverting conversation, and he made her laugh easily.

But the laughter had another effect. It made her increasingly aware of him, of the attraction she felt for him. Last night's kiss had seared itself into her memory, along with the totally novel sensation of sitting on a man's lap. She had felt his desire for her, a secret and guilty pleasure. She wasn't sure he had wanted her to notice that.

How would she know, with her limited experience? Men were a mystery to her, she realized, and she had only herself to blame for that.

But mystery or not, there was nothing mysterious about the feelings he was evoking in her. She tried to look at her plate, but her gaze kept drifting back to him, drinking him in. She wondered vaguely if she was using him as an excuse not to think about all the hard and scary stuff of the past day but didn't believe that was true.

From the instant she set eyes on him, she had noticed how darkly handsome he was. Exotic. She had felt a pull toward him, unlike anything she had ever felt before.

From that first instant, he had been turning her common sense and protective shields into shredded paper.

How did he do that?

He had finished eating and glanced up to catch her staring at him. A faint smile framed his mouth.

"You keep looking at me like that, and I may grab you again. I'm sure you don't like being manhandled."

She didn't. Except for last night, when she hadn't minded it at all. Feeling her cheeks grow hot, she dropped her gaze. "Sorry."

"Oh, don't be sorry, *chica*. I like that expression in your eyes. I like the way it makes me feel. It makes me imagine all the ways I'd like to make love to you."

She drew a sharp breath and dared to look at him. Inside her, everything went crazy, then started to melt into a hot ache. A throbbing she *did* know began between her thighs, so strong that she felt she couldn't stand it if someone or something didn't touch her there. She shifted on her chair, trying to ease it, but even the pressure of her jeans wasn't enough.

Sensations and needs she'd been forcing herself to ignore for years refused to be ignored. Instead of fearing them, she wished she knew what to do about them.

"You don't have to be scared," he said quietly. The smile had vanished. "But if you want to explore this, *you* have to take the next step. I won't grab you again."

Her breath stuck in her throat. Her heart speeded up from a steady, heavy beat to pounding as if she were running a marathon. Fear and desire warred in her as never before.

She had to take the next step? She didn't know how.

What was the next step? Imagine being her age and knowing less that the average high schooler. All her fault. She'd been denying this side of herself for a long, long time. Because she feared it. Because it would bring her close to a man.

She had done an amazing job of shutting down her desires, making them almost nonexistent. Then this guy shows up and it was game over?

She wished she could get mad at him for eliciting these feelings and making her so confused. But it wasn't his fault she'd been hiding inside herself for so long. The only question now was whether she had any real courage left.

The kind of courage that would help her take the next step. She felt an urge to just run from this, but she'd been running for a long time, and apparently her safety had been illusory. Was she going to run again, this time from something she truly wanted?

He sat there completely still. She studied his olive-skinned face, his dark eyes, his high cheekbones and strong jaw. He had made her see herself through his eyes, made her recognize what she was doing to herself, yet he was still here.

"If you had a brain," she whispered, "you'd be heading for the hills right now."

"Why?"

"Because I'm so messed up."

He shook his head slightly. "I don't think you're messed up. I think you took the best path you knew to deal with some terrible things. The question now is, do you want to change that path? It won't be easy."

No, it wouldn't. But it was beginning to seem necessary. Living a half life wouldn't satisfy her forever. Or if it did, she was going to reach the finish line wondering if she'd even run the race.

"I've never..." She couldn't force the words out.

"I know." His face gentled, but he offered her no escape.

She had to make the next move, or none at all. What did she really want? That was the question.

Then the answer pushed past all her questions and concerns, and it was utterly clear: she wanted him. And she wanted the experience. But mostly she wanted him.

On legs that felt at once weak and strong, she stood and walked around the table. When she reached his side, she looked down at him and he looked up. Waiting.

She could still run.

But then she reached out and laid her hand on his shoulder. It felt so strong beneath her fingers, and through his shirt she could feel his warmth.

"Austin?"

"Yes?"

She felt so awkward. She felt frightened, almost like the day she had gone with her friends to a swimming hole and they were jumping off a tree limb that hung out over the water. She could still remember sitting there, telling herself to jump, while her body remained frozen. Beneath her, kids who had already jumped into the water splashed and played. But then it was her turn, and she froze, unable to move. Then something inside her had said, "Just do it." She had jumped.

Just do it.

She trailed her shaking hand down his powerful arm until she found his hand where it rested on the table. He turned it over at once and welcomed her grasp. She felt as if there was almost no air in the room.

And still he waited. For what? Finally, daringly, she gave his hand a little tug.

He stood then, wrapping her gently in his strength. "You can always say no, *querida*. At any time, at any point."

Then he kissed her, gently at first, seeking her response. Heat flared in her instantly, as if it had smoldered for so long it only needed a breath of air to ignite a wildfire.

As his tongue painted the sensitive tissues inside her mouth, shivers of longing ran through her. Reaching up, she wrapped her arms around his shoulders and hung on for dear life. Already he was taking her places she hadn't even visited with last night's kiss.

Nerve endings awoke to fresh life. Every part of her became acutely aware of him pressed against her. She felt the soft fabric of his shirt beneath her hands. The hardness of his entire length against her, an utterly new and confounding sensation.

It felt so good, so very good, just to be held close and kissed. Earlier that morning, she had come up against his hard body as they practiced self-defense, but it hadn't been the same. Her attention had been focused on her moves, not so much on him.

Now she forgot everything except him, and as he stoked the fires in her, first with his kisses to her mouth, then with kisses that trailed over her cheek, a gentle nip to her earlobe followed by more kisses along the column of her neck, she grew bolder. She ran her hands over his shoulders, then down his back, feeling his muscles move beneath her touches. Each new sensation poured waves of heat through her body, making her self-aware in a new way.

Her breasts ached for touches she had never really imagined. Her body cried out to be borne down beneath his weight. The flesh between her legs seemed to develop a life of its own, pulsing so hard it almost hurt.

She sagged into him, needing to be impossibly close. He smelled so good, of fresh air, of man, of soap and even the dinner they had just shared. As he trailed his mouth along her neck, causing her to shiver, she reciprocated and felt him shudder in response as she found the prickly skin he probably hadn't shaved since much earlier. She liked the difference.

Then he startled her, making a quiet exclamation she couldn't understand. Spanish? It almost tripped her out of the moment, but not quite, because he astonished her by sweeping her off her feet and carrying her back toward her bedroom.

Swept off her feet, she thought hazily. She hadn't really believed men did that. Apparently, Austin did. She clung to his shoulders, even as he lowered her to her bed.

"Easy, *querida*," he murmured. "We have all the time in the world."

A little bubble of happiness rose in her, as she wondered who he was trying to remind of that: himself or her. All the time in the world? She didn't know if she wanted to wait that long to discover what lay ahead.

Impatience now goaded her, having driven out the last of her fears.

He sat on the edge of the bed and pulled off his boots. Then he turned to her and got rid of her sneakers and socks. So little and yet so much. Only then did he stretch out beside her, propping his head on his hand and smiling down at her. For the first time she started to feel really nervous. Excited but nervous. Little bubbles of anxiety popped in her stomach, not quite drowned by the other awakening hungers.

"So beautiful," he murmured, running his fingertips along her cheek and neck. Delight poured through her.

"Not your type," she reminded him, amazed that she could speak at all when her entire body seemed full of demands she couldn't even name.

"Oh, very much my type," he said. "Very much. A few weeks ago would you have imagined yourself about to take a Latino lover?"

She felt a smile dawn on her face. "I never thought of taking even an Anglo lover."

His face sobered. "I know. Just be sure, Corey. Please. This is a huge step."

She dared to lift her hand to cup his cheek, enjoying the feel of his stubble. Enjoying a sense of freedom to reach out and touch him. All new and delightful sensations. "Be my first, Austin." She didn't dare ask for more than that.

He bent to kiss her again, this time so deeply that she felt as if he would enter her very soul. The kiss carried her away on a tide of longing so strong that when he broke it she was amazed to realize he had unbuttoned her shirt.

For an instant, beneath his gaze, she felt shy. He didn't give her long to continue feeling that way. With a twist, he released the front catch on her bra and her breasts spilled free. She bit her lip and closed her eyes, but then she heard him catch his breath.

"Perfect," he murmured. "You are perfect. Now lie as still as you can while I show you how perfect."

His hand, slightly roughened, cupped one of her breasts, lifting it and squeezing it gently. She could barely breathe now as fresh rivers of heat flowed through her. Then his thumb brushed her nipple and she arched helplessly, need elevating to heights she had never imagined.

"Shh, shh," he whispered as his thumb continued to taunt her and tease her. "Just feel. Just feel the wonder."

She couldn't do anything at all except feel. Thought vanished to some distant horizon and every cell in her focused on his touch. Each brush of his thumb ratcheted her longing, stoking the fire that seemed to have no limits.

She almost cried out when he released her, but then he cupped her other breast and repeated his caresses. She had never guessed the sensitivity of her nipples, not once. Now she knew, and she loved it.

A helpless cry escaped her when he replaced his thumb with his mouth, drawing her into his wet warmth, then flicking her with his tongue. She grabbed his head, as if fearing he would draw away, but as soon as she did, he sucked even more strongly, as if he would pull her into himself.

She would have liked nothing more. With each flick of his tongue, everything inside her tightened, answering his rhythm with growing hunger. Anticipation dizzied her as her body began to respond with helpless, gentle movements. It seemed to know the way, even if she did not.

She moaned softly as he released her, afraid he was going to disappear. Her eyes fluttered open to see him sit up and cast aside his own shirt.

He had a beautiful chest, and her body reacted to the sight instantly with a deep clenching. Smooth skin, bronzed as if sun-kissed, strong layers of muscle that rippled as he moved. She needed no encouragement to reach up and run her hands over him, awestruck by the sensation of his warm skin beneath her palms. She was awed by the freedom as he allowed her to explore his planes, angles and hollows.

How had she ever thought she could live without this?

He smiled sleepily, letting her touch him as she chose while running his own hand over her swollen breasts and down across her stomach. The caresses only deepened her excitement, causing her breaths to come in gasps.

Then he lay over her, propped on his arms, looking down into her eyes for a second before he bent his head and began to kiss every inch of her. All she could do was cling to his shoulders as if she feared falling. Or losing him.

But he didn't vanish. With lips and tongue he covered her in kisses that aroused her until she thought she couldn't stand any more. Instinctively, she tried to re-ciprocate, running her hands over whatever she could reach of his shoulders and back, but never did he come close enough for her to kiss him as he kissed her.

He painted her with fire, driving everything from her world except him and the eruption he was build-ing inside her. The throbbing, pulsing ache between her thighs became nearly painful in its strength. Her heart hammered wildly. She needed…oh, heavens, she barely knew what she needed.

He pulled away, and this time she cried out in protest.

"Easy, *mi querida*. There's more."

Oh, man was there more. He ditched his pants, show-ing her for the very first time a man in full arousal. She nearly gasped. He was so big, and she suddenly felt very small and vulnerable. He waited a moment, letting her see, then caught her hand and wrapped it around his staff.

She gasped, hardly able to believe that his skin felt silken, or that something that felt so soft could also feel as hard as steel. He moved her hand on him, showing her, and she watched as he sucked air and threw his head back. A huge sense of power filled her. She could make him react like that?

But he didn't give her long to learn him. He had more to show her. When he tugged away her pants and un-derwear, she felt no shyness this time, only eagerness. Every cell in her body was demanding more.

"New surprises," he murmured.

He lifted her knees and then spread them wide, kneeling between them. She threw her arms over her eyes, afraid suddenly, but the fear didn't last long.

The gentlest of caresses traced her lips, driving fear away and replacing it with more amazed hunger. That a touch so light… Her mind spun away.

Over and over he drew his fingertips lightly across her most secret flesh, teasing her to the brink of insanity. Her hips began to rise and fall helplessly, responding to the lightest touches.

"You are exquisite," he whispered, filling her with a wonder that nearly matched her need. Then, gently, he parted her petals. The sensation of cool air down there overwhelmed her. Never had she felt so exposed or helpless, and she was loving it. Loving it.

He found a knot of nerve endings so sensitive that when he touched it she cried out. The sensations that filled her nearly shattered her. She cried out his name, needing, wanting and having no words for it.

"A moment," he said gently. "A moment."

She pried her eyes open to see him roll on a condom, and wished she could have done it herself.

"Are you sure?"

She managed a nod, wanting to sink back into the lava that was pouring so hotly through her.

"There will be a little pain…"

She felt him nudge at her with his hardness, then a tearing sensation that caused her to gasp and dig her nails into the bed.

"It'll pass," he said, lowering himself over her as he entered fully. He cupped her face and sprinkled more kisses on her. "It will pass."

It did, too, and as jarring as the pain had been, it vanished quickly in the heat he rebuilt by kissing her, by sucking on her breasts, just by the very weight and feel of him between her legs.

When it faded completely, she was again consumed by need, and tentatively lifted her hips to bring him even closer. At once he started to move in her, taking her completely to another world as he pumped, first gently and then more strongly.

His head lowered, a long sigh escaped him, then a moan. The sound of his moan added to the pleasure building in her. She began to fly upward like a rocket on its way to the moon. As every sensation seemed to grow harder, her body seemed to grow softer until she hovered on a precipice she had never known existed. Her nails dug into his shoulders, her head arched back. A mindless plea began a drumbeat in her head, in her body. She almost feared she might never find what lay over the lip of this pinnacle.

Then she tumbled, falling endlessly as satisfaction gripped her repeatedly, each pulse of her body sending a new wave through her. She became a thousand glowing embers of sheer pleasure.

She felt him pump into her one more time, hard. Then his back arched and a deep groan escaped him.

Moments later he sagged onto her. She felt replete, weak and oh, so happy.

A long breath escaped her at last, and she settled back to earth in his arms.

Chapter 9

Austin wrapped Corey in his arms and held her close beneath the covers. If she could have purred, he suspected she would have. He had enough experience to know that he had truly pleased her. Honestly, he probably would have purred, too, if he could. Other lovers, other times, other places, nothing quite matched what he had just shared with this woman.

He wanted to luxuriate with her in this, but he wasn't the sort who could lose track of reality for too long. That had helped keep him alive for six years. But right now he was asking himself only one question: Had he just made the biggest mistake of his life?

This woman had given him an infinitely precious gift and he knew it. But in his way, he had barged right in, first telling her how she was hiding, then taking her to bed. While she might be feeling wonderful at the moment, and she seemed to be, it remained that he might just have added to the scars she already bore.

He'd shoved past her walls, breaking down her carefully constructed defenses, at least where he was concerned. He wasn't sure if idiocy had pushed him, or desire, but either way he might have weakened something she truly needed.

He didn't feel very good about himself right then. Sooner or later he was going to have to go back to work. Back to D.C. What would that do to her? She'd let one man into her tower and then he took off?

God, it had been killing him to watch her live in that prison, but now he'd yanked at least one bar out and he had no way of knowing if he'd made her less safe by doing it.

She stirred and snuggled closer. He immediately tightened his arms around her. One special woman. Maybe he just needed to focus on that part.

"I'd like to do that again," she murmured.

He brushed her hair back from her face. "Me, too, *querida.*"

"What's that mean, *querida?*"

"It derives from the verb *querer.* To want, to need, to desire. So you can translate it as dear, or darling, or more bluntly, woman that I desire."

Her lips curved. "Mmm, I like that."

"It's a common endearment between couples."

"I like that, too."

Couples, he thought. Were they a couple? She probably thought so. Maybe they were. He'd certainly spent enough time trying to get into Rapunzel's tower. The only question he hadn't asked himself was why.

Sighing at his own stupidity, he held her close and caressed her, thinking that he'd better get himself sorted out fast, before he made things worse for her.

He suddenly remembered something his uncle had

said to him one summer when he was sixteen and visiting the *finca*. He'd been exchanging longing looks with the daughter of a neighbor, a beautiful girl of fifteen. Her dark eyes had snapped at him, and if she'd ever escaped the watchful eye of her *dueña*, something might have happened between them. But then his uncle took him aside and gave him a warning. "You can't have a one-night stand with a virgin."

Hell.

Cuddling with Austin felt so good, and Corey was savoring every instant of it. He had showed her a beautiful new world, and she wanted to replay every moment of it in her mind, over and over. She loved lying with him like this, skin on skin. Who would have ever thought it could feel so delicious?

She also experienced a newfound sense of freedom. No more pretenses, everything was out in the open now. She could reach out and touch him anytime she wanted. She no longer needed to hang back or hold back. She felt as if she could fly, as if she were weightless. The cage and the fears that had cramped her for so long seemed to have vanished.

At least for now. Tomorrow would come, and with it all the fears and worries. Nor was she deluded. Austin had come here for a place to get away and sort himself out—not that he struck her as needing a whole lot of sorting—and he would be leaving. Three months, Gage had said. She had no reason to believe that was going to change.

She assured herself she could handle the situation,

that she would treasure this time with him and move on. There was no need for it to be anything more than a fling and she'd keep her heart guarded. She certainly had enough experience with that.

Confident of her ability to handle whatever happened, perhaps foolishly so, she turned her head to look up at him and realized that his face reflected tension.

"Is something wrong?" she asked. Her glow began to fade rapidly.

"No," he said swiftly, and dropped a kiss on her forehead. "I'm lying here with a beautiful woman enjoying an incredible afterglow."

Exactly the right thing to say, but she didn't believe him. She hesitated, wondering if she should just accept his words at face value or press the issue. She didn't have a whole lot of experience with relationships of this kind. Well, no experience, to be precise. But she was also a grown woman and no fool. Nor had she ever been one, even as a child, to accept a pat on the head and vague reassurance.

Sighing, she sat up, clutching the coverlet to her breasts.

"Corey?"

"Just don't lie to me, Austin. I may be only twenty-five, but I've had plenty of experience with the downside of life. All I want is truth, not soothing nothings."

"Nothings? I wasn't lying."

"You weren't exactly being truthful, either. Something is bothering you."

"Amazing."

"What is?"

"I'm not usually easy to read. In fact, I've worked very hard not to be."

"So tell me." She waited, her heart skipping a few beats. Maybe she was a terrible lover. How would she know? She had no experience by which to measure. Nerves began to turn her stomach over. "Austin?"

"It was wonderful. It was beautiful. You're fantastic and I want to make love to you again. Unfortunately, I'm having a belated attack of guilt."

"For what? I thought we just had a great time."

"We did. But was it right? You gave me something precious, Corey, but maybe I shouldn't have accepted it."

She began to feel confused. "Why not? You gave me plenty of opportunity to say no."

"That doesn't change the fact that you deserve someone with something to offer you. I have to go back to Washington eventually. How's that going to make you feel? Like you've been used?"

Her jaw dropped in surprise as she understood the route his mind had taken. Guilt? For the pleasure they had just shared because he couldn't make her promises of any kind? That gave her his measure more clearly than anything could have. Her nervousness eased in a wave of warmth toward him.

"You're remarkable," she said.

"Me? Not really."

"Yes, really. I may have lived in a cave most of my life, but I gather the vast majority of men wouldn't feel the least bit of guilt. So, relax. I have no regrets."

His face seemed to say that he hoped she didn't have any later, but then it smoothed over and he smiled. "I guess we'll see. Are you hungry? Because much as I'd like to go right on holding you, my stomach is rumbling."

He reached out before she could move, though, and drew her down on his chest, brushing her hair back with his hands, then pulling her close for a deep kiss. When he let her catch her breath again, his dark eyes sparkled. "Snack? Then more of you."

One of the things Austin had noticed about this house was how heavily curtained the windows were. Upstairs they let in light, but down here they darkened the house completely. He hadn't really thought about it until tonight, assuming they were insulation.

But now they struck him differently. Evidently she didn't want anyone at any time to be able to look in her windows. In the time he'd been here, he'd only seen her open any of them once. At the back of his mind he'd assumed that because she was gone so much, she didn't think about it.

Now it struck him as a sign, maybe because of those damn notes. Then another thought hit him.

Every night at a reasonable hour, he'd been turning on the lights upstairs. But not tonight. If someone was watching her, stalking her, that was more information than he wanted them to have.

While she pulled out some leftovers and started a fresh pot of coffee, he excused himself to dash upstairs. Once there, he followed his usual habit in the way he turned on the lights. Then he made a point of picking up a book and starting to flip through it, casting his shadow clearly on the thinner curtains. After a minute he wandered away as if going to settle in with a book.

He hadn't any idea if anyone was watching, none whatsoever. But it seemed like a good idea not to take foolish chances. Little by little he'd been working himself back into form as an agent, but right now he decided he needed to speed up the recovery quite a bit.

Like mother, like daughter could mean almost anything. Unfortunately, to him it sounded like a potentially deadly threat, although he didn't want to say so to Corey. He didn't know for certain, so there was no point in scaring her more than she already was. But to him those words meant less that she was like her mother, than that she was going to die like her mother. He'd gotten the sense that Gage saw them the same way but hadn't wanted to say so where Corey might overhear.

Making his way slowly back down the stairs, knowing full well that Corey's mind was going to be in a much happier place than his, he tried to push such thoughts away. He didn't want to ruin this night for her, not even a little bit, by bringing ugly reality into it. Not *that* ugly reality, anyway. She'd come back to it soon enough.

So he could give her one night, at least one, during which she could feel prized and special and not afraid of anything.

It might be a fool's paradise, but everyone needed one from time to time.

Corey smiled to herself as she heard Austin coming down the stairs. She'd already heated a few things in the microwave, and more was on the way. A feast was beginning to appear on the table.

"I think," Austin said as he entered the kitchen, "I need to learn to cook for less than a dozen."

"But the leftovers are so scrumptious. Didn't you cook for yourself in Mexico?"

"Rarely. I needed to become a familiar sight, so I ate at cantinas, and kiosks, places where I could be seen. Also places where I could hear gossip."

"I never thought about all that must go into doing what you did. You really had to burrow in."

"That's a good word for it."

She popped the last of the tamales out of the microwave and placed them on the table. "Is this an old recipe, too?"

"Yes. Five to eight thousand years old. Portable food. Used by workers and by armies."

"It's kind of remarkable," she said, joining him at the table with steaming cups of coffee. "In use for so long."

"I'm sure a lot of things we eat stretch back a long way. Roast beast, for example. I'll bet cavemen were inventing barbecue sauces."

She laughed. "You're probably right."

At least he was smiling at her, not looking haunted as he had for a few minutes earlier. She didn't want him to feel guilty or in any way disturbed by their lovemaking. For her it had been a wondrous experience and she wanted it to stay that way, not become a cause for angst. And mostly, she wanted to try it again and again. That wasn't very likely if he started berating himself for taking advantage of her.

But she honestly didn't know how to address the issue. She hated her lack of experience in this arena for the first time. Just hated it. She didn't know the right things to do or say.

Lovemaking seemed to have given her an appetite, and eating gave her an excuse not to talk. Which was good, she decided. With each passing minute she felt increasingly insecure, afraid she'd say or do the wrong thing.

How did she know this man even liked her? Or that he'd enjoyed making love to her? She'd heard men didn't need much more than a willing body to get what they wanted. Maybe for him it had been utterly pedestrian. How would she know?

She'd just shared one of life's most intimate experiences with Austin, and here she was feeling smaller and more afraid by the minute. The devils of insecurity began to sting her with their pitchforks, reminding her of all she didn't know, all she had never done, which made her a poor judge of what had just happened.

For her it had been amazing. But what about him? Maybe he hoped she'd just leave it at this and not bug him. Maybe he just wanted to move on.

And she feared that if she opened her mouth she'd put her foot in it.

A short while later he said, "Corey, don't do this."

She looked up from her miserable thoughts. "Do what?"

"You're pulling inside yourself again. I can almost see you shrinking. What are you afraid of?"

Herself. Him. Her cheeks began to grow hot. The

doing had been new enough. Talking about it seemed beyond her.

A gleam came to his eyes. "Ah," he said, sounding as if he got it.

"Ah, what?"

"You're asking yourself questions. Were you good enough? Was I pleased? Do I want to make love to you again?"

Now her cheeks felt so hot she wanted to put ice on them. A slow, warm smile grew on his face. "You were wonderful. I enjoyed every minute of it, and if you'll have me, I'll prove it again. You pleased me more than you can probably imagine."

She couldn't help it. She pressed her hands to her cheeks to try to cool them. He laughed kindly. "Relax, *querida*. Say and ask whatever you want. I've got a thick skin."

"You don't need one with me," she managed to say. "It's just…well, this is all so new to me I don't even know how to talk about it."

"I didn't know there was a special way. Say whatever occurs to you. I am."

A wave of relief washed through her, not because he had given her permission to say whatever she wanted, but because he had assured her that he was saying what was on his mind, too.

He leaned across the table and trailed his finger along her cheek. She dropped her hands.

"There's only one first time, Corey. For anyone. It's special. So go ahead and say anything about it you want."

"I was just…" She really didn't want to admit how

insecure she had been growing, but he'd already figured out that part. "I keep replaying it in my head. I never want to forget an instant."

His entire face softened. "Nobody's ever said anything that sweet to me before. If I start pounding my chest like a gorilla, I hope you'll excuse me."

That surprised a giggle out of her. "Gorilla?"

"It's always possible. You just made me feel really good. Very studly."

She had to laugh again at his absurdity. God, she loved the way he could make her laugh. "You *are* studly." And that was the truth, she thought. Something about him in particular. She knew of lots of attractive men around town, but none had ever awakened a smidgen of what Austin had awakened in her. Maybe it was his innate confidence. Maybe it was the sense he could take care of himself in any situation. Maybe it was the fact he could get into cooking and exchanging recipes and not feel the least uncomfortable. He could even joke about wearing a frilly apron.

It was as if he felt he had nothing left to prove. Maybe he didn't. She wished she could feel that way.

The only shadow that crossed her mind was after they cleared away the food and he led her back to her bedroom.

"The lights are on upstairs," she said.

"Leave them," he murmured. "Just leave them on."

But she didn't miss the fact that later he went up to turn them off, then came back to her side.

Did he think they were being watched? Before the ice

could begin to freeze her insides, though, he once again drew her into his arms.

"Now," he said, "let me show you the ways I can love you."

He not only showed her how he could love her, but also how to reciprocate. She couldn't decide which was the more dizzying experience, what he did to her with his mouth and hands, or what he showed her to do with hers.

The latter, she finally decided. He appeared to have no inhibitions at all, but when he lay back and gave himself to her to do with as she pleased, she felt an incredible sense of delighted power.

It was like petting a lion, she thought dreamily as she ran first her hands and then her mouth over his angles and planes. He was so strong and big in every sense, and she loved feeling him quiver helplessly under her touch. He mostly allowed her to find her own way, so she paid close attention to his responses, seeking those things that made him groan.

Like his small brown nipples. They drew her, and when she finally dared to close her mouth over one, she discovered that they were as sensitive as her own. Not only did he groan, but he clutched her head gently and held her close.

"You can do that forever," he muttered.

Joy zinged through her as she realized what she could give him. Emboldened, she continued her exploration, loving the way he writhed in pleasure but didn't take command as he had earlier. Remembering the pleasures he had taught her with his lips and tongue, she reluctantly moved from his responsive nipples, down across his flat hard belly to the core of his manhood.

Stiff hairs tickled her nose, but she hardly noticed them. The aroma overpowered her, pleasing her with its rich muskiness. She nuzzled him and felt him buck. Then she reached for his staff, so hard and strong yet so incredibly silky and smooth. She ran her fingers lightly over it, loving the way it responded to each touch. Listening to him nearly pant as she carried him higher and higher. Her own desires were rising apace with his, making her insides tighten with hunger, pulsing with need.

Swept away on a tide of her own feelings, she then did something she had heard about but had never believed she would do.

She closed her mouth over him and mimicked the movements he had earlier made inside her.

It was like setting off a rocket. If he had wanted to delay, he couldn't. Moments later she felt him jet, hot and salty, into her mouth.

Before she could react, he startled her by turning her over. He kissed her moist mouth, then slid down over her, tucking his head between her legs while he reached up with his fingers to tease her nipples.

She reached the pinnacle so fast under the strokes of his tongue that passion left her dizzy.

Then it left her feeling like a warm, happy puddle.

It might have been a courtesy call, the man across town told himself as he sat in front of his computer. The message had been meant to unnerve Corey, but it had been deliberately opaque. So maybe the sheriff had just showed up because he'd brought that guy to room with her. Just to check on things.

The visit had come late at night, the sheriff had come from home. Yeah, it had probably just been a friendly visit. Not a response to the note. He didn't want Corey to guess until the last minute. He wanted her to wonder. He hoped she was thinking about what might have gotten her mother killed.

Relax, he ordered himself. Relax. Corey still hadn't done anything different...well, except for that trip to the gym today. Maybe she was a little uneasy. He didn't mind that. But then she'd gone and opened her store as if nothing had changed.

What he needed to focus on was that even though she had a man living in her house now, nothing had changed. He still couldn't believe she had let the guy run home instead of offering him a ride.

Well, what could you expect from an unnatural man-hater? Like mother, like daughter indeed. She'd inherited her deviance, and maybe he shouldn't blame her for that, but he could blame her for giving in to it. She didn't have to indulge herself this way.

Look at him. He controlled everything in his life, allowing no overindulgence of any kind. Not in his relationships, not in his drinking, not in his eating. Corey showed no moderation at all. With her it was only women all the time. All the claptrap about her taking in roomers, he didn't believe it. She took in her lovers. They stayed awhile, then moved on. But he didn't know of a one of them that had married. As far as he could tell, the last woman she'd had live with her for two years hadn't even dated.

So it was as clear as the nose on his face.

The only thing he had to decide now was when. And which note he would send her as a final note, the one he really wanted to scare her. Nobody would be able to trace it, and if someone thought it was a real threat, he intended to make sure they couldn't do anything about it.

Fact was, if the sheriff got involved, he could wait it out. The person who would pay for the waiting was Corey. She would know she wasn't safe.

He wondered idly if she'd run to Denver like her mother. No, he decided. She would stay right here because she knew what had happened to her mother in Denver. She wouldn't risk running.

The trap was tightening, and she was probably only beginning to suspect it.

Satisfied, he allowed himself another sip of beer and sat staring at the last sentence on the screen.

She deserved it. So do you.

That would do it.

When morning came it was hard to tell because of the heavy curtains. Only the quiet buzz of the alarm clock alerted them.

Corey would have been happy to stay in bed all day, but she had a sewing class this morning and had to open the store. Austin settled the issue, sweeping her out of bed in his arms and carrying her laughing into her small bathroom. There, standing in the tub, he lathered her until she had to grab his shoulders to keep from collapsing.

"Hold on to that thought," he said, grinning. "There's tonight."

But tonight was a long way away. Corey sighed but smiled, liking that he'd given her something to look forward to. Could life get any better?

But bit by bit, reality crept in. His smile faded. Her happiness began to flee. In the kitchen, the memory of the notes returned, hitting her as hard as a punch. She'd managed to forget them for a little while, but now they zoomed to the forefront of her mind, filling her with unease. She had the inescapable sense that someone was hunting her. Following her. Watching her. Intending far worse than a prank. Seemingly innocent, the threat of those notes once again hit her.

"Corey? What's wrong?

She felt a superstitious dread of even mentioning those notes, as if she could push them out of reality by denying them. Oh, she was good at denial. She'd been engaging in it for years. "What name did you go by in Mexico?"

"Tino," he said. "I went by Tino, a common nickname." He crossed the floor to where she stood leaning against the counter, and caught her chin, making her look at him. "What's going on? You're not really looking like this because you're wondering about my name."

She started to shake her head, but he wouldn't release her chin.

"Corey?"

"It's the notes," she admitted finally. "It all just

kind of hit me again. What the hell does it mean, 'Like mother, like daughter'?"

He hesitated, then released her chin to embrace her. "It means," he said slowly, "that we're going to have to solve a murder."

Chapter 10

An overwhelming feeling flooded her, although she couldn't tell if it was fear or anger. It just flooded her. She twisted out of his grasp, ready to fight.

"What are you talking about?" she demanded. "The police couldn't figure out my mother's murder eighteen years ago. What makes you think you can do it now?" Before he could answer, she glanced at her watch and said in a steely voice, "I've got to get to work."

Grabbing her tote and a sweater, she walked out without looking back. Solve a murder? Really? As if the Denver police hadn't done their jobs when the case was fresh? Dig into that all over again now?

That was when she realized that fear was driving her not anger. She didn't want to dig up all that again. She didn't want to have to retrace the most painful path of her life. She was terrified that doing so might awaken memories she didn't want to have. That it might cast her back into the darkness she had been struggling with for so long.

Her chest tightened until she felt she couldn't draw in air. She had to slow her pace as her heart hammered loudly enough to deafen her. How could he even suggest such a thing? It was madness, and it was mean.

After last night, it only seemed meaner. He'd opened up something soft and trusting inside her, a place that had never opened before, and then he slammed her with this?

The notes were troubling, yes. Even a bit scary. But to think he could solve the murder of her mother after all this time and all the effort put into it seemed like pure hubris. Dangerous hubris. Nobody was as aware as she that she lived her life on a carefully balanced point surrounded by a moat full of monsters.

She knew why she didn't remember, and knew equally well why she didn't *want* to remember. Maybe he wasn't talking about poking into that blank space in her memory, but to start trying to recall things or answer questions might only tip her into that inky moat that surrounded part of her life.

She couldn't afford that. They'd have to find this tormentor some other way, or she'd just have to live with those unnerving notes.

There was no other way.

She reached the front door of her business and unlocked it with a sense of relief. Familiar faces would be arriving soon. She went to the bay window to check the displays, and forced herself to go through the motions of preparing for the sewing circle. When school was out and the ranches were busy, it was mostly a group of older women, but during the school year the store would swell with younger women whose children were in school. It was always a group full of good conversation. The way she felt right now, she wasn't sure she'd be able to keep up her end.

Damn Austin, she thought. It was as if last night had never happened. See if she would trust a man ever again.

Lift her to a pinnacle of joy and happiness, then trash it all with a couple of words?

Damn him, she thought again, and turned to greet the first customer of the day.

Well, that had gone swimmingly, Austin thought after he cleaned up the kitchen and headed to meet the sheriff. Although maybe going to visit Dalton might not be smart. Yes, everyone around seemed to think he was a friend of Gage's, but his paranoia was reaching new heights.

That last note had flipped some switch inside him. So much for finding a way back to ordinary life. Once again he walked the streets as a man on a covert mission, and any one of these people around him might be the threat.

He shouldn't have let Corey walk to work on her own, yet he knew as well as anybody that changing routine could give away information. He had no proof that someone was watching Corey, no proof that she was actually being stalked, but if something changed radically, it could precipitate action. Until he had some sense of the shape of the threat here, he didn't want this guy to have any idea that his notes were having a serious impact.

He didn't see how dogging Corey's steps could help. It might expose her to swift action at the first opportunity. Or it might push the problem further down the road. Hell, he hadn't the foggiest idea what kind of person would even do something like this.

The criminals he dealt with were more like a cross between gangs and businessmen. They didn't play these kinds of games. The guy sending these notes was savoring something. Whether it was the idea of frightening Corey, or even that he was enjoying his private knowledge of what had happened to Corey's mother, Austin didn't know. There was something measured in this, too, something being carefully doled out in those notes. A control freak?

Ten minutes later, he and Gage were having coffee together at Maude's. The place was properly known as The City Diner, as the sign out front proclaimed, but he'd swiftly learned that the locals referred to it by the owner's name: Maude's.

The place was only moderately busy at this hour, giving them privacy to talk and sufficient noise to prevent eavesdropping.

"So you want the whole file on Olivia Donohue?"

Austin nodded. "That last note shoved me into high gear. This guy knows something about the murder. Whether he's going to try to hurt Corey... Well, I'm getting a bad feeling about that."

"It grows on you," Gage remarked. He picked up his mug. "No prints, by the way. None. And that makes me even more uneasy."

Austin sat very still. He'd been hoping against hope that there'd been prints on that note. Not because they'd necessarily lead them to this guy, but because it would remove him from the category of major threat. If the perp was being careful enough not to leave any evidence, then he'd just moved himself into a whole new class.

"Nothing else, either," Gage continued. "I'd have been happy to find even a cat hair."

"Something," Austin agreed. "This level of caution…" He left his sentence unfinished.

"I know." Gage sighed, rubbed his chin and signaled for more coffee. In the manner to which Austin had rapidly become accustomed, Maude stomped over, poured with a grunt, then marched away. No friendly chitchat from her.

"Working a cold case is hell," Gage remarked. "It's hard to rustle up anything that hasn't already been chewed over. Really, all you've got to count on is fresh eyes."

"That could be enough."

"Hope springs eternal." He rested his elbows on the table, leaning in a bit. "There was some talk about Olivia back when."

Austin's attention pricked. "What kind?"

"That she was a lesbian. Didn't date much in high school, I hear. But then she up and got pregnant and the gossip pretty much stopped. I wasn't clued in to all that back then, since I was pretty much dealing with my own demons. I only remember it vaguely, but you know how small towns are. Somebody's a little different, and folks start coming up with reasons."

"Would that have been a problem here?"

"Hell, yeah. It would have been a problem a lot of places. Folks have gotten more tolerant, even here, but yeah, it would have been uncomfortable. I don't recall hearing her giving people a reason to wonder. She just didn't date much. Like that's a crime."

"Corey doesn't date at all. Are folks talking like that about her?"

Gage shook his head. "After what that girl's been through, people seem more than willing to cut her any slack she needs or wants. They get that she's still frightened."

Austin raised his brows. "I hope they don't tell her that."

"Why would they? They feel a lot of sympathy for her and they like her. She's pretty popular with the sewing and quilting crowd, too. Sometimes I think more people get to her shop during a week than go to church."

Austin laughed, but none of this was helping him get any closer to the problem. As if he realized it, Gage sighed and sipped more coffee, then fell into reflection. "I'll get as much information out of Denver as I can. After all this time, maybe they won't feel like we're stepping on their toes."

Austin was all too familiar with that reaction. Jurisdiction mattered.

"Something that's really bugging me," Gage said after a moment. "There was no physical evidence at the scene of Olivia's murder, other than her and Corey, of course. No hairs, no skin flakes. Some fibers that could have come from anything—a cotton thread from a white T-shirt, a stray denim fiber or two, but nothing else."

Austin felt his heart stop. "Not one thing?"

"Nothing the least bit useful. He must have shaved himself all over pretty good and climbed into freshly laundered clothes. Whatever he was wearing on his feet didn't even track in anything that didn't come from right outside the apartment. One of the crime scene techs figures he wore disposable booties over his shoes, gloves and maybe a ski mask. Hell, for all anyone knows he might have been wearing a Tyvek overall."

Austin felt ice creep along his skin. "Completely and carefully premeditated."

"Exactly. Which tells us only that he wanted to kill Olivia Donohue."

"So he must have known her."

"If I can get the report, you'll read all about it. They checked all her known associates, even up here. Nothing. Everyone, amazingly enough, had an alibi. It would have been easier to deal with if there'd ever been another murder that fit this M.O. But there wasn't, not before or since. A crime scene that clean stands out like a sore thumb."

Gage paused. "For your ears only. Corey doesn't know this and I don't want her to know unless there's a damn good reason. In Olivia's papers, the cops found a receipt from a fertility clinic. Corey's father was a vial of sperm."

There went that possibility, Austin thought. No angry ex. "I won't tell her," he said. "She's lost enough. She seems comfortable about not knowing who her father was. I'm not sure how she'd feel about this."

"Me, neither."

"I mean, I suppose it could be easier knowing there's no guy out there who just didn't want you, but that's a boat I don't want to rock. It hasn't struck me as very high on her list of concerns." But what did he know? He hardly knew the woman, he'd bedded her last night— which he was still pondering as possibly his greatest act of stupidity—but that didn't mean he really knew what Corey thought about anything.

But who ever did know another person fully? You could spend a lifetime getting to really know someone, and then still know only part of them

Gage eased out of the booth and tossed some bills on the table. "I've got the coffee. I'll get in touch with Denver."

"Thanks."

Austin sat there for a while, nursing his coffee and thinking. Not even Maude's clomping by penetrated his deep well of thought. No father. A crime scene so clean it was memorable. Which brought him right back to those notes. They were clean, too. Not a hint or a clue on them except that they were mailed in town.

That meant the murderer was stalking Corey. But why in the hell would he do that? Just to scare her? Or to let her know he was coming, that he intended her to die the same way her mother had?

Austin had met some sick twists in his life, but this one took the cake. He had trained himself to remain calm on the job, but right now he was feeling anything but calm. A surprisingly cold anger filled him. Cold as the Arctic wastelands. He no longer had the least doubt what this guy wanted to do. The question about that had vanished.

The question now was what he was going to do about Corey to make her safe.

* * *

Early-autumn twilights lingered, not as long as at the height of the summer, but long enough. When Corey closed up her shop, there was still enough light to walk home by. Her day had been busy, filled with women she liked, and gradually she had shed her earlier anger at Austin and decided she had overreacted. After all, if he asked questions she didn't want to answer, all she had to say was no. She'd been a child when she had learned to evade those questions, and she hadn't lost the ability.

A lot of people were out on the still-warm evening. In the winter a lot of shops closed around six, but until then many stayed open later. It was kind of like an evening promenade, folks getting out for a postprandial stroll, kids tagging along in hopes of a stop for ice cream or another treat. The tiny ice-cream shop sold a lot of frozen yogurt these days, but inside it still looked as if it had stepped out of another time. Which it had. Once it had been the soda fountain. Now it offered ice cream, yogurt and smoothies.

Corey realized she was feeling pretty good. Almost without noticing it, she was humming a cheerful tune as she walked, pausing to speak occasionally to someone she knew. Without giving it much thought, she headed straight for the ice-cream shop. When she came out, she had a quart of rich vanilla ice cream, some nuts and a bottle of hot fudge.

She didn't know whether Austin liked ice cream, or even which kind, so she hoped she'd picked a flavor he wouldn't object to.

It was hard to remember that only this morning she

had been mad at him and frightened by what he'd said. Somewhere along the way today, she had fallen more often into memories of the night they had shared. So here she came, bearing gifts.

Maybe it was stupid of her, but it wasn't as if the guy had been deliberately mean to her, even if it had felt that way for a little while. No, he'd been expressing concern. He was a cop. Of course his first thought would be about solving her mother's murder. Man of action and all that.

She was still smiling when she arrived home and entered. She could hear Austin moving around upstairs.

"Austin?"

"Yeah?"

"You'd better hurry before the ice cream melts."

Then she went to the kitchen and started getting out bowls and spoons. She heard him trot down the stairs and enter the kitchen.

"Ice cream?"

"Vanilla," she answered. "I hope you like it. I also bought nuts to put on it, and some hot fudge topping if you like."

Then she turned and saw him standing there in jeans and a black T-shirt, his fingers jammed into his front pockets. "Really? I love ice cream."

"Maybe I should have gotten you the kind with jalapeños in it."

His face lightened and he laughed. "To what do I owe this?"

"It's an apology for getting mad at you this morning. Plus, I wanted ice cream."

"I'm sorry I made you mad."

"Actually, I think I got afraid. I never did get that completely sorted out. Nuts? Topping?"

He wanted everything and helped as much as he could. Soon they both had big bowls at the table.

"This is one of humankind's greatest inventions," he remarked as he lifted the spoon to his mouth.

"Did you know the Earl of Sandwich invented chocolate ice cream?"

That raised both his dark brows. "I thought it was sandwiches."

"That was his descendant. No, I read recently that the first Earl of Sandwich invented chocolate ice cream."

"Well, I've been known to take cocoa powder and sprinkle it over a bowl of vanilla ice cream. It's great. The Earl of Sandwich, huh? Those guys must have really been into food."

"Actually, I gather he was on some board of trade that was trying to find uses for things from the colonies. And what he made was more of a frozen drink than what we think of as ice cream."

"Who cares? I'm sure it was a great idea. Chocolate wasn't always eaten sweetened. It still isn't in some places."

"You're neat," she said suddenly.

"What?"

"How many men will discuss recipes? You're neat."

He laughed, shaking his head.

"Actually," she said after a few more mouthfuls, "I bet humans have been making iced drinks and other stuff ever since we noticed snow and ice could be useful."

"It wouldn't surprise me. How did your day go?"

"Very busy. It was nice." She hesitated. "I'm sorry I walked out on you like that. I got too upset."

"I'm not blaming you. It probably did seem like a cockeyed statement."

"It wasn't that it was cockeyed." She nibbled on her lower lip, looking down into her bowl. Had she really eaten that much? "It's that I don't think we'll ever know. Unless…"

"Unless what?" he prompted finally.

"Unless the guy who's sending these notes is the man who murdered my mother."

There it lay, Austin thought. The heart of the question, a live grenade between them. The only question was whether he should pull the pin or conceal his concerns from her.

The urge to protect her warred in him because there were two routes to follow. He could shield her from his suspicions, or he could guard her by warning her about the danger. Either one might not save her from whatever her tormentor planned. But which would make her safer?

On the face of it, it seemed like a stupid question. Knowledge was always a better shield than ignorance. But after what this woman had been through, he didn't want to terrify her again. Hadn't she been through enough?

Of course she had, but it apparently wasn't over yet. It was always possible some sick twist just thought this was funny, but the lack of evidence on those notes combined with the lack of evidence at the original crime scene made that important. Too important to ignore. Humans just left detritus wherever they went, from hairs to skin cells, from clothing fibers to the stuff they tracked on their shoes. A clean crime scene was a feat, and now those notes were too clean. A definite link.

Corey broke the silence. "You think this guy wants to kill me, too."

She had pulled the pin on the grenade. Had she done it because she wanted him to deny it? He met her gaze, found it steady, and anyway, he didn't want to lie to her. As far as he was concerned, if he never told another lie in his life, he'd feel pretty good about it.

"It's crossed my mind and Gage's."

Those brilliant blue eyes of hers closed. She dropped her spoon into the bowl where it began to sink into softening ice cream. "I knew it," she whispered.

"Knew what?"

"I'm really good at denial," she said, her voice thin. "But at some level, I knew it, anyway. One note I could dismiss, but not quite. Before Gage brought you here, I actually got the shakes from just reading it. I tried to tell myself a friend was pulling a prank, but I couldn't believe it. Something about it didn't seem like a joke. That's why I didn't throw it away. I knew."

He wanted to reach for her, to scoop her into his arms and try to hide her within his strength, but he figured that wouldn't work at all. Just more denial, and she had clearly moved beyond that.

Nor did he know exactly what to say. Any words of comfort that occurred to him sounded hollow even inside his own head.

Then her eyes opened and he glimpsed the steely resolve that had gotten her through an incredible lifetime of pain and fear. "Okay. I guess nobody knows why, but this guy wants to kill me. That's the reason for that bit about *like mother, like daughter*. He wants to do the same thing to me. I just wish I knew why."

"Knowing might help us identify him."

"What else do you know that I don't? What made you and Gage think this was possible?"

"Lack of evidence." He explained about how clean the Denver crime scene was, how difficult it was to achieve that, and linked it to the notes that were every bit as clean.

Her faced had paled, but she nodded. "It does seem unlikely that they'd get that way by accident. But that doesn't give us any way to find out who's writing the notes. What are we going to do? Stake out every mail drop in town looking for someone to mail something to me? Assuming there's even another one."

"I'm going to reread the Denver police file. Sometimes a pair of fresh eyes can catch something."

For an instant, he thought he saw panic flutter over her face. "You're going to Denver?"

He shook his head quickly. "No, Gage is going to get a copy of the full file if he can."

"And in the meantime?"

"I'm honestly not sure this guy is ready to act. He's leading you toward something, but I'm not sure he's there yet. The notes have been amazingly vague."

"Not vague enough," she muttered.

"Only when combined with the absolute lack of evidence. Like Gage said, he'd have been happy to find a cat hair."

"It's really that rare to leave nothing behind?"

"Have you ever seen a clean room? Maybe on TV or in a movie? They cover up completely for a reason. It's almost impossible for people not to leave some kind of residue behind. Skin constantly flakes, hair is always falling out. When we talk we spray sputum, even if only minuscule amounts. This guy has gone to extreme lengths to leave nothing in his wake."

"Except my dead mother."

Austin felt a shaft of pain pierce his heart. "Except for her," he agreed quietly. "I'm so sorry, Corey."

"Yeah, well. It's too late for sorry." Then she paused. "I'm not blaming you. It's just that…" She paused again. "I wonder if my mother got notes, too. If that's why she left for Denver."

"Did anyone ever say why?"

"My grandmother said she wanted more opportunity than this town could provide. She didn't want to go into the family business. My aunt…" Corey hesitated.

Austin forced himself to wait patiently. Under no circumstances was he going to beat on Corey's memory. That was the last thing she needed.

"Just before she died, my aunt told me something. She said my mom went to Denver because she couldn't be herself here."

"Did she say why not?" But he already knew, or at least suspected, the answer. Somehow he didn't think the rumors about Olivia had been entirely wrong.

"My aunt said my mother was a lesbian. That she

could never have the kind of life she wanted in a small town. Apparently having me had quieted the talk about her, but my aunt said my mother could never have a girlfriend here. Never live the way she wanted to."

"What did you think about that?"

"Frankly?" Corey's eyes seemed to burn. "That it's nobody else's business how someone chooses to live unless they're hurting someone else. Nobody should have to feel unwelcome for loving who they want. Nobody should have to move hundreds of miles away just to be themselves." Her statements were practically a challenge.

"I agree with you," he said quietly.

"Anyway, I don't know if it's true. She *did* have me. I look a lot like her, so I know I'm not adopted. But…I don't know. My aunt was on some pretty strong medication at that point, just trying to survive her days. She might have been telling the truth, or she might have been guessing. Either way, I don't care. My mother was who she was, and nobody had a right to kill her for any reason."

Ice cream sat melting in bowls, the house had grown extraordinarily quiet, and Austin sat there wishing he knew how to handle the situation. He was great at some things, but dealing with a woman who was looking down the dark path of her past…hell, he couldn't even tell if she was upset or just remembering. She didn't look very well, but he suspected that the time for comfort had passed years ago. Now she was at the just-dealing-with-it part.

"'Like mother, like daughter,'" she said. "How alike

could we possibly be? I barely remember her. Does he have it in for blue eyes?"

He didn't want to say the thing at the top of his mind. There was no way to know for sure about Olivia at this late stage, but if that had been some kind of hate crime, why would the guy want to take out Corey now? Because she didn't date? Because…

Well, of course. Not only did she not date, but she rented rooms to women only, which most people would think to be perfectly sensible for a woman living alone. But this guy…

Damn.

He wondered if he should drag Corey out of here now, hold her hand as they walked down the street, give her a passionate kiss in the middle of the courthouse square, and hope that he could deflect this guy completely.

Except for one thing. It would leave Olivia's murder unsolved and leave Corey wondering for the rest of her life if her mother's murderer was still out there. The shadow would never be gone. She'd never be fully free of the nightmare.

No, that wasn't going to work unless he thought that leaving Corey in the same hellish prison of fear would be okay. He didn't think it would be okay at all.

So what now?

"Would it help," he asked carefully, "to know that your mother's murderer was behind bars?"

After a moment of thought, she nodded. "You see how I live. Sheesh, Austin, you painted it pretty clearly. I'm living in a prison myself. Afraid. Trusting almost no one, at least when it comes to men. It's not something I can turn off like a switch, obviously."

"But would catching him do it?"

"How can I know? But it would sure help."

He nodded, thinking. "How much of your fear comes from what you can't remember? How much comes from the fact that the culprit could still be out there? Do you have any reason at all to think he would want to come after you?"

"Well, now I do," she said irritably.

"I meant before. All these years. Think about it. Have you been afraid that he might have a reason to come after you?"

"Yes," she answered. "Yes."

"Why?"

"Because I might remember, and if I remembered I could identify him."

That made a whole bunch of sense to him. Remembering that night would not only be horrific, but remembering might put her at risk. This was starting to make a whole lot of sense, at least with regard to Corey. The reason her mother was murdered didn't worry her as much as being able to identify the killer.

So in some way she had chosen to go through life afraid of all men, rather than risk herself by remembering the one man, the murderer.

A brilliant move on the part of a small child's mind. Truly brilliant. Her amnesia protected her twice over. But it had also crippled her in important ways she couldn't have imagined when she began taking this self-protective path.

After all his talk about how she was in a prison of her own making, he sat there stymied, with absolutely no idea what would be best for Corey. Talking about getting her out of her shell was easy. Actually facing the reason for it made it a whole lot more difficult.

"I'm sorry for the way I talked about you hiding," he offered finally. "Cheap psychology. I should just keep my mouth shut."

She gave him a wan smile. "You were right. It wasn't cheap psychology, it was something I needed to face. It comes in bits and pieces, Austin. It's not like it can all be handled or identified at once. How else do you think I learned how to get out of visiting that therapist? Learning bits and pieces of telling her what she wanted to hear to convince herself I was okay. Everybody wanted to believe it."

"I'm sure they did."

"But I'm not, am I? I even deluded myself after a while. I wanted nothing but my shop, the women I've made friends with and a safe little home to come back to every night." She froze and for an instant looked like a frightened rabbit.

"Corey?"

"It just occurred to me. If this guy wanted to kill me because he was afraid I'd remember him, he should have done it a long time ago. Besides, like you said, he was probably covered from head to foot."

"The Denver cops were pretty sure of it."

"So I couldn't have recognized him, anyway, even if I remembered. There's got to be another reason…"

He let his suspicions lie. He didn't want to add any

more to her already huge concerns. Bad enough that
she knew now she was probably being stalked by her
mother's killer.

"Why?" she whispered.

She jumped up suddenly and began to pace the
kitchen rapidly. "Oh, I get it. I really get it."

"Get what?"

"My mom's decision to move. It was just a few months
before she was killed. I'll bet you anything that having
me didn't put this monster off her trail. Why would it?
There was never a father in the picture, and you can get
pregnant lots of ways. I bet she was getting these notes,
too. I bet she figured the only way she could shake the
guy was to leave town. My God!"

"Corey..." But what could he say? He shut his mouth
and waited, wondering where she would go.

She looked at him, her eyes sparking with anger, but
something else, as well. "Maybe she was a lesbian. She
sure never told anyone a thing about where I came from.
She went away for a month or so and came back pregnant. Why would she do that? To quiet the talk?"

"Maybe," he said gently, "she really, really wanted
a child."

She paused midstride and finally nodded. "She did.
Both my grandmother and aunt were definite about that.
But how odd, to go away and come back pregnant. Almost nobody does that. So let's just say for the sake of argument that having me quieted the gossip, but this creep
wasn't buying it. Maybe when she didn't date after that,
he decided he was right. Something sure made her up

and take off quickly. My aunt said she was gone a week or so after she explained the move. Just gone."

"But nobody knows any more than that?"

"Nothing that anyone shared."

"Maybe I'll find something about it in the police file."

"I don't know. When I talked to Gage about the case in high school, he said they didn't seem to have a thing."

"Okay." He was still amazed that she had tried to delve into the murder. That had to have taken a lot of courage, given that her mind had erased it all. So she had tried to open a Pandora's box once before. Gutsy lady.

"Will they tell you more?"

"Since Gage is requesting the complete file, we might get every single thing Denver's got."

She nodded and began pacing again. "I know I'm taking huge leaps here. I have no proof for any of this. But say my mom left to escape being harassed by this guy. Maybe she was getting afraid. Regardless, two months later she was killed. Which leaves me. If he was afraid of me remembering him, he should have come after me a long time ago. Then there's that last note."

"'Like mother, like daughter,'" he repeated.

"Exactly. What if he's a nut and has decided I must be like my mother. That I'm a lesbian. God knows, it could easily look like it. It would probably never occur to this demon that I avoid men because of *him*." She swore quietly and finally sank back onto her chair. "Tell me I'm crazy."

He couldn't. The way she was adding it up was the only way it could begin to make sense. Whether or not her mother was a lesbian, whether or not this fruitcake thought Corey was, he plainly was after her for the same reason, like mother, like daughter.

She took his silence as her answer, evidently. She nodded slowly. "Okay, I'm not totally in left field."

Time to walk carefully. He couldn't imagine the emotions that must be coursing through her now, or what pitfalls might lie right ahead. "Maybe not," he said.

"Well, I'm onto something."

"I'd tend to agree. But there's still a lot we don't know. We can't know."

"Of course not. But his linking her to me in this way…" She trailed off. "Maybe it's too tidy. But it fits. All I know is, I don't want to imagine how this guy must have scared my mother to make her take off like that. It was so sudden, her decision to move. I know that for sure because both my grandmother and aunt commented on it. To them it seemed to come out of nowhere, and once it did, she packed and left. I get that she might have been thinking about it for some time, but not to say anything to her family?"

"It does seem odd, but the only family I know really well is my own." He tried to lighten the moment because to him it looked as if she was edging into a bad place. Little by little she was battering at the past, and each thing she brought up was more scary. "In my family, a decision to move involves at least five people and weeks, if not months, of discussion."

"I think I'd like your family." But it sounded as if she was hardly attentive.

"You would," he said confidently. "Mention you want a new place to live and you'll have a bunch of people checking out housing for you. And when moving day comes, forget it. Every able-bodied person and every available truck will show up."

"That must be nice."

"It could be annoying, too, depending on your nature. It doesn't happen without tons of advice."

At least she managed a wan smile. But then, to his horror, a tear trickled down her cheek.

"Corey?"

"Can you imagine?" she asked, her voice wavering, "how afraid she must have been to leave that quickly? To take a child and move to a big city where she didn't know anyone? She'd lived her entire life here, Austin. All of it. It must have been so hard to leave."

He'd reached his limit. He couldn't just sit there anymore and let her walk her past alone. Rising, he scooped her up and carried her to the living room where he sat with her on his lap and wrapped her in the tightest of hugs.

"You're not alone," he said quietly. "I won't let that happen."

He expected her to dissolve into tears, but she didn't. A couple more large drops escaped her eyes, then she seemed to relax into his hug and accept the comfort he was offering. It didn't seem like much, but it was all he had.

A long time passed. His hunger for her returned, but he couldn't think of a worse possible time. Not when she was trying to handle a whole bunch of stuff that he figured had just shaken her whole world. Things she hadn't thought about before, maybe had never guessed at, were front and center, and they needed tending more than he did.

Finally, she spoke, her head still resting on his shoulder, her eyes closed.

"We could go make love in the town square."

He would have laughed if he hadn't understood exactly what she meant. "I thought of that."

"So what stopped you?"

Ah, hell, back to the bad stuff. "First, we don't know why he's after you. We're assuming. He could have another reason. Second, how safe will you feel if we merely put him off? I couldn't guarantee that he'd never get a wild idea again. If I thought it would make a difference, I'd marry you tomorrow."

"Very generous of you." She sighed and slowly opened her eyes. Even though she had barely cried, they were reddened.

"Basically, we have two options here. You decide which one you want to pursue."

She sniffled once. "Okay."

"We can carry on in public and shame the porn industry as far as you want in the hopes he'll give up on you. In the hopes that we're not wrong about his motivation. He moves on and leaves you alone."

"Maybe," she qualified.

"Maybe," he agreed.

"And the other option?"

"We get ready and let him play his game out. Catch him and put him where he belongs. The only problem with that one is that we really don't know what he wants here. Just to scare you? Maybe. He might not even be the guy who killed your mother."

"True." Lifting an arm, she wiped away the drying tears. "We really *are* blind here."

"Pretty much."

"That doesn't help."

"No."

She lay quietly in his arms while minutes ticked by. Then she startled him. "I'm tired of hiding. Of being afraid. I'm over it. I've been missing a lot of life, a lot of good things, because I've been hiding from the past, hiding from fears I can't even name. I guess I shouldn't have been so eager to get out of therapy."

"Oh, I can understand that. You were afraid your doc was going to take you places that terrified you."

"And all I did by being so smart was create a cage of fear. I get it. You were sure right about that. Well, I'm tired of it. I don't want to live with that anymore. So...we let this game play out, like you said. We hope we catch the guy and put him away. Even if he isn't the man who killed my mother, he's still tormenting me. A real sadist. So let him pull whatever it is he wants to pull. At least I can get rid of him."

"This could be really risky. You could get hurt or worse. You're sure?"

"I couldn't be more positive."

He felt so proud of her then. Despite the way she'd been living, he'd never figured her for a real coward. She'd moved on, she'd moved ahead, she'd run a successful business where just anyone could walk in the door. It took strength to do all that in the face of her fears.

No, she was no coward. She was a coper, and that was a huge difference. The thing was, coping skills developed in childhood weren't always the right ones for adulthood, and she was facing that. Bravely, too.

His heart swelled and he hugged her even closer so that he could drop a kiss on her forehead. Yet he felt obliged to remind her once again. "This could be dangerous."

"I know. But I'm tired of living half a life."

Then she totally took his breath away. Slipping her arm up around his neck, she kissed him hard. "Make love to me, Austin. Please."

He drew back a little to study her face. He didn't want to be just a momentary escape. He wanted something more, a real pairing, a meaningful coupling. He didn't want to be used like a drug.

But what he saw in her face, for the first time since early this morning, was passion. Real passion. No desperation. No fear. Just a complete and total look of desire.

She pushed his shoulder playfully. "Did you think you could hold me on your lap and not get a reaction?"

"Corey?"

She smiled faintly. "I'm not losing my mind, and I'm not running. I want you. The mess will still be there in the morning, but right now, all I want is you."

He hoped like hell that she wasn't fooling them both.

Chapter 11

First Austin ran up the stairs to turn on lights and pretend he was settling in. This time he explained his reasoning to her and she nodded.

When he came back down, he found her totally naked on her bed, temptation personified as she lay on her side and smiled at him. "You're gorgeous," he said, his breath catching in his throat. "Exquisite. Beautiful."

"So are you," she answered. "Or at least you will be when you get rid of those clothes."

Standing beside the bed, he stripped rapidly. Then, realizing she was drinking him in with her eyes, he waited a few moments, holding back his urge to pounce.

Then she saw something and frowned. He tensed immediately until she sat up and scooted over so she could touch his side. "They really did hurt you."

"Let's not think about that. I'm fine now." The beating had left some external scars on his torso where skin had split because of the kicks. "I figure I'm lucky that they left my head alone."

"I guess that's one way to look at it. I'm sorry I didn't notice last night." While she was exploring him.

"I think we were preoccupied. I intend to get that preoccupied again right now."

She looked up at him, a giggle escaped her and she lay down and rolled away. He hit the bed in one leap and grabbed her, causing her to shriek playfully. A second later he had her pinned beneath him, and was staring down into her laughing blue eyes.

"Rapunzel, Rapunzel, let down your hair," he whispered.

"I think I already have." An instant of shyness appeared to overtake her, then she gave herself up to him, wrapping her arms around his neck and her legs around his hips. Oh, damn, he was going to go off like a rocket.

"Just a sec," he said hoarsely. "Protection. Expect no quarter this time, *querida.*"

"Give me none," she murmured. She attempted to help with the condom, which only made him crazier. He didn't know what was happening between them, and right then he wasn't going to think about it. All he knew was that never in his life had he gotten this hot this fast. Well, okay, not since he was in his teens.

She made him feel that way again, young and hungry and so very impatient. He lifted himself on one arm and plunged his hand down between them, stroking her petals. A low moan escaped her and she arched toward his touch. Sliding a finger into her, he found her moist and ready. Nor did she wince.

That was his last coherent thought. He slid into her, claiming her with every inch of him, and pumped them toward the heavens. All he cared was that she take this ride with him, and everything in the way she moved, groaned and sighed said she was right there. His moans joined hers, sounds that only inflamed him more.

He was mindless by the time he reached the peak. He felt the shudders rip through her, heard her cry of completion, felt her buck up hard against him. Then he let go, jetting into her and feeling as if he turned inside out. He exploded into a ball of blinding light.

Collapsing on her, both of them sweaty and panting, he didn't want to move. He could have stayed there forever. But reality wouldn't allow it. Cussing silently, he climbed out of bed to take care of business, then returned.

She looked dazed, he thought as he pulled the covers over them and drew her close. Well, he felt stunned. In the usual way, he didn't compare his lovers, but this one got to him in an unprecedented way.

Holding her, he could feel her fragility. She was fine-boned, delicate in her build, yet he'd seen her physical strength at the gym. She wouldn't be a pushover even for a large man.

But those thoughts drifted away as he continued to hold her. She felt so relaxed against him, and he decided that's why she felt so fragile. Protectiveness surged in him. At that moment he'd have gone to slay the dragon in her moat. He'd have taken up his sword and gone to battle wearing her scarf.

And he'd read too many fairy tales in his youth, he thought. A quiet laugh escaped him.

"What's so funny?" Corey asked lazily.

"I'm feeling like St. George ready to battle a dragon on your behalf. Ready to carry your scarf into battle."

She rose and pushed herself over until she was resting her head on his chest. "St. George, huh?"

"I can be silly."

"Good. But I kind of like it. You've been slaying one dragon or another since you got here."

He wished it were true. Reaching up, he ran his fingers through her hair. "Why do you wear you hair up almost all the time?"

"It gets in the way at work. Sometimes I think about cutting it."

"But then it won't get long enough for me to climb up into your tower room."

Now it was her turn to laugh. "You do have a fanciful mind."

"Does it bother you?"

"I like it. It's playful and fun. So you see me as Rapunzel?"

"Sometimes. My first impression was a Viking princess."

"Hmm, I think I like that better than being the lady locked in a tower."

"What was your first impression of me?"

"After my initial discomfort of your being a strange man, you mean?"

"Yeah, once I was no longer a dragon."

She rubbed her cheek against him. "Handsome. Exotic. Sorry, I wasn't ready to see you as St. George."

"I can understand that." Especially since she hadn't wanted him there at all.

"But what I liked most about you was the way you were so comfortable with me. It couldn't have felt very good to know I didn't want you here. But you just made yourself at home and you cooked your way in."

He laughed again and squeezed her. "It was nice to be able to cook again. And you realize we haven't eaten tonight. Most of our ice cream is sitting in a melted puddle right now. Although my mother would insist that's not food."

"It has calories, right?" But she laughed with him. "I think we're still loaded with leftovers. If you keep cooking like this, I'll have to get a freezer."

His hand hesitated for a fraction of a second as he stroked her hair. Was she suggesting they had a future? He hoped not. There was too much uncertainty right now. She might turn to him for safety, and while he didn't want to be needed only as a bodyguard, he didn't know what he would do if it was more. Regardless, sooner or later, he'd have to return to work. What then? The cards weren't looking good.

His uncle had warned him about one-night stands with virgins. Maybe she was investing too much of herself because they'd made love. On the other hand, he might be doing the same thing in his own way. He finally spoke hesitantly. "You know I have to go back to Washington, eventually."

"I know. But right now I'm all into living for the moment. For all I know I could be dead tomorrow."

That thought pierced him worse than it should have. He'd felt fear before, but nothing like he felt at that moment. "I won't let it happen," he vowed.

"We'll see." Surprising him, she sat up. "Do you know your stomach is growling? Let's go find food."

* * *

Her job kept her so busy, Corey thought, that it seemed as if they spent most of their time together cooking and eating. And now making love.

She really liked the lovemaking. Imagine having missed that all these years. Well, she liked the cooking and eating, too, but it was a limited life experience. They couldn't go anywhere together now, if they were to follow the course she had chosen, so any chance of finding out what it was like to take a long walk with him, or see a movie, or laze around in the backyard on a sunny afternoon—all of those things were precluded.

And just as he had said, he had to go back to Washington eventually. Her life was here, his was elsewhere, and she suspected they were sharing a bubble of time when the fates had brought them together. Eventually they would go their own ways.

She could think clinically about it, but in her heart felt the foreshadowing of loss. She was really going to miss him, this man who had managed to get past her barriers and all the protections she had built around herself.

Maybe what she needed to do was raise all those barriers again, and quickly. Before she got really hurt.

Easy enough to say, she thought as she helped reheat the delicacies that Austin had cooked. The thing was, did she really want to back away from the most glorious experience of her life?

Hell, no, she thought. Everything had a price. She ought to know that well enough by now. But what she had shared with Austin over the past day or so? No, she didn't want to end it prematurely by ducking back into her safe little cave.

When Austin had to leave, she'd deal with it and far better than she had dealt with every other loss in her life, all thanks to Austin. In fact, if she honestly thought about it, life seemed to be a series of losses. But Austin had shown her a whole new world, and she wasn't going to give it up because she feared the future.

In her experience, fearing the future hadn't gotten her anywhere at all, or saved her any pain. All it had done was lock her away from a lot of life.

Then life had found her, anyway. With Austin. With the stalker. Apparently living in a carefully constructed cocoon was no defense. Sooner or later you paid the price of living.

She thought about those notes and the conclusions they had reached while Austin rummaged about, cleaning up the ice-cream mess and laying out fresh plates and flatware. She'd made the right decision there, she decided. She couldn't live the rest of her life wondering when this jerk would start bothering her again. Evidently he had some unfinished business with her. She couldn't be absolutely certain what it was, but she was stubborn enough to do whatever it took to end this. She'd sacrificed too much of her life to nameless terrors. This was not going to become another one.

"You look very determined," Austin said as they sat at the table.

"I am. I was thinking it would be nice to take a walk with you after we eat. Just a simple, ordinary walk. But we can't do that right now. It makes me mad."

"Good." He gave her one of his great smiles. "Mad is better than a lot of other things."

"I guess you'd know."

"I think I said once before that anger can be a fuel. Very powerful if harnessed right."

"Well, I'm harnessing it now. I want this nut unmasked. I want to know if he killed my mother. And I want him out of my life for good."

"Check, check and check," he said. "I don't know if he's your mother's murderer, but we'll get him and find out."

"So sure of that?"

His face hardened. "I usually achieve my goals. One way or another, we're going to get this guy."

She wished she were as sure. He'd warned her it would be risky. If this man was the murderer, he probably wanted to kill her, too.

In that moment, she had a memory flash across her mind, a vivid, horrifying image. "A ghost killed Mommy."

She barely heard herself speak because the world seemed to be spinning away.

Austin caught her just before she tipped onto the floor.

A ghost killed Mommy? Oh, God, she was remembering, the one thing he had hoped wouldn't come out of this. A child's mind had been so seriously traumatized it had forgotten, utterly forgotten. In this he agreed with the therapist who had told her she didn't need to remember.

He shifted his hold on her and carried her to the living room, where he laid her on the couch, then knelt beside her, waiting. He was sure she'd be fine soon. Fainting didn't last long.

But his mind was now racing at top speed. She'd remembered something, and now she was going to have to deal with it unless her mind successfully locked it away again. Damn it all to hell, he wanted to get his hands around the throat of this guy. The impulse to violence wasn't native to him, but he was feeling it now.

Her eyelids fluttered.

"Corey?"

"Austin?" For a few seconds she looked almost dreamy, then a frown knit her brow. "What happened?"

"You fainted." He tensed, waiting to see if she still remembered or if the image had once again been locked away.

Then her eyes widened. She remembered.

"Oh, my God," she whispered.

"You remembered something, didn't you?"

"A ghost killed Mommy?" She repeated the words, then her entire face twisted into a grimace of pain. He started to reach for her, then hesitated. He didn't want to frighten her more if she was locked in a memory.

"Oh, God," she repeated, her voice taut with pain. "A man. He was all covered in white. He looked like a ghost. But a ghost couldn't have killed her."

A man in a Tyvek coverall could have, though. At last Austin dared to reach for her hand. He was relieved when she grasped him as if he were a lifeline, her grip almost painful.

"I'm here," he said. Useless words, but intended to draw her out of the well and back into the present.

For a few moments she didn't respond. Then she said quietly, "That's it. That's all I can remember."

When she burst into tears he was ready. He leaned over her and slipped his arms around her, holding her tight. "It'll be okay, *mi querida*. It'll be okay."

Empty promises, he thought almost bitterly. A well of hate opened in him, hate for her nameless, faceless tormentor. Was he amused to think she might be terrified? Did he get his jollies out of threatening young women? He'd met some contemptible people during his time undercover, and this guy was fitting squarely into the class of people the world would be better off without.

She shed too many tears to kiss them all away, although he tried. She cried until exhaustion claimed her, her sobs dying away into hiccups of shattered breath. Finally, even that trailed away. He figured she must feel utterly wrung out.

He went on holding her, willing her to come back, and felt immense relief when her arms at last stole around him. Her embrace was weak, but at least she was reaching for him. Her return had begun.

But her cry would remain with him forever. It had emerged from the maimed child still within her, in a child's phrasing. For an instant, Corey had been seven again.

He hoped that would never happen again.

* * *

Austin lifted her from the couch and carried her back to bed. He pulled away her robe, ditched his jeans, then climbed in with her, tangling their limbs together. She felt him, felt his heat, strength and reality, but part of her still seemed far away. The part that remembered the man who had killed her mother, a snapshot in her mind, just a single frozen image.

"I'm afraid," she murmured a long time later.

"Of what?" He ran his hand along her back reassuringly.

"Of remembering more. That was bad enough. I don't have to remember the murder, do I?"

Even as the words were torn from deep within her, she knew it was a question no one could answer. She could no more stop the memories if they decided to return than prevent the amnesia after her mother's murder had happened. Her subconscious was in control of this, had always been in control. She couldn't flip the lever to guarantee forgetfulness any more than she could have prevented it in the first place. That single photo image that her mind had dug up had cast her back into a terror beyond description. She didn't need any more of that. Or at least she didn't think she did.

"I don't know," Austin answered presently. "I hope not."

She chewed her lower lip. "But maybe I could remember something useful."

"I doubt it. You already told me what we suspected, about how he managed to leave no evidence behind. Since you said he was a ghost, my guess is that his face was covered, too. So what could you possibly remember? His eyes?"

She screwed her eyes shut. "There was a screen over his eyes."

"Like a beekeeper suit?"

"Yes." Her eyes popped open. "Something like that."

"Okay. Corey?"

"Yes?"

"Don't push at it. Please. I'm inclined to agree that you don't need to remember the rest."

"Me, too. But I can't seem to escape the image of him. It's hanging there. How do I banish it?"

He didn't have an answer for that. Right now he was definitely feeling pretty useless. Finally, he said, "You've got to be exhausted. If you can sleep, sleep. It might help put some distance between you and the memory."

At least he hoped it would. Eventually she did fall into slumber, but he kept watch over her, anyway, alert for any sign of distress. After that blast out of nowhere, she might have nightmares.

But eventually he slept, too.

When Corey opened her eyes, she found Austin propped on his elbow, watching her.

"Feel any better?" he asked.

It was like trying to find a sore tooth. She prodded around inside. The image of the "ghost" seemed to have receded. It was still there, but didn't grip her as it had last night. "I think so."

She glanced at the clock. "Oh, man, I need to get to the shop."

"How about having someone run it for the day. Someone you trust?"

"There're so many people…"

"Corey, do you ever get sick?"

She sighed and turned back to him. "I'll call Maureen. She fills in for me on occasion."

"Great idea."

"Except for one thing. This is changing the pattern you didn't want to change."

"You've been sick before, right? Besides, I think you're fragile today."

She didn't like the idea of being fragile, but had to admit he had a point. What if she had another memory at work? She'd freak out all her customers and friends. She called Maureen, claiming she had a really bad headache. Maureen, as usual, was only too glad to fill in.

"I ought to hire her," Corey said as she hung up. "I'm getting to the point where I think I could afford an assistant."

"Tell me about her."

Talking about Maureen got them all the way out of bed and into the kitchen for coffee. Maureen had been a friend of the family forever, and now that she was retired she nearly lived at the shop. She taught some of the sewing and knitting classes because she enjoyed it, and participated in most of the circles. She also had four rambunctious grandchildren whom Corey adored.

Gage called Austin before they were on their second cups of coffee, just about the time Austin was suggesting he go and pick up something from the bakery for breakfast. Corey was glad of the interruption because she didn't want to be alone. Not at all. For some reason, that memory, abbreviated though it was, had scared her even more than the notes, and they were creepy enough.

Maybe she was afraid that she'd remember something else, something awful, and feared that it might happen when she was all alone. Or maybe she was more afraid of that creep out there than she had thought.

All the tough talk about dealing with him sounded like a whole bunch of bravado right now. Deal with him how? They didn't even have a plan. Until he decided to act, there was no way to know who he was. How did you prepare for that?

"Thanks," Austin said into his cell phone. "Could you do me a favor and pick up some rolls or something at the bakery for our breakfast? Corey's staying home today. I'll explain when you get here."

Relief flooded her. At least for now she didn't have to be alone. Then a thought occurred to her. "Won't Gage coming over here let this guy know we're worried about the notes? And that the police are involved? I thought we wanted to avoid that."

Austin shook his head. "There's no perfect plan for this one. If Gage scares him off, we can't prevent it. Somehow I don't think that's going to happen."

"Why?"

She watched him think it over, waiting impatiently.

When he spoke, he did so slowly. "The notes aren't a threat per se. Not yet. Plus, it was Gage who brought me here. If he's paying that close attention, then there's no reason to assume Gage isn't just dropping by to see me. If he thinks otherwise, it might push him to act quickly rather than withdraw. Whatever he's up to, Corey, he apparently thinks it's time to do this. If he was going to stop, why wouldn't he have stopped when I moved in? When Gage brought me here. How would he know that wasn't about his first note?"

She nodded slowly. "You think he feels compelled?"

"I'm wondering. Besides, none of it matters if he thinks he can get to you safely. And we're going to make it look that way, aren't we?"

She felt her heart stop. "We are?"

"I thought that's what we were discussing last night. Tomorrow you go back to normal activity. Tomorrow you act like nothing's going on. But you won't be alone. Regardless, judging by his timing on these notes, you should get another one soon. They've been coming closer together."

"If you can judge by three notes, yes."

"Then if we haven't scared him off, I think we can expect another one by the end of the week. If it doesn't come...well, we'll have to wait and see."

"I hate those words."

He smiled. "Most of us do."

Gage arrived twenty minutes later with a big bag of croissants, bagels and doughnuts. "Whatever you don't want will make my deputies happy for the rest of the day," he answered when Corey remarked how much he'd brought.

She brought out plates and poured coffee, trying not to notice that her muscles pretty much felt like soft rubber. The croissant she chose and lightly buttered melted in her mouth. Gage and Austin went for the doughnuts.

"I got the files from the Denver P.D.," Gage said. "Everything they have, according to them. It's way too much for me to bring over here, especially if you think there's any chance this guy might be watching. You'll have to come read them at my office."

"Did you review the documents?"

"Last night. Nothing important that I could see. This guy was a ghost."

Corey dropped her croissant, and felt an icy shudder run through her.

"What?" Gage asked.

"Corey remembered something last night," Austin answered. "She said a ghost killed her mother. From her description it sounded like the culprit was wearing a beekeeper suit."

Gage arched one eyebrow. "I'm sorry for my choice of word, Corey."

She shook her head, but her mouth had gone dry and now her hands were shaking. "I don't want to remember any more of it."

"Of course not," Gage said swiftly. "Of course you don't. There's no need to. Some things are best forgotten. Are you okay?"

She managed to lift her coffee without spilling it and wet her mouth. "I will be."

Gage hesitated, watching her, then turned to Austin. "Maybe we shouldn't discuss this right now."

"No!" The word burst from Corey. "I'm right in the middle of this. How much protection does ignorance give me?"

Neither man said anything for a couple of minutes.

They waited until she was able to once again nibble at the croissant and drink her coffee. God, she hated feeling like this, as if she were in a dark tunnel surrounded by demons, unable to know which way to run.

But even as she nearly caved to her fears, she remembered the little girl who had hidden in a closet and refused to talk for days. Was she going back to that? Did she even want to?

"Hell, no," she said aloud. "If this is the same creep who killed my mother, I want him caught. I don't care what the risk is. I'm not going to let him ruin the rest of my life."

Coming in on the middle of her mental conversation must have surprised them, but both of them caught on quickly.

"Well," said Gage, "there's one thing I can promise you. He won't be able to run around town in a beekeeper's suit."

"Which means," Austin said, "that he'll leave evidence."

"If he attacks me." Corey could no longer even pretend that wasn't this guy's goal. The notes made no sense any other way.

Silence fell again, then Austin spoke. "There's no other way to get him."

"I get that. Believe me, I get that. I've had enough. I want this done and over with. God, I'm at risk sitting in my own house, working in my own shop, all because I don't know who he is or what he's planning to do. So let's get on with it because I'm so sick of this. There's no reason not to think he's the man who killed my mother.

No reason at all. These notes are too directed. Remember the first one? *I remember you but you don't remember me.* That's no joke. He meant it. He was there."

Austin nodded slowly. "That may be the most important of the notes, after all."

"Viewed from this perspective, I have to agree," said Gage. "Nothing strong enough to take to the police. No evident threat. But maybe that first note said it all."

"I want him to pay for what he did," Corey said. Strength had returned to her, and she stood up. "Oh, man, do I want him to pay. He killed her and locked me up in a cage of terror all these years. Living half a life. And now he thinks it's amusing to taunt me? Scare me again? I don't think so."

She faced the men. "I don't care why he did it. All I want is to take him down. And if that means I have to wiggle like a worm on a hook and put myself in danger, then I'm damn well going to do it."

Austin was looking at her with something between admiration and concern. "Hold your horses there, Corey. We can't go at this foolishly."

"Then give me a plan. I have had enough."

Chapter 12

"The simpler the plan, the less likely it is to get screwed up," Austin said. "We go with what we originally talked about. You and I appear to go our separate ways. Gage can't heighten any kind of security around you because it might be noticed. No change there. I'll have to keep a loose circle around you myself. I can do that by pretending to job hunt while you're at work. If he was paying any attention to me at all when I first arrived, then he would have noticed I often went to Mahoney's in the evening. I suggest that I resume that habit. I'll look like I'm out of the picture, but I can slip out the back and start circling again. Besides, how many people can he keep an eye on at one time? He sees me go into the bar, he'll assume I'm there for a couple of hours. I'll arrange to do that right around your closing time."

Corey and Gage nodded.

"He's most likely to strike when you're alone. Obviously. So let's pinpoint the times of greatest risk."

"Sunday afternoon at the shop," Corey said. "When I close up at night. Walking home late."

"Not so much walking home," Gage remarked. "There are still a lot of people on the streets."

She nodded, thinking about it. "You're right. I'm mostly alone in the shop on Sunday afternoon, although someone could walk in, and then again when I close in the evening. I usually spend about half an hour tidying up and taking out the trash."

"The alley would be a great place for him to wait," Austin remarked. "I saw it when I took the trash out for you that one time. Be sure you don't go out there unprepared."

"Should I get a gun?" she asked.

Austin and Gage exchanged looks. "Unfortunately," Austin said almost gently, "that makes the situation even more dangerous. You don't want to inadvertently arm *him*."

"He's going to come armed," Corey said. "He stabbed my mother. That's probably what he wants to do to me. Besides, if someone fired a gun in that alley, you could hear it all over town."

"People would come running," Gage agreed. "Lots of people." He drummed his fingers on the tabletop. "I want to think some more about this. I know I can't put any kind of watch on Corey, not officially. Hell, word would leak out. It always does. So even if he didn't notice increased patrols, he'd probably hear about it. Damn grapevine."

Then he looked at Corey. "You still up on all that self-defense you studied in high school?"

"She's still plenty good," Austin said. "As I learned at the gym on Sunday."

Gage smiled faintly. "Good."

"I'm going to work," Corey announced. She was starting to feel as if she was waiting for her own execution. Maybe she was, but the only way to deal with this was to stay busy. In fact, it felt good to have the decision made, even if was only to wait for this murderer to act. Facing it all made her feel stronger than just worrying about what might be going on, what might happen.

She really *was* fed up. She quickly cleaned up and changed into her work slacks and polo. When she came out, the two men were still at the table.

Austin spoke. "We're going to go to Gage's office to review the file."

"Good idea," she said briskly. "Let me know if you come up with any details or a better plan."

She stepped out the door, sewing bag in her arms, and headed for her shop. This time, though, she had one hand inside the bag and it clutched a very sharp, very strong metal knitting needle.

There were different ways to be armed.

"What got into her?" Gage asked Austin as they drove toward the sheriff's office.

"Memory. For a while last night I was afraid it would get the better of her, but from what I'm seeing now I guess it galvanized her instead. Maybe a guy dressed like a beekeeper isn't as frightening as not remembering him at all."

"Maybe. All I know is that I do not like this. Period. I would give my left arm to have a bead on the guy so she didn't have to take this risk."

"I'd give more than that," Austin replied.

Gage shot him a sharp look. "Like that, is it?"

"I don't know. I've got a job to go back to. She's got a life here. I just know I wouldn't hesitate to step between her and a bullet."

"Whether she knows it or not, a few people around here pretty much feel the same. I just wish I knew how to put that to use."

"Grapevine?"

"We put light to shame with the speed of gossip around here. And if anybody's ever figured out how to keep a secret, I don't know about it."

Austin laughed. "Well, you wouldn't, if they kept a secret. But I get your drift."

He thought of himself as a Righteous Man, devoted to fighting the worst of sins, saving his community from moral pollution. Since no one else would do it, the task fell squarely on his shoulders. Not that he minded.

The time was approaching to cleanse the town. His neighbors were good people, and didn't deserve to have to live with a pervert among them. Their children didn't deserve to be exposed.

Not much longer now.

Briefly, that morning, he thought there might be a hitch, a need to delay. The sheriff had gone to her house. Was the law worried about his little notes? He was sure he hadn't written anything to worry them. Worry *her,* yes, but not them. The notes looked like a prank. A little nastiness that had no meaning.

He'd been very careful about that. But she knew who she was, she knew her own perversion, and her fear must be growing.

If the sheriff was worried, though, he could wait a while. He could always wait if necessary. He was the arrow in the bow, ready, but until he unleashed himself, nothing need happen.

He saw Corey come out and walk to work as she always did. Alone. The others didn't come with her. A short while later the sheriff and his friend came out and headed downtown. He saw them laugh together in the car.

So it was all right. It would happen.

Back at home, he debated about the last note. He had intended to send it today or tomorrow, to put the last shaft of terror into her heart. But maybe it would give away too much. She would know why he had come for her. He could tell her.

Maybe the note would have more impact if it arrived after she was dead. Then the whole town would talk about it and understand they had a protector.

He studied the words on his screen. *She deserved it. So do you.*

Maybe something a little stronger, if it was going to arrive after she died. Something clearer. Certainly the way it read now might be enough to get the sheriff's attention.

On the other hand, it didn't explain much.

He sighed, rubbing his temples as his head began to ache. He had expected to have to make adjustments to his plan, but this one stumped him.

Before or after?

Worded differently?

Damn, he wished he could have a beer, but it was too early.

One last note, his pièce de résistance. He needed to plan this very carefully.

Of one thing he was absolutely certain, though. Corey's remaining days were few.

The evening quilting circle had been canceled because one of the women needed to go to Casper for the birth of a new grandchild, and another was stuck at home with two children who had colds.

Since she had very little traffic in the evenings while the sewing groups met, Corey decided she should close up early. Maureen had left at four because she needed to babysit.

So even if Corey hadn't come in at all, the shop would have closed early. She made the decision easily. There were too many other things going on in her life right now to hang around here for another few hours to help possibly no one. She quickly cleaned, Maureen had already taken out the trash, and after only fifteen minutes she was locking the front door and heading home.

She didn't know if Austin was around somewhere as he had promised, and she wasn't especially worried about it. It was still really early, there were plenty of people on the streets.

One thing she knew for certain, she absolutely wanted to get home to Austin.

This was a totally new experience for her, and she found herself smiling, even though she really had little to smile about. She'd seen many of her friends fall in love, or at least develop crushes, but she'd never had the experience herself.

For the first time she understood why they became so preoccupied and let so much else slip. All day long her thoughts had been filled with Austin. She wanted to see him. She wanted to kiss him. She wanted…Austin.

A definite preoccupation going on here. Maybe not for the good, but better than thinking all day about that shard of memory that had returned to her last night.

She was also feeling relieved because she hadn't recovered any more of her memory. Maybe that would be it. She didn't think she ever wanted to remember exactly what that guy had done to her mother. Hearing the details had been bad enough.

Then another thought struck her and dropped a weight on her shoulders. Was she hiding behind thoughts of Austin? Turning him into another security blanket? She had certainly developed enough of those protections over the years, and she didn't want to think she was now using him as another barrier.

How could she even be sure? Looking back over her life, she had a full appreciation of the games her mind could play, the defenses it could build. It was a master strategist at preventing her from dealing with the intolerable.

Here she'd been so determined this morning to face this down, whatever it turned out to be, whatever the risks involved, and now she was running home in hopes of seeing a man?

A man who had promised her nothing, who would be

leaving in a couple of months. Certainly before the next semester, Gage had said. Three months, he had said.

So what the hell was she thinking? Was she thinking at all or just reacting?

Then, almost bitterly, she remembered that she could be dead in a few days. How could she know? She was taking a huge risk here, a risk she needed to take, but what if she couldn't deal with this guy? What if Austin didn't get there quickly enough? It was possible. She might be on her own just long enough to get her throat slashed.

Damn, she hated the direction her thoughts were taking. She couldn't seem to straighten them out for more than a few minutes at a time. Determination one minute, absolute certainty, and then massive confusion all over again.

Like it or not, she had to face the fact that she'd spent most of her life reacting. Just reacting. The only things she really thought through had to do with her business. Everything else was based in emotional traumas.

She was a mess.

When she got home, Austin was already there. He smelled as if he'd just stepped in, radiating fresh air.

"Hi," he said, and smiled. "I visited the grocer again."

"What are we doing this time?"

"It's all ready. He showed me how to make galumpki. Galopki? Danged if I remember. He also called it something else. Anyway, they're basically stuffed cabbage rolls. He was already making it, and I rolled a few myself for practice and guess what he sent home with me? Dinner. It's simmering on the stove right now."

She sniffed and finally picked up the scent of toma-toes. "You must have just started it."

"Yeah. I wasn't expecting you so early." He stepped toward her. "Did something happen? You don't look so good."

"I'm not. I'm a mess. But nothing happened. I'm going to change."

At least he didn't press her or follow her as she headed to her bedroom. She changed into her favorite jeans, a cotton sweater and slippers. He was going to want to know why she was a mess, but how could she explain to him what she couldn't explain to herself?

She was feeling a little cranky by the time she re-turned to the kitchen. A fresh cup of coffee was waiting for her, along with a slice of Danish.

"My family believes that food always helps," he re-marked. "Dig in."

Well, at least he didn't ask. She drank half the cof-fee and finished the Danish before she realized she *was* feeling better. "Your family's right."

He laughed. "Not always." He checked the pot sim-mering on the stove, then joined her.

She spoke before he could question her. "Did you learn anything from reading the files?"

"No, sorry to say. I'll give them credit for leaving no stone unturned, but they didn't find a thing to give them direction. No one saw anything, no one heard anything. No forensic evidence other than that the killer had to be right-handed and that he used a common hunting knife. No way to track it."

She shuddered, and for an instant she glimpsed blood

in her mind. A memory? Or simply an image conjured by what he said? She couldn't tell.

"Corey?" All of a sudden Austin was squatting beside her, looking at her with concern. "You just paled. What's wrong?"

"Mental imagery," she answered. "I don't know if it was a flashback or just something I created when you talked about the stabbing."

He swore quietly and reached up to run his fingertips along her cheek. "I'd like to kill this man with my bare hands."

"Join the club." Then she turned her head and looked straight at him. "Have you killed anyone before?"

"Never had to. Thank God. But I'm beginning to change my view."

"Me, too," she mumbled.

He brushed her cheek again. "You didn't look very good when you got home, either. What's going on, Corey?"

"Self-examination," she admitted. How far did she want to go with this? Explaining the train of her thoughts to him would leave her utterly exposed. No secrets, no safe little emotional hidey-hole. Did she trust him enough to express her doubts about herself?

But as she looked into his dark eyes, she realized that she did. They had shared a deep intimacy already, but sharing her thoughts and feelings was an even bigger intimacy, one that seriously frightened her.

He waited, showing a patience that was truly amazing, leaving it to her to decide whether she wanted to explain. Finally, she took her courage in both hands and decided to tell him. He was always truthful with her, and would be truthful about this. Maybe a little honesty would settle the mess inside her.

"I closed up early. The quilting circle was canceled and there didn't seem to be any reason to hang around. I might not even have one customer at this time of day."

He nodded.

"But it wasn't just that. I wanted to get back to you. I've been thinking about you all day."

"Same here," he said.

Her heart skipped, then began a rapid tattoo. She liked that he was thinking about her, but that didn't necessarily mean a thing. He could have been having thoughts very far from hers.

"Anyway, it suddenly struck me that I'd spent all day thinking about you and not about the murderer."

"That should be a good thing, right?"

"Maybe. But that's when I started to feel messed up. Austin, if there's any example on this planet of the tricks and games the mind can play, I'm it. So I started to wonder if I was feeling all those things because I was turning you into a security blanket."

"Ah."

Much to her dismay, he rose and turned away. He checked the pot again, then shook his head. "It's never going to simmer if I don't leave it alone."

At last he pulled a chair around so that he could sit catty-corner from her. "Okay. I have to admit I've wondered about the same thing. You've got a lot of stuff to sort out, and I know you will. I don't want to hinder that in any way. Not even a little bit. But it's important to me that you know your own mind and heart."

"You're leaving," she pointed out.

"I do have to go back to Washington. For how long is a decision I don't need to make right now. And you know what?"

"What?"

"You don't have to make a decision right now, either. In fact, there's no real decision to make yet. So stop worrying about it and let's just enjoy what we have, why ever we have it. Plenty of time later to get smart. Right now we have something big on our plates."

It wasn't exactly what she wanted to hear, but it didn't crush her, either. He was acknowledging her right to be confused about them and reminding her they had a killer to deal with first.

Gazing at him, an ache of longing blossomed in her so intense that it hurt. "I want you," she said bluntly.

"I want you, too. I'm on fire for you."

"Can the cabbage rolls wait an hour or so?"

The smile returned to his eyes. "I'm betting they'll cook a whole lot better if I don't hover."

Between them, there was no more uncertainty. After the past two nights, they came together with confidence and the comfort of familiarity. But sureness didn't dim the flare of passion in the least. If anything, from Corey's perspective, it heightened it. She didn't have to wonder, to become anxious, to question her own skills. No, Austin made it perfectly clear how much he enjoyed her explorations.

Emboldened, she became a tigress, wanting to give him everything she could, seeking new ways to make him captive to desire. It absolutely delighted her to make him writhe and groan. It made her feel powerful for the first time in her life. Holding him totally in thrall was matched by absolutely no other experience she had known.

But just as she thought he was about to climax, he reared up and rolled her onto her back. "Your turn," he whispered.

If she had any modesty left, she lost it as he dragged his mouth and tongue over her body, even urging her onto her stomach to teach her about places she never would have imagined being part of lovemaking. But there was no mistaking the thrill she felt as he spread her cheeks and touched her gently.

Passion caused her to quiver, as if she was shivering violently, and made her call his name, pleading with him not to wait.

But he made her wait a while longer, driving her ever higher up the mountain until she thought she couldn't take any more. Only then did he pull her toward him and plunge into her warm, moist depths. It was as if that part of her had been aching forever to be stretched and filled.

With her back to him, he held her hips as he pumped into her womanly center. Then, just as she was peaking, he leaned forward on her and clasped her breasts, pinching her nipples.

She shot over the top as if fired from a gun, so fast and so hard it approached pain and left her dizzy with satisfaction. Dimly she felt him shudder and follow her to completion.

It was a long time before she returned to the moment. He lay on her, both of them breathing like runners, damp from the exertion.

And it felt so damn good.

"You're amazing," he murmured later as they lay in a limp tangle face-to-face. He sprinkled kisses on her forehead as she nuzzled his shoulder.

"Bet you say that to all the girls," she tried to joke.

"I'm not joking, and I've never said that before."

She tilted her head up, trying to see him in the dimly lit room. His expression had grown stern.

"Don't say things like that," he said quietly. "Don't put yourself down. I won't have it. You're an amazing lover. Period. Now say thank-you."

"Thank you." She had a crazy urge to giggle but swallowed it.

"Now, believe it," he continued. "Because it's true."

"But—"

He stirred and laid a finger over her lips. "You give yourself totally to the experience. Every bit of you is involved. You try to find every way possible to please me, and you accept everything I offer you. So not only are you gorgeous, but you're amazing."

Warmth settled into her heart and she smiled. Something in her life that she hadn't messed up. That felt pretty darn good.

Suddenly he lifted his head and sniffed. "Um…I hope

I'm not burning that galopki or whatever it is. Does the air smell scorched?"

"I can't smell it. All I can smell is us."

"Keep saying things like that and dinner *will* burn." Grinning now, he pushed her back. "I better check it. I hope you're getting hungry."

She watched him climb from the bed and pull on his jeans. The house felt a little chilly, but he didn't bother with shoes or a shirt.

He was magnificent. She could get used to this, she thought. All too easily.

She pulled back from that precipice, reminding herself that he'd be leaving soon, and hit the bathroom for a quick shower. Well, he might go, but he'd leave a whole lot of good memories behind him.

When she emerged from the bathroom, toweling her hair, he was sitting on the edge of the bed, pulling his boots on.

"Something wrong?" she asked. She didn't even notice anymore that she was standing there naked in front of him. It seemed natural and right.

He smiled, running his eyes over her, drinking her in. "Only that we'd better eat soon or dinner will be ruined. And if you stand there like Temptation personified, that's a distinct possibility."

Then he rose, grabbed her for a swift kiss and headed for the kitchen. The silly grin remained on her face while she dressed and was still there when she reached the kitchen.

He'd set the table, and steaming cabbage rolls filled

a bowl in the middle. He held her chair out for her, then sat as close as he could while he served them.

"After this mess is over," he said, "I'd like to take you somewhere. Assuming you can get away."

Startled, she stopped slicing the cabbage roll with her fork and looked at him. "Where?"

"Anywhere you want to go. Mexican pyramids. You said you wanted to see them. We could go to my family's *finca* and use it as a base of operations. Or we could go to San Antonio. I love that town."

"That would be great. What brought this on?"

"Your comment about how we can't even take an ordinary walk. You're right. We spend all our time together doing this. I'd like to broaden the view a bit. Could you find a way to get away?"

"I'm sure. I was thinking today about hiring Maureen. I have no doubt she could manage for a while."

"Good. We'll discuss where you want to go later."

Amazement filled her once again. He was talking as if they might have a future. Although, honesty compelled her to admit he was talking about taking a trip, not about years down the road. She liked the proposal, anyway. At least he wasn't in a hurry to get away from her. "I'm surprised you'd want to go back to Mexico this soon."

He shrugged. "We wouldn't be going anywhere near the border towns. The *finca* is south of Mexico City, almost in the Yucatán. Right in the heart of Mayan country."

"I've always wondered what happened to the Maya."

"They're still there. Lots of them. They abandoned

their cities, but they didn't vanish. Millions still speak the language and they're quite proud of their heritage."

After dinner and cleanup, they took coffee into the living room. Austin opened his arm, inviting Corey to sit beside him on the couch, and she snuggled in happily.

If only this could last. Deep inside, though, she knew she was enjoying an idyll out of time. The stalker was still out there. Austin would be leaving. Talk of taking her on a trip was nice, but she doubted it would come to pass.

She didn't want the shadows to creep in, but they crept in, anyway. Little by little, they stole her contentment and began to replace it with dread.

She was scared. All that brave talk about dealing with this guy was exactly that, brave talk. The reality of it would be very different, and while she didn't want to think that way, she knew perfectly well that she might not survive a confrontation with her stalker. And much as that frightened her, she was equally frightened by the possibility that the creep might stop, might go completely silent, might withdraw into the shadows and leave her wondering if she'd ever be safe.

Life had been full of enough fear. She really *was* getting tired of it. She wanted a normal life, one where she wasn't hiding from memories, from the past, from any of it. She wanted to be able to take that trip with Austin, and if not with him, then with someone else someday.

On the surface, her life looked normal enough, but working twelve-hour days, and working seven days a week, wasn't a full life. She came home to an empty house, worn-out because she needed to be worn-out. Because she had never shed the terror of a long-ago night she couldn't even fully remember.

Even Maude, who never seemed to leave her diner, had managed to marry and have two daughters. Corey couldn't manage even that because of an overpowering fear of men. A fear that honestly didn't make sense to her, but one she had never been able to overcome.

Not until Austin. She wondered if he had broken that wall down for good, or if he'd leave and she'd be afraid of men again.

The only way to get past that was to deal with this guy, no matter how scary it was. For the sake of her future, if nothing else, she had to defang him, demystify him, turn him into the ugly but mortal being he was.

A ghost killed her mother? No wonder she had problems. The murder was bad enough, but the childish interpretation of the killer made it worse. How could you catch a ghost? How could you stop one?

"Penny for your thoughts," Austin said.

"I was just thinking about that memory I had last night. That a ghost killed my mother. I can understand why it seemed that way to me when I was seven, but maybe it was the worst-possible interpretation."

"I think that whole event had to classify as the worst-possible thing for you to witness. But what do you mean?"

"I made him supernatural. How do you defend against that?"

"Good question," he agreed. A minute or so passed before he spoke again. "Are you feeling differently about him now?"

"Not really. Somewhere deep inside I'm still endowing him with crazy power. I need to stop that. Obviously he's just a man."

"Obviously. But something being obvious doesn't always help. So let's talk about how we're going to get this guy."

"How can we do that when I don't even know how or when he'll come."

"We agreed earlier on your most vulnerable times. Gage and I talked more after you left. On the off chance that he might be concerned about me, I'm going to go to Mahoney's in the evening and buy a beer. Then I'll slip out the back and get to your place before you close. You won't see me, okay? I don't intend to be seen by anyone."

"Okay."

"But I'll be there. And if you want the truth, I think you can probably handle him yourself."

"Me?" Her eyes widened and her stomach flipped nervously.

"I saw you in the gym on Sunday. But it's more than that. You're not a child anymore. You won't be taken by surprise. And he's eighteen years older now."

She turned to look at him. "I hadn't thought about that."

"Well, think about it now. You're in your prime physically. He's past his, even if he's keeping in shape. You're going to have speed and reflexes on your side, and you're pretty good at using them. I saw it. You don't really need me. I'm just backup."

She almost gaped at him, but then it was as if some kind of earthquake took place in her, shaking out dust and some of her fear, to replace it with confidence. "You believe in me that much?"

"Yes. I do."

"Wow." The warmth that flooded her, then turned her insides into something approximating melted chocolate. "No one ever believed in me that much."

"Not even your grandmother?"

"She tried, but I know she always saw me as a bird with a broken wing. She tried to protect me from nearly everything."

"I understand the impulse. I'd do the same if I could. But that isn't very good for you, is it?"

"Maybe it wasn't. I was always made to feel fragile in some way. Broken. And I was broken."

"In some ways. Given what you went through, it's not surprising. But you're grown up now, and you're a very capable woman." He paused. "I'm sorry if I gave you a different feeling when I pressed you about hiding. Damn, I just wanted to get past your walls. But you know something?"

"What?"

"I never saw you as weak in any way. You did what you had to do in order to survive a terrible trauma. That's not weakness, Corey. That's strength. Hell, you even had the strength to protect yourself from the dangers you perceived in therapy. The strength to put on a facade to ease the worries of your family."

"Pretense isn't strength."

"Sometimes it is. You were not only protecting yourself, but have you considered that you were also protecting your family?"

She drew a sharp breath. "No."

"Yes," he said firmly. "You made them believe you were okay so they wouldn't worry too much. That was protection. You're an amazing woman. Then, despite a very reasonable fear of men, you let me in. That fear would have been unreasonable only if you'd known who the murderer was. But you didn't. He could have been anyone. I told you before, I think you were very smart."

He had shone a whole new light on her, and she turned what he said around in her mind, feeling stronger by the minute.

"I can do this," she announced.

"You can," he agreed. "Now, can I take you to bed again?"

Chapter 13

The Righteous Man decided to wait on the note. He could send it right before he took care of the pervert and restored decency to Conard County. It would make his message clear then but not get the cops involved beforehand. He even considered lengthening the note, to make sure everyone knew that he had cleaned the trash and sin from the community.

But perhaps that was self-serving. He shouldn't aggrandize himself for doing the right thing. No one should.

But it tempted him. No one had understood why he'd killed Olivia, except Olivia. That should be enough, but considering the terrible thing he had to do, and the burden he bore guarding this town from evil, didn't someone need to understand that he was protecting them and their children?

He wrestled with his thoughts for a while, writing various notes. Some sounded too much like self-justification. He needed none other than that he was doing the right thing. Some sounded preachy, and he knew folks wouldn't appreciate that tone from someone who didn't belong in the pulpit at church.

He just wanted them to understand they had a protector, someone who was looking out for them. Sort of like Batman, maybe.

That thought drew him up short. Talk about aggrandizing himself. He was no superhero, but an ordinary man trying to serve his neighbors.

Halfway through his daily beer, he realized that he was wrestling with a temptation of his own: to feel important and special.

Not good. It would diminish his purity of action and intent. Doing the right thing deserved no special attention or praise. He must do it for no other reason than that it needed to be done.

Maybe he shouldn't even send a final note. But no, he needed to leave some message. Some mark that there had been a reason for this. He wouldn't want anyone to think he was just a common murderer, even if they didn't fully understand why he was doing this. That would be bad. People at least had to understand there was a reason. Otherwise they might think he was the sinner and not understand anything at all of his grand mission.

He called up the message he had originally intended to send and edited it. *Your mother deserved it. You do, too.*

That would at least put them on the right trail as they looked for a reason. He had almost no doubt that they would figure it out. Neither mother nor daughter dated. They hung out with women.

He took another pull on his beer and smiled. Yes, that would do. They would figure it out.

* * *

Corey had a restless night. Horrific images plagued her dreams, waking her repeatedly. Each time she jerked awake with a gasp, Austin was right there, holding her.

When he questioned her about her nightmares, she finally tried to explain. "They're not really nightmares. I just keep getting these awful, bloody images. The instant I have one, it jerks me awake."

"Are you remembering?"

"I don't know," she admitted, wishing she could burrow into him. "I have no way to know. It could all just be my imagination."

"I doubt it," he said grimly. "Your memory is waking. I hope it stops. Do you want to get up?"

"For a little while," she decided. "I need my sleep or I'm never going to get through the day. Maybe I can shake this dream off."

So once again they sat in the kitchen, this time with warm milk and cookies. She barely touched her cookie, but she drank her milk, hoping it would make her sleepy.

"What exactly are you seeing?"

She shuddered. "So much blood. Lakes of blood. How could there be so much?"

He didn't answer, and she thought she understood why. He didn't want to prod her memories. But she wasn't sure they hadn't already been prodded. God, morning couldn't come quickly enough.

But as for whether she was remembering something real, or her mind was distorting things in her sleep, she had no idea. "I still don't want to remember," she said presently.

"I hope you don't. I don't see how it could do a damn bit of good."

She agreed with that. She knew the things that mattered, that her mother had been stabbed to death. She didn't need to remember it. Not for any reason. Nothing would change, essential facts would remain the same.

It wouldn't even help her face the criminal who had killed her mother.

"Let's not go back to bed," Austin said when she finished her milk. "Maybe we can get comfortable together on the couch. It might change what your mind is doing."

It was worth a try, she thought. So he stretched out and had her lie on top of him, between his legs, her head pillowed on his chest. She felt surrounded by him and safe.

It did help. No more images interrupted her sleep.

In the morning, he reminded her of the plan. He'd go to Mahoney's, order a drink, play darts for a while and then as her closing time approached he'd leave through the back door.

She had only one question. "Do you think it'll be tonight?"

"Probably not. I get the feeling he's taking a bit of sadistic pleasure in toying with you. Besides, we haven't gotten another note."

"Maybe there won't be one."

"He hasn't exactly said anything definitive about why he's doing this. From the looks of the others, I'd guess he plans to make sure you know first."

"Like my mother knew."

He hesitated, taking her hand. "We don't know what she knew. All we can do is speculate."

"I can't imagine any other reason she just up and took me to Denver. Something was scaring her."

"Maybe. Or maybe your aunt was right. Maybe she felt she just couldn't live the kind of life she wanted here."

"I suppose," Corey said. But something deep inside her disagreed, and she didn't know why. Something left over from somewhere, either from the night of her mother's murder, or something she'd heard at some other point. Her mother had fled to hide.

That thought didn't exactly bolster her as she walked to work.

The day had developed a slight nip, a hint that winter was getting closer. Ordinarily she loved days like these, but she didn't really notice it that morning. She wrapped her arms around herself and clutched the knitting needle hidden in her bag.

So Austin didn't think it would be today. She almost hoped he was wrong. Her nerves were starting to feel stretched as tight as a drum skin. First the inchoate threat of the notes, then the realization that she might be the next intended victim of a killer with a knife.

She hadn't been kidding when she said she'd had enough. She wanted this settled, the sooner the better. Waiting without knowing where the end point was didn't agree with her.

Like her aunt's death from cancer. God, that had been nerve-wrenching agony, watching her suffering, wondering every morning if she'd still be alive, wondering if every good night would be the last one. Much as she had grieved, there'd been an undeniable sense of relief when it was over. Her aunt had been freed of pain, and the endless watching and fearing had drawn to its conclusion.

She felt much the same way right now. Just get it done with.

Business filled her day. It seemed as if the door never stopped opening, the bell over it never stopped tinkling. She moved from room to room, wishing she could settle enough to join one group or another, whether it was making embroidered butterflies for the quilt, or preparing the colored pieces for it. She tried to join the knitting circle for a while, but she just couldn't count stitches. A couple of the women remarked that she seemed edgy about something. She replied with a forced laugh. "Just antsy."

Antsy didn't begin to cover it. Dread crept ceaselessly along her nerves, and from time to time massive anxiety filled her.

Not today, Austin had said. Part of her hoped he was right, and part of her, the biggest part of her, just wanted it over before she went home.

She caught sight of Austin a couple of times through her front window. He was walking in and out of little shops, as if he was indeed job hunting.

Then she didn't see him again and knew he must be moving on to the rest of the plan.

The last group of the day came through. About a dozen women had started a project to make appliquéd holiday sweatshirts for the kindergarten through third grade at the elementary school. They were having a great time with the task, and a bit of early holiday spirit seemed to fill the place. While they worked, they talked about their next project, making Christmas-tree ornaments.

Corey reminded them she'd need a list of supplies in the next week or two so she could start ordering them.

Then they trailed out the door, and she decided to lock up behind them and turned her sign to Closed. As she saw the women out, though, she realized for the first time that the evenings were shortening again. Soon she'd be walking home in the dark.

If she was still around to walk home in the dark. Grimly she set about cleaning and getting ready to take out the trash.

Not tonight, Austin had said. All of a sudden she hoped he was right.

The Righteous Man decided to check one last thing before he acted. That guy staying with Corey still troubled him, although given the way she had let him run home from the college Sunday morning while she drove, he supposed it wasn't a concern. Besides, he hadn't seen them spend any time together.

Regardless, he'd noticed the guy sometimes went to Mahoney's, so he waited outside for a few, trying not to check his watch too often. At last the guy showed up and went inside. The man waited a couple of minutes and then followed him in.

Drink. Then darts. He watched Corey's tenant get into a friendly squabble with another guy over who was going to use the blue darts.

Okay, he was here for a while.

Time to go.

* * *

Austin was getting edgy. He had been trying to reassure Corey when he told her the guy wouldn't act tonight, but that didn't mean he believed it. Nothing about this situation was predictable. Not one damn thing, and he hated it. It had been easier to maneuver his way through Mexican cartels.

He glanced at his watch and saw Corey must be closing up. He had to get to the empty building behind Corey's place quickly. He was sure the alley would be the point of attack. Any other place and it might draw too much attention.

He was slipping out the back door when he ran into a drunk urinating against the wall. "Hey, man," he said as he tried to pass, "there's a urinal inside."

The last thing he expected was for the man to turn and punch him in the jaw. For a drunk, the guy landed a good solid punch. Because he hadn't expected it, Austin stumbled and felt his head hit the brick wall.

Oh, hell, he thought as he sank into blackness.

Corey putted around as long as she could. It only made sense to give Austin every extra minute she could to get here. But finally it was nearly dark outside, and she couldn't find any other excuse to linger. He had to be out there in the vacant house across the alley.

She could do this.

She picked up the biggest, strongest, sharpest knitting needle she could find, then hesitated, wondering if it would be better to take her box cutter. She didn't know how she could carry both of them in addition to the trash can.

She studied the situation for a moment, then stuck the box cutter in the pocket of her apron. She clutched the knitting needle hard against the side of the can and went to the back door.

She drew a few deep breaths, steadying herself. Summoning every ounce of courage she had. If this was it, at least it would be over.

She hit the bar. It was a fire door, so it was always locked from the outside, but until she bolted it from the inside, she could always open it. She pushed it open a few inches, then put the doorstop in place so it couldn't close behind her. She supposed it didn't matter. She always had her shop keys in her apron and could still get back in from the front.

She poked her head out. The darkening alley was utterly still and silent. She even peered around behind the door and saw no one.

Feeling marginally better, she opened the door farther and carried the can to the bin and dumped it.

When she turned around, she gasped.

A man stood there. He had appeared out of nowhere, like the ghost she had once thought him. He wore no big white coverall this time, though, although he had a nylon stocking over his head. Very little of him was exposed.

"C-can I help you?" she asked.

"No, but I'm going to save you," he answered.

She'd seen him around. She knew that voice. God, she wished she could recall his name. But she knew him all right. He lived here.

"Save me from what?"

"Sin," he answered.

Her grip tightened on the knitting needle. "Leave me alone."

"No." He stepped toward her.

Grabbing the edge of the metal wastebasket, with more strength than she would have believed she had, she swung it at him. She wanted his head, but got his shoulder.

It didn't stop him at all. Now she was down to her knitting needle and the box cutter in her pocket.

Then she gasped again. In an instant he whipped out an ugly hunting knife with a blade so highly polished it caught the vanishing light and sparkled.

"That wasn't very nice."

She pulled out the box cutter, extending the blade. "I'll scream."

"Too late."

He swung the knife toward her neck. Instinct made her duck just in time and he missed her. Her adrenaline hit hyperdrive. It filled her with strength and banished fear. She didn't even wonder where Austin was.

As she straightened, she managed to kick out with her left leg. She caught him in the thigh, but she didn't manage to get his knee.

Focus! The command was loud in her head. From somewhere in the distance she heard pounding footsteps. He didn't seem to hear them at all.

He jabbed at her this time, and she managed to jump to the side. The blade missed her, but she didn't miss him. Driving forward with her right arm, she jabbed him with the knitting needle right in the soft part of his stomach.

God, he was possessed! He didn't even seem to feel it. Instead, he edged closer and readied another swing with the knife. She whirled out of line with his swing and used the box cutter savagely on his arm. This time she got a reaction. He dropped the knife.

"You," she said in a tight angry voice, "killed my mother."

"She deserved it."

"Nobody deserves to be murdered. Except possibly you."

He pulled out yet another knife, holding it in his other hand. She didn't draw away, but moved into the fight, aware she could take a fatal wound but beyond caring.

Her needle took another jab at his midsection. He was ready this time, though, and turned away from the box cutter. He wasn't going to be disarmed again.

So she took another swipe with it, this time at his face. Savage satisfaction filled her as blood started to stream down his face.

"Next," she said, "is your throat."

At that point he bellowed and barged straight toward her, knife high.

All of sudden she was no longer alone. A fist came out of the darkness, hitting the guy's left arm from underneath, driving it upward. The second knife fell.

Then she realized Austin had taken over. He wasted no time pummeling the man to the ground. "Call the police," he said to Corey.

She hesitated only a moment, watching as Austin punched the guy again.

Then she ran inside and dialed 911. She heard the sirens even before she hung up.

Then she dashed back outside and saw her mother's killer lying facedown on the filthy pavement. Austin was tying his hands behind him with plastic cuffs.

"You will never believe," he said, "why I was late. I'm sorry. But you seemed to have things pretty well in hand."

"I still want to cut his throat."

Austin looked up then. "No, you don't," he said gently. "You have enough bad memories."

"This might be a good memory."

"I doubt it." But he pulled the guy's head back. "Have at it if you want. Before the cops arrive."

The adrenaline deserted her as swiftly as it had arrived. She started shaking, dropped the box cutter and slid down the wall until she was sitting.

"No," she said. "You're right."

She stared at the monster, knowing for sure now that there was nothing supernatural about him. An ordinary man. Sick, but ordinary.

Oddly, she felt as if the last of a very old weight lifted from her shoulders.

The rest of the night and the next day passed in a blinding whirl. Corey answered questions. The guy was in jail. She sat at the sheriff's office, sometimes nodding off in a chair. Velma, the dispatcher, finally showed her to a cot in the back.

It didn't help. The minute she lay down, everything returned, all of it, in excruciating detail. Finally she went back out front because at least out there she wasn't alone with memory. Other people came and went, talking about the past night, talking about other things. It helped.

Austin sat nearby, taking his turn at answering questions. He'd apologized again for being late, and explained what had happened.

One of those weird things in life, being knocked out by a drunk in an alley. He'd had to have a couple of staples in his scalp.

She, however, was untouched physically, but she felt she'd gone miles away emotionally and mentally. She wondered if they would let her go home. Maybe she could crawl into bed with Austin and find her way back.

In the late afternoon, he stepped outside to take a phone call. When he returned, he squatted in front of her.

"Are you going to be okay?" he asked as he took her hands in his.

"Eventually. I think I'm exhausted or something."

"You're still in shock, too. It'll be okay." He squeezed her hands. "I have some bad news. I've got to catch a flight for Washington tonight."

Her heart stopped. "Tonight?"

He nodded. "They need some more information, and I can't do it over the phone."

"Will you be gone long?" Dimly she realized she didn't even have the right to ask that.

"I don't know exactly, but I promise I'll be back. We have a trip to take, remember?"

Then he leaned forward, and heedless of everyone in the room, he kissed her. "Trust me," he murmured.

"I do."

Then he rose, shared a few words with Gage, and left. It was Gage who took her home finally.

Austin wouldn't be back, she told herself. Why would he? He had come here to find his footing in normal life again, and all she had done was get him wrapped up in her abnormal life. He'd be a fool to come back.

Besides, their paths in life couldn't possibly meet. Her work was here, his was there. He'd been kind to her, he'd helped her in a lot of ways, but she could see absolutely no reason he would really want a basket case like her.

He'd be wise to stay away, and she'd be wise to stop thinking of him.

Trust him? Of course she trusted him. But what she trusted him to do was what he believed would be best for both of them. And she could think of a whole lot of reasons he might think avoiding her would be best.

She'd looked at herself and didn't much like what she had found. She needed to change the habits of a lifetime, and who'd want to put up with that?

Never had the house or her life felt as empty as they did now.

Chapter 14

Coming back to Conard City was neither the hardest nor the easiest thing Austin had ever done. He was definitely edgy, though, wondering how Corey would welcome him.

Over the past month, he'd called a number of times, and with each call he felt her withdrawing more. She had less to say, she sounded cooler and more distant. The barriers were rising again, and he had only himself and his job to blame.

He still had the house key, so he let himself in. All his stuff was exactly where he had left it. He supposed that was a good sign, that she hadn't just boxed it all up and donated it.

He glanced at his watch and saw that she would be home soon. He thought about opening her curtains, but the night was chilly and dark already, and they probably provided insulation. The house was cool, as if the heat wasn't on, and he wondered if he should look for the thermostat.

He did nothing. Finally he made a pot of coffee and sat at the table waiting for judgment. Waiting for his Viking princess to return, probably all covered in frost.

She had every right to feel he had abandoned her, despite his calls. After all, no promises had been made, and his departure had been sudden, as if he just wanted to get away.

But one way or another, he wanted this settled. He wanted her to understand why he'd had to go. Why he'd come back.

At long last the front door opened. He heard her freeze just inside the door.

"I'm in the kitchen," he called out so she didn't have to wonder why she smelled coffee and who was in her house.

He heard her drop the mail on the hall table and hang her jacket on the coat tree inside the door. Her footsteps sounded heavy with reluctance. He'd done that to her by bailing at exactly the worst time possible.

But there was something else, too. He needed to be sure she didn't just want him for a security blanket. Better not to be wanted at all. He hoped the month had given her lots of time to sort things out, regardless of how it went for him. He'd figured out a lot himself.

She appeared in the doorway at last, and his first look at her expression made his chest tighten. Cold, distant. She'd thrown him out of her life. Now he was just a loose end she wanted to tie off.

"Hi," she said finally.

"Want some coffee? You look cold."

Her hesitation was visible. "Sure," she said finally. She entered the kitchen slowly and sat across the table from where he was seated.

"How are things going?" he asked her. He needed her to speak, to engage in any way possible.

"All right."

"The guy we caught?"

At that her face animated a little. "They found enough stuff on his computer to charge him with my mother's murder and my attempted murder. He was writing letters he apparently wanted to send to people around town. Longer than the ones he sent me. In fact, I got just one more note two days later."

"What did it say?"

"'Your mother deserved it. You do, too.'"

"God!" He could only shake his head. "What the hell got into him?"

"Apparently Lew Cumbers felt he needed to clean up the streets of this town. He knew my mother was a lesbian, and when she ran with me to Denver he followed her. Then, just before you arrived, he decided I was another pervert, too. His word, not mine."

"How did he reach that brilliant conclusion?"

"Like we thought. I never dated. I confined my friendships mostly to women. I only rented the apartment upstairs to women. He thought they were actually my lovers."

Austin could only shake his head. "What a sick creep."

"Especially the part about keeping this town safe. It seems he had delusions of being a hero of some kind."

"I am so sorry."

"Me, too. But it's over now."

She barely looked at him, and he felt an ache in his heart. "Do you hate me now?"

That startled her. "I don't hate you," she said, glancing at him. "I get you have a job and all of that."

"But it was a horrible time for me to leave. I wished I could postpone it, but I couldn't."

"Why not?"

The question challenged him, but he had an answer. "Nobody's supposed to know this, so keep it under your hat."

She gave a stiff nod.

"I was under subpoena to testify at some closed-door congressional hearings. You don't keep those guys waiting."

At last he had her attention. It was a step in the right direction, but as he sat there feeling more frightened by the minute, he understood something. He kept it to himself. It might only make things worse.

"Really? *You* had to do that?"

"Yeah, little old me. I guess I was expensive, for one thing. Putting someone undercover often is. They wanted me to justify what I'd done. Then my bosses wanted me to justify the whole operation, not just my part of it. So we had to answer endless questions about the efficacy of ATF's role south of the border."

"How did it come out?"

"I may never know. I'm out of the loop now, unless they come up with more questions. That's part of the reason I had to stay so long." Was that a softening he saw in her? A slight thaw of the autumn frost? He couldn't be sure. Not for the first time in his life, he wished he could read minds.

Finally, she said something that seemed to come out of the blue. "You didn't have to come back just to keep your promise."

Fear began escalating to something like panic, and he didn't panic easily. How had she twisted this around in her mind? "Of course I did. I always keep my promises. What's more, it's a promise I wanted to keep."

Her gaze flickered toward him, then slid away again. He'd lost her. He'd really lost her. She'd found a way to leave him in her past, and he didn't matter any longer. He felt gut-punched and didn't know what to do about it.

Maybe he should just get up and leave, write this all off. But he couldn't make himself do that. He had to find a way to get through.

"This month has been hell," he said finally, emphatically.

Startled, she looked at him again. "All those hearings?"

"They didn't even come close to calling you and listening to you grow more and more withdrawn. Did you build your walls again? Climb back into your tower and draw up your hair so I can't reach you?"

"How dare you!" she said sharply.

"No, how dare you! When I was busy getting behind your walls, you were busy getting behind mine, whether you know it or not. I spent every minute of the last month, except when I had to focus on work, thinking about getting back to you. And all the while I could hear Rapunzel closing off her tower."

"I am *not* Rapunzel."

"No, you're definitely not. You're not even the Viking princess I originally saw you as. You deal by hiding. I should have expected it."

"That's not fair. I fought that guy. I took that risk."

"Is that the last risk you'll ever take?"

Fire flashed in her blue eyes now, better than the ice that had been there before. "Damn you, Austin. You're here for a few weeks and then you vanish."

"I didn't vanish. I called. And you really didn't want to talk to me, did you? Why? Were you afraid of me? What have I ever done to make you afraid of me?"

"You battered down my defenses and then you hurt me. Isn't that enough?"

"I never intended to hurt you. And while we're on the subject of me going away, there's something you need to understand. I'm taking a desk job in Denver, but that doesn't mean I'll never need to be away for a few weeks at a time when something blows up. It's part of my life, even if I don't ever again go undercover. And I won't. But I'll still need to help with operations that make me leave for a few weeks. If that's going to cause a problem, maybe we should end this now."

"End what, exactly?"

He stilled, hammering down his emotions, realizing that she had just revealed the crux. She had no idea that she meant anything at all to him. He'd blown into her life for a few weeks, then vanished. His only promise had been that he would come back. But he hadn't said why. He hadn't told her anything that a woman could cling to. He hadn't given her any assurance of the important things.

"Estoy estupido," he said succinctly.

"What?"

"I'm stupid. You know, I once had an uncle who gave me some very wise advice about not messing around with virgins."

"What does that have to do with anything?"

"You haven't learned to read between the lines."

She gaped at him, but he'd reached the end of talking. He came around the table, lifted her in his arms and carried her back toward her bedroom.

"Austin! I didn't agree…"

"I'm through using words. Let's talk this way."

If she had struggled, or actually told him to stop, he would have. She didn't, though, so he stripped them both and carried her down onto her bed.

He was past finesse. He'd been dreaming of being with this woman for an entire month. He let every bit of his hunger show, even when it made him a little rough, and he sure as hell hurried. She didn't complain, though, and soon the room was full of sighs and moans and the musk of their lovemaking. When at last he entered her, he pumped so hard he dimly wondered if he were bruising her. It didn't stop him. It was as if he needed to tell her something that no words could.

She climaxed at the same instant he did, but he continued to hold on to her, buried deeply within her because if there was one thing of which he had become absolutely certain, it was that he would never, ever let go of her easily.

* * *

Corey lay sated and stunned beneath his weight. Despite the chill in the house, perspiration slicked her and beads of it ran down her cheeks.

What had just happened? Near violence, she suspected, but so full of pleasure and satisfaction that she felt utterly limp. She would have cried out if he had tried to move away. She needed him on her, needed him in her, and all the time she'd spent assuring herself that she was just fine and that it was okay that Austin was probably gone for good melted away.

She raised her shaking arms to grip his shoulders, holding him even nearer.

"I didn't want to cling," she whispered.

For an instant he didn't move. Then he raised his head. His first remark stunned her. "Why do you keep this place so damn dark?"

He twisted, found the bedside lamp and switched it on. Then he propped himself on his elbows and held her face between his hands. "Cling?"

Her cheeks colored enough to burn. "Cling," she repeated. "I may not have been with a man before you, but I'm not totally uneducated. I know sex doesn't mean the same thing to men and women. We tend to get attached. Men don't. The last thing I wanted you to feel was that I thought you owed me something. That I was clinging to you when you didn't want me."

"Oh, boy," he said, followed by some words in Spanish that she suspected she was glad she couldn't understand.

"That may be true some of the time," he said after

a moment. "It sure as hell wasn't true this time. Cling away, *querida*. I'd like it."

"Then...you want to be here?"

"I wouldn't be here for any other reason. I spent an entire month missing you so much, I felt like my heart had been torn out. If there's one thing I'm absolutely certain of at this point, it's that I'm in love with you." And there was the thing he had figured out but had been afraid to mention earlier.

She caught her breath, then felt the smile dawn on her face. "I love you, too."

"Good." He kissed her soundly. "Now that we've taken care of that, how about we plan our trip to Mexico. I want to introduce you to my family."

"That sounds awfully serious."

"Oh, it is. Very serious." But he was smiling. "However, that's as far as I want to go right now. We need more time together. I want you to lose all your doubts."

She suspected she already had, but she was so happy right then, she figured she could play it his way.

A month later they sat on the top step of the Pyramid of the Moon and looked down the broad avenue at all the pyramids of varying size.

"Once," he said, "these pyramids were covered with mica. It would have made them gleam almost like glass. And the only place to get mica in large quantities was Brazil, two thousand miles away. Can you imagine it?"

She narrowed her eyes as she leaned against his shoulder and tried to envision it. "What happened?"

"Some supposed restorer removed what was left of it.

Turns out he was less of a restorer and more of a reno-vator. Anyway, look at the avenue, too. Some scientists believe a large part of it was filled with water. Just imag-ine how this place must have shone."

"It's amazing," she agreed. "Awe-inspiring. I want to stay for a long, long time. I just can't soak it all in."

"Teotihuacán is overwhelming," he agreed. "I lost count of the times I came here, and every time I found something new. Chichén Itzá is like that, as well. Maybe I should take you to some of the smaller sites. Easier to grasp."

She laughed. "I am having the best time of my life. Being overwhelmed by this is a good thing."

He smiled and wrapped his arm around her. "We don't really know who built this city. It might have pre-dated Mayan culture."

"I love a mystery."

"There are plenty around here." Then he said some-thing that clearly wasn't Spanish. *"Lak'ech Ala K'in."*

She turned her head to look at him. "What's that?"

"A Mayan greeting. It means roughly, *I am you and you are me.*"

"Oh, I love that," she breathed.

"Kinda creates a different perspective, doesn't it?"

"Absolutely. Say it again?" So he did and she tried to imitate him. It wasn't exactly easy. "I need to practice."

"I'd love to give you a whole lot of time to practice. But I mean it, *querida.* I am you and you are me. Will you be my wife?"

Part of her had expected this, especially when she quickly realized that introducing her to his family was no casual thing for the Mendez family. Still, joy exploded in her, depriving her of breath and thought and speech.

"I know the whole package is a bit daunting," he said lightly as his dark eyes scanned her face. "Two and a half cultures…"

"Half?" She had found her breath again.

"Some of my family are Mayan. So two and a half. At least. And I realize that I have more cousins than any one human should have, more aunts and uncles…well, I wouldn't be surprised if you wanted to run."

"I don't want to run." The smile dawning on her face grew wider and wider until her cheeks hurt, but she didn't care. She reached up to cup his face. "I love you."

"Te amo," he replied.

"I love your family, too."

"Ah, *mi amor,* you've only seen their best side. Wait till you see the fights, the spats, the bickering…"

She laughed, the joy filling every inch of her, the day more beautiful and perfect than any she had ever known. "We can always go hide at my place."

"True. Are you going to answer me? I'm dying here, Corey."

"Don't do that." She leaned in and kissed him with all the love she felt for him. *"Te amo.* I will be your wife." Then she threw her arms around him and felt his close around her.

"Hey, *ten cuidado.* Be careful. These steps are narrow and I don't want us to slide down them."

She drew back and looked at the distance they had climbed. It had been hard going, but now they were here, and she wanted this moment to be frozen in amber.

"I don't think I could fall down if I tried right now. I feel like I have wings."

"Let's not test that theory." But he was smiling, too. His dark eyes danced. "Forever, my love. Forever."

"Forever," she agreed.

"You do know I'll only be home on weekends."

"You told me."

"You're okay with that?"

"I thought I just let you know. And you're okay with kids?"

He kissed her long and hard. "As many as you want. The cousins need more cousins."

She tipped her head back, laughing again in her joy. "I have never, ever been happier!"

She had barely realized that there were other tourists around, but when he called one over, the man came with a huge smile. "You two look happy."

"I think," Austin answered, "that we're the happiest people who ever sat up here. My lady just accepted my proposal." He held up the camera he had brought along. "Would you capture the moment for us?"

The man took the camera and Austin turned to her again, seizing her mouth in a kiss that completed the healing of her soul.

* * * * *

A sneaky peek at next month…

INTRIGUE…

BREATHTAKING ROMANTIC SUSPENSE

My wish list for next month's titles…

In stores from 18th April 2014:

☐ Sawyer – Delores Fossen

& The District – Carol Ericson

☐ Scene of the Crime: Return to Mystic Lake
  – Carla Cassidy

& Navy SEAL Surrender – Angi Morgan

☐ Lawless – HelenKay Dimon

& The Bodyguard – Lena Diaz

Romantic Suspense

☐ Cavanaugh Undercover – Marie Ferrarella

Available at WHSmith, Tesco, Asda, Eason, Amazon and Apple

Just can't wait?

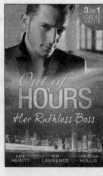

Join the Mills & Boon Book Club

Want to read more **Intrigue** books?
We're offering you **2 more** absolutely **FREE!**

We'll also treat you to these fabulous extras:

- 🌹 **Exclusive offers and much more!**
- 🌹 **FREE home delivery**
- 🌹 **FREE books and gifts with our special rewards scheme**

Get your free books now!

visit www.millsandboon.co.uk/bookclub
or call Customer Relations on 020 8288 2888

The World of Mills & Boon®

There's a Mills & Boon® series that's perfect for you. We publish ten series and, with new titles every month, you never have to wait long for your favourite to come along.

By Request
Relive the romance with the best of the best
12 stories every month

Cherish
Experience the ultimate rush of falling in love
12 new stories every month

Desire
Passionate and dramatic love stories
6 new stories every month

n o c t u r n e™
An exhilarating underworld of dark desires
Up to 3 new stories every mo

Discover more romance at

www.millsandboon.co.uk

- ❤ WIN great prizes in our exclusive competitions

- ❤ BUY new titles before they hit the shops

- ❤ BROWSE new books and REVIEW your favourites

- ❤ SAVE on new books with the Mills & Boon® Bookclub™

- ❤ DISCOVER new authors

PLUS, to chat about your favourite reads, get the latest news and find special offers:

- 📘 Find us on facebook.com/millsandboon
- 🐦 Follow us on twitter.com/millsandboonuk
- ❤ Sign up to our newsletter at millsandboon.co.uk